CLAIMED

GATEKEEPERS OF THE GODS

JENNIFER CHANCE

OLIVERHEBERBOOKS

For Cathy, Frani, Laurie and Sandy
May your lives always be filled with romance.

Prologue

The gates to Olympus never failed to impress.

Stefan Mihal assessed the iron and copper bars that made up the primary entry point to the realm of the gods. To either side, the long, curved wall of white marble extended away into the shadows. Only a few lonely torches lit the heavily carved surface.

Despite the scant illumination, the sculpted images of gods and monsters seemed to leap from the wall to assert their bygone dominance. They all were there, somewhere. Zeus, Hera, Poseidon, Athena, centaurs, nymphs, chimeras, Pegasus, and even the Sphinx. Gods high and low and the creatures that supported, adored and reflected them. They all converged on a wall that would've been one of the seven wonders of the ancient world...if anyone had ever known about it.

Nothing appeared to be moving beyond the bars. All Stefan could see was a thick, primeval forest choked with shadows and the weight of history. Everything seemed exactly as it should, exactly as it had for the past two hundred and fifty years he'd been making this trek to these hallowed gates.

1

But, as he knew more than most, appearances could be deceiving.

Olympus never slept.

Stefan lifted a hand as he approached, an unnecessary but familiar salute to honor the gate's welcome of his presence. Ordinary mortals couldn't set foot in Olympus without an invitation. Demigods could. They retained their all-access pass to the realm of the gods whether they committed themselves to the long-lived service to their patron deity, or chose to honor their heritage through a human life well lived.

The gates opened inward with barely a murmur, the murk of the forest beyond darkening as he passed through. He continued, unperturbed. He could see nothing in front of him but blackness, but he felt the pressure of the whispers, the excited murmuring. He carried no offering; he didn't need one. The gods were always starved for company.

The gates swung back into place with the softest click. At that moment, the space before him lit up, revealing the true nature of what lay just beyond the gates of Olympus: the receiving gallery of the gods.

Beneath him, a jewel-inlaid mosaic floor burst with an internal fire that extended to a semi-circle of carved, golden thrones mounted on white marble pedestals. More steps rose up behind the thrones, standing room for any of the minor gods or mythological creatures that might be interested in whoever breached the gates. Often, the gallery remained cloaked in shadow, leaving the mortal supplicant to state their business and be judged anonymously. Today, it was packed—but not solely with gods.

Sea nymphs in their legged form crowded the space behind the thrones, males and females of breathtaking beauty, their skin ranging from pale azure to translucent blue-green to deepest midnight. Their eyes were unusually large in their fine-boned faces, their lips full and lush. The hair of both genders tumbled in a thick tide over their shoulders, manes of blond, deep chestnut, or inky black. Though sea nymphs had no need of clothing in the depths of the ocean, they delighted in adornment, like all Olympians. For this audience, they were gowned in shimmering fabric caught up with tiny bits of shipwreck treasures—ancient amulets, golden clips—or with shells and dried coral clasps.

In the center of the gallery, Hermes sprawled on the throne usually reserved for Zeus...because of course he did. The messenger god feigned disinterest at Stefan's approach, staring at the ceiling with his legs draped over the armrests of Zeus's throne. But no one would be fooled into thinking that he wasn't already thoroughly enjoying himself.

Built tall, lean, and deceptively strong, Hermes was beautiful, of course—most gods were unless they intended to strike fear in a human—but his beauty seemed to be merely part of a game for him. His sunny blond locks spilled with surfer-boy ease to his shoulders, and his dark eyes snapped with fierce delight. A grin played at the edges of his sculpted lips, and the wings of his sandals fluttered with a restlessness that belied the god's permanent excitement.

As Stefan stopped in the middle of the mosaic floor, Hermes spun to face him, swinging his legs around to rest his feet on the floor. He leaned forward and flapped his hands when Stefan began to take a knee in honor of his patron deity.

"Stop-stop-stop! There's no need for that. Spill everything—all of it!" Hermes gestured expansively at the nymphs, who were clearly his invited guests. "And then I'll share what these beauties know. Poseidon never uses his army well enough, but we can be glad he isn't paying much attention to the world beyond our iron gates. He'd be *pissed*."

Stefan grimaced. It was a familiar refrain of Hermes, especially in the past century or so. "Earth wasn't made for the gods to live in, but for humans. It's not yours to rule."

"But you all are doing such a terrible *job* of it!" Hermes's sandal wings folded flat with irritation against his heels as he leaned forward again. "If you don't want to stir up Poseidon's attention, maybe try not to bleach all the coral in the sea or coat the entire ocean floor with plastic. It's rude. And so unnecessary. We can *help*."

Stefan's brows lifted, but he didn't pursue the topic. Hermes had all ten of his fingers on various pulses of humanity, though he contented himself with remaining behind the gates of Olympus, at least for now. If that ever changed, however...

Not Stefan's problem today. "Typhon's influence is growing," he informed the god. "We performed a thorough search of the yacht of a recent troublesome guest of the Crown and uncovered his connections to a syndicate of similarly wealthy business moguls spread throughout Europe, Africa, and Asia. The Americas are less swayed by the ancient gods."

"Heathens," muttered Hermes. He tented his hands. "But why Typhon? His pull wasn't strong even before Zeus dropped Mt. Etna on his sorry ass. Surely he has no power now."

"I would've said the same thing until recent events forced me to look into it more deeply. Mt. Etna has been particularly active of late, emitting vortex rings that have galvanized Typhon's followers and drawn new recruits. And he is a monster god. You may not have been keeping up with popular culture recently—"

"Please. Monitoring world media is *literally* the only thing we can do from this side of these infernal gates."

Stefan smiled. "Then you know the current popular fascination with monsters. Who better to feed this than..."

"The literal god of monsters." Hermes sat back in his

borrowed throne. "I like it. If Typhon wasn't such an unmitigated ass, I'd applaud him. Alas."

He pinned Stefan with a gaze. "That's not the only news out of Oûros these days. How goes the queen's attempt to infuse her castle with romance?"

Stefan narrowed his eyes on his god. "That's not uppermost in her mind."

"Please," Hermes scoffed. "Have you not been paying attention? Queen Catherine has had to do *something* to keep her mind off her lost son, and what she's chosen couldn't please Eros more. The new Crown Prince Kristos has a bride, and that insufferable by-blow of Zeus has his hands full with—what's her name?"

"Lauren Grant," Stefan said repressively. "But Queen Catherine—"

"Has now ordered you to go to Turkey, of all the godsforsaken places, and I'll bet she's asked you to bring another of the Americans along. Am I right? I know I'm right." He sighed expressively, sagging back in the throne again and crossing his legs. "I'm going to lose you to Windsurfing Barbie, aren't I?"

"No." Stefan could feel his pulse jumping in his jaw. "The American provides a credible cover for an exploratory mission. We go in, we look around, we get out. If you—any of you—have any information you could share to help guide our search, we'd appreciate it."

He'd pitched his voice louder to include the sea nymphs in the gallery, and they responded with the chirruping whistles of their native tongue. Hermes straightened, the grin back on his face.

"They know nothing of Ari, like always—it's as if the boy was spirited away by another god, if you ask me, and dropped into the middle of nowhere. He's not dead—I would have known. But he's caught up in some darkness I can't penetrate from here."

Stefan nodded. One of Hermes's many roles was as a psychopomp, guiding souls across the River Styx and into the Underworld at the end of their lives. It had been the only reason why Stefan had held out hope for Ari to still be alive after all these months, despite the decision by the Crown to move forward with installing Kristos as crown prince in place of his missing brother. The people of Oûros needed the assurance that the royal family was stable.

However, Stefan hadn't missed the fact that Ari's wrist-watch had turned up within a bare week of Kristos's accession ball. Not all the gods were ready for the royal family to move on, it seemed.

"What do they know that they can share?" he prompted, favoring the nymphs with a smile. As usual, the nearest ones to him giggled and preened, male and female alike. Nymphs liked attention almost as much as the gods.

"There's been a lot of activity in Alaçati in the past several days. Particularly south of the city. The port has been full of international traffic for some sporting event, but the event has happened before with less activity. There's something going on beyond entertainment."

"Any sign of Typhon?"

"No," Hermes confirmed the chirruping dissent of the nymphs. Like any demigod of Hermes, Stefan could easily translate any language—even the native tongue of these ancient creatures—but he allowed his patron to continue. "That doesn't mean he's not involved, just that he hasn't shown his hand. And they think he is involved. There've been deliveries to the Port Alaçatı Marina that are problematic. Live animals and maybe creatures who are not exactly animals. They're sent into the city and never seen again."

"How long has this been going on?"

Hermes spread his hands at the chorus of dismayed and defensive chirruping. "For months. And stop scowling. The nymphs were looking for a golden prince, not a cargo of the damned."

Stefan worked to school his face. "How could any of those creatures escape Olympus?"

"Same way as always," Hermes shrugged. "The gates to Olympus are barred, but the Underworld? That's Hades's realm. If he lets a few nasty bits slip out on occasion, we don't raise a fuss. They can't survive in the modern world for longer than a few weeks at a go. The air is poison to them. But if your goal was to use them for sport, they're dead anyway."

"As you say." Stefan didn't like any of this, but he couldn't ignore it. "And there's been a new delivery since Ari's watch was recovered?"

Another wave of murmurs and chirps. "Several, it would seem. Again, no clue of what, exactly, but—it's alive. I will say, I'm looking forward to hearing of your adventure. You'll be back with a full report, I expect?"

"Of course," Stefan said, recognizing the dismissal in his patron's words. He bowed his head in respect, but when he lifted it again, he was surprised to find Hermes staring at him, his dark eyes curiously intent.

"Have a care with Windsurfing Barbie," Hermes said, already growing more diffuse as his focus waned. "She strays too close to the veil at her peril, and Hades has always had a soft spot for any fire that burns so bright."

Stefan bristled. "What's that supposed to mean?" Acting on instinct, he reached out to keep the mercurial god from disappearing, but it was already too late. The forest hissed, darkness swirled around him, and his grasping, outstretched hand banged into the unforgiving iron bars of the gates of Olympus—now once more shut tight.

He turned on his heel and strode back into the night.

One

Nicki Clark inched her fingers along the thick ridge of the stone wall, grateful as always that the capital city of Oûros had a deep and abiding love for ornamental frescoes over every door, window and empty roofline. She hadn't tried escaping the palace at this particular point before, but the descent so far had been easy.

Getting down the last several feet would be more of a trick.

"One...two..." she muttered, planting her right foot solidly as she eased her way down. She didn't have to jump the entire distance, not yet. The wall was smoother below this point, but it was nevertheless hewn out of thousands-year-old chunks of stone. She could keep going for at least another yard, then drop. Her shoes were sturdy and her grip strong. Besides, she'd already done this a dozen times since she'd first been trapped inside the gilded palace of Oûros like a caged lion.

She shimmied downward, her heart rate picking up. She'd only glimpsed this specific four feet of wall from down the alley when she'd been out shopping the day before with Emmaline, Frani, and Lauren. It'd looked promising, but the space below her was currently hung with early morning shadows, and she couldn't see beyond the next small jut of stone.

She swung a foot out experimentally—

And nearly fell off the wall when it was forcibly stopped by someone's hard grasp. A grasp that was infuriatingly familiar.

Nicki gave her foot a hard shake. "Back off, Stefan."

The diplomatic ambassador of the royal family of Oûros—and hello, a *demigod*, whatever the hell that meant—held fast.

"If you insist on clambering over walls to escape the confines of the royal palace, you should at least do a better job picking your locations," Stefan said in his cool, superior voice. When he wanted, like now, he could speak English without so much as a trace of the thick accent she'd heard him use when he spoke his native tongue. As usual, she wished he would stick to Oûrois so she didn't have to listen to his complaints about every detail of her existence.

"So far as I can tell, there's nothing beneath me but you. And if you have your hand on my foot, it's not a far drop. So go away."

"I'll catch you."

Nicki took a moment to rest her head against the cool stone. Solid rock was more reasonable than Stefan when he got that tone. She knew it well, having heard it virtually every time they'd spoken in the past few weeks. From practically the first time they'd met during Emmaline's epic falling-in-love-with-a-fairytale-prince adventure, he'd formed completely pointless and aggravating opinions about what was appropriate for her. Which would have been nervy enough, except the guy wasn't exactly in a position to judge.

Still, judge he did. Worse, rather than moving on to torment one of the other women of their group, Stefan had fixated on her. He constantly dogged her steps, showing up every time she'd thought she'd fled the palace, berating her every decision from running routes to climbing gear.

She knew he wasn't going to go away. And if she was honest, she didn't want him to—not entirely. First off, the guy was seriously easy on the eyes, at least when he wasn't irritating the crap out of her. Secondly, she'd recently learned from a breathless and starry-eyed Emmaline that the kingdom of Oûros wasn't just your average fairytale kingdom set in a Mediterranean paradise, but something straight up out of a freaking Greek *myth*, with Olympic gods and a gateway to Olympus and nymphs and tridents and *demigods*. That information ratcheted up Stefan several degrees on her interest-o-meter.

Emmaline was absolutely sure Stefan was a demigod—but a demigod of what, exactly—or who? Apollo? No, Stefan was too sneaky. Poseidon? Meh. He possessed not a single tattoo. Nicki was pretty sure tattoos were a requirement of any demigod of Poseidon.

Was there a Greek god of condescension? Now *that* was a possibility.

Either way, questions, she had them. And this seemed like a good time to start asking.

"Fine." Without any further warning, Nicki kicked her foot free of Stefan's hold and pushed away from the wall. He was expecting the movement, and he caught her easily, dropping her lightly to her feet.

As usual, the touch of Stefan's hands on Nicki's arms electrified her. How had he found her so early, though? The sun was barely up over the ridgeline of the mountains ringing this seaside idyll, and the Oûrois weren't known for being early risers, other than the fishermen.

Stefan wasn't dressed for fishing.

She took in his hard body encased in long spandex shorts and a short-sleeved racing top, the outfit doing nothing to hide the fact that he had muscles on top of muscles, for all that he cut an aristocratically slender figure in a tuxedo. He couldn't be planning on running with her, either—she'd told no one she was going to attempt this particular avenue of escape.

But Stefan *had* known, apparently. He always seemed to know. The bastard.

The bastard in question remained way too close to Nicki as she drew in an unsteady breath, his gaze raking her face. She stared back, taking the opportunity to memorize the man's impossibly beautiful features—light-colored hair and honey-tanned skin, piercing gray-blue eyes, angled cheeks and hard jaw. He was quite a few years older than the other members of the royal family she'd met—Prince Kristos was maybe twenty-six, and Dimitri, the captain of the country's security force, appeared to be about the same age. But Stefan looked like he'd seen some things. She clocked him at thirty-five years old, easy. He was quick, competent, experienced—and someone who could take care of himself.

That pretty much made him perfect in Nicki's book. But that book might as well be a fairy tale, because eventually, she *would* escape this royal city with her friends in tow and get back on their trip through Europe. By then, Stefan would be only a memory.

She wanted him to be a fantastic memory, though. Which meant he needed to stop judging her every chance he could.

No dice. "You're breathing too fast," he informed her tersely. "What's wrong?"

"You're blocking all the oxygen in this alley." Nicki stepped back, already changing her mind about interrogating the guy. Demigod or not, right now, she just wanted to ditch him. "How'd you know I'd be here?"

"It wasn't too difficult." He smirked. "You've escaped via nearly every other likely avenue in the palace. Your itinerary yesterday suggested you'd be walking through the old city, which would have afforded you a view of this wall." He gestured down the cobblestoned street. The courtyard where they'd shopped yesterday for yet another round of wedding paraphernalia for Emmaline and Prince Kristos was less than a hundred feet away.

"You had someone *spying* on me?" she demanded. "One of the guards?"

Stefan drew up to his full six foot two inches, which put him nearly a foot taller than her, and Nicki rolled her eyes. She wasn't a huge fan of her height, but it did allow her to be light and quick. She was also wiry enough to shimmy over walls, up trees and through tight spots that most people couldn't manage.

None of that helped her right now, however, as Stefan loomed. "I didn't need to have anyone spying on you," he said, his voice taking on the clipped edge she enjoyed provoking so much. "You're a guest of the royal family of Oûros. As such, your safety is our number one concern."

"Got it."

Without any further warning, Nicki took another step and turned sharply away, her feet digging into the cobblestones as she launched herself down the narrow alley. Stefan immediately gave chase, but not ten steps away, Nicki saw what she thought she'd glimpsed earlier—another alley, barely wide enough for a child to scrape through.

She dove into the tight corridor and grinned as Stefan shouted something filthy-sounding in Oûrois. He took off again down the main alley, though, and she knew she wouldn't have much time. The city was riddled with these tiny passages, but they all eventually ended up dumping either into the main courtyard of the town or one of the smaller streets that led to the sea.

She bet Stefan would pick the courtyard—Nicki had run on

the beach twice already this week, and she typically mixed things up more than that. Which Stefan would know, because, despite his demigodly outrage, he *totally* had been spying on her.

The moment she cleared the narrow space, Nicki turned in the opposite direction, jumping over short walls and skirting fountains and public wells, the quaint architecture of the city blurring by her as she raced through more streets and down additional narrow walkways. She had traversed the capital city of Oûros way too many times to count, and she had an affinity for directions and maps and knowing where she was quickly and certainly. That skill had served her well in her job, and it definitely helped today as she sought to shake her most persistent tail.

She succeeded.

Laughing as the full brunt of the Mediterranean sun hit her, Nicki burst out of the last little cluster of buildings and onto the wide, fine sand of Oûros's famed Royal Beach. Had they really been stuck here two full weeks? This morning, it felt like she was seeing it all for the first time.

She fairly flew by a collection of fishing nets and headed straight for the packed sand at the water's edge, which would definitely be easier on her ankles. Her gaze filled with the gorgeous blue-green Aegean Sea, and she drew in a deep, cleansing breath, tasting the salt and sun and heat. She had the whole beach to herself, and she bent into her run, mentally choosing her destination as—

A sudden weight thudded against her right shoulder. It wasn't enough to down her, certainly not enough to cause pain, but a thick drape of fisherman's net had somehow wrapped its way around her body and was everywhere. She turned, then turned again as she fought to get herself free. While cresting a small dune, she saw the flash of Stefan's running shirt too late as the man leapt toward her.

"Got you—" he crowed. Then his arms were around her, and the two of them were rolling in the thick sand, the net somehow growing to three times its normal size as she fought to escape.

"Don't move—don't move!" Stefan laughed. "You'll only make it worse."

But she couldn't make it worse—she couldn't.

Because Stefan was lying on top of her...and her heart felt like it was about to explode.

Two

"You cheated!"

Nicki Clark's gasp was so affronted, so outraged, that Stefan couldn't help but gloat a moment longer than was strictly necessary to prove his point. She was the most infuriating woman he'd ever encountered—and he'd encountered quite a few in his generations of serving the royal family. Never, though, was there anyone as confident in ways that she manifestly shouldn't be confident. Not in her beauty, her brains, or even her ingenuity, either—Nicki Clark thought she was a lion in the body of a mouse.

And she was constantly trying to prove she was right.

"Get off me," she sputtered, and he moved willingly enough to the side, but he wasn't quick about freeing her from the thick ropes. To her credit, she didn't struggle. Instead, she went wholly quiet, her breathing evening out though he could tell her pulse was racing.

Racing...a little too fast, he thought. The same as it had in the corridor by the palace wall.

Concern instantly flushed the momentary surge of triumph out of his system. "Are you hurt?" he asked, reaching for her, but Nicki flinched away from his hand, in that peculiar manner she had. He'd seen many women who'd borne the brunt of a man's violence—this wasn't that. She wasn't ducking away from his attack, but from his offer of aid. It had taken him days to realize that distinction, while she and her friends had been guests of the royal family. If anything, it made her more intriguing to him.

Now she glared down at the web of netting with which he'd ensnared her. "I always see it thrown at people's feet, tripping them up," she said, reaching out one long-fingered hand and expertly picking up the edge of the net that would most quickly free her. The woman's mind worked like that, he'd learned too. She didn't flail. She didn't flop. When she was out of her depth she slowed down her mind and body, and her next choice was almost always the right one.

"I wasn't trying to hurt you, but to stop you." Stefan leaned back to watch her pick her own way out of the netting. This morning Nicki wore barely enough clothing for decency, but she did it in such a way that it wasn't intended as a means to attract men. In truth, she could outrun most of the men of Oûros if she caught them off guard—including him, though he was getting better at not being caught off guard. Her legs were powerful for all their short stature, corded with muscle beneath smooth, tanned skin. Her core was tight—not thick with muscle as he would have expected, but steady and firm. Her arms were lean and toned, burnished bronze by the sun despite the suntan lotion she liberally applied. She was too young to be weathered, but he'd caught himself imagining what another twenty—thirty years out in the elements would do to her face, her skin, her shiny, red-gold hair. She would be stunning in her older years, fierce and free.

He couldn't imagine Nicki old, however. He could never get past the woman's bright laughter and flashing eyes...nor the way she danced on his every last nerve, deliberately flaunting any rule she encountered.

"Yeah, well, you weren't trying to help me either," Nicki scoffed, flinging off the last of the net from her upper body. Her legs remained trapped by the trailing edge of the net caught beneath him, but she sank back on the small dune, apparently content to remain in the sun. A tightness in his gut he hadn't realized he'd been holding eased.

As he was about to ask again if she was hurt, Nicki made a face. "You know, if you want to kiss me so badly, you don't have to throw a net on me. You could just ask."

Stefan didn't react to her taunt. Nicki Clark spoke with the offhand assurance of a woman who knew that men didn't find her sensually alluring so much as startlingly attractive, her bold, fervent grasp on life so shocking and vibrant that it took most people by surprise. She used the reaction she caused as a shield, he suspected. But a shield from what?

And the woman *was* pretty, by any standards. With her burnished red hair, currently tangled in a sand-caked ponytail, her green eyes, and fresh, open face, she could—and had—turned heads both in the city and inside the palace. He'd watched others react to her, men and women alike naturally gravitating to her sunny demeanor and smiling at her brashness. Even the older, more established officials had unbent around her, in the way one did with someone who would be leaving soon. Nicki Clark didn't fit, but you found yourself wishing she could.

She eyed him. "See? You're thinking about it. Probably should get it over with." She settled back into the sand, her eyes drifting shut as if she didn't have a care in the world. "Again."

Her own skin flushed with the last word, and he found himself easing closer, despite the hard control with which he willed his body not to respond. He had kissed Nicki once, in the palace pool. She'd been determined to beat him in a lap endurance test, and he'd broken first, knowing he was expected in the throne room of the palace. She'd surged out of the water with such delighted enthusiasm that he hadn't thought, simply grabbed her and kissed her hard.

She, as usual, had given as good as she'd gotten, leaning into the kiss with a passion that shouldn't have surprised him, but somehow had.

Then she'd laughed it off as she laughed everything off, and he'd been left feeling...slightly uncertain.

And he never felt uncertain.

It was that memory of uncertainty that urged him forward now. As his shadow fell over Nicki's face, her smug expression faltered—not a lot, but enough for him to know he'd gotten her attention.

"You want me to kiss you?" he murmured.

Her breath hitched—and a surge of adrenaline shot through his body, priming him for action. Nicki Clark was like a lit fuse. He didn't know when she would spark out of control, but he wanted to be the one who started the fireworks.

That was dangerous, and stupid.

And so was he, when she was around.

"I have to say, I enjoyed feeling your body up against mine when you kissed me by the pool," he continued, watching the stain of a blush creep up her face. "You surprised me then."

He could tell the moment she lost her nerve. Her eyes flashed open and she gave him a big smile, as if the entire conversation were a joke she was wrapping up.

"I'm a surprising girl," she said, angling her head away from him to peer down at her legs. "I'm pretty sure I'm also going to be a crippled girl if you don't get these nets off me though. I'm about to lose circulation."

He moved enough to free her legs, but as she scooted backward out of the cocoon of netting, he caught her hand. The movement apparently startled her so much that she let him turn her wrist to his mouth. Holding her hand firmly in his grip, he bent forward and pressed his lips against her inner wrist. Her pulse was jumping again, and there was no mistaking the quick intake of breath as Nicki inhaled, her entire body going still.

"You taste like sunshine," he murmured against her skin, and he didn't mistake the shudder that rippled through her. "I haven't tasted sunshine in some time, I'm afraid."

"I—"

He lifted his head. Nicki's eyes had widened, her mouth soft and inviting, her skin flushed.

"I want to taste more of it, if you don't mind."

Not waiting for her to counter, he leaned forward and brushed her lips with his.

Three

Nicki's head felt too light and her legs too heavy as Stefan deepened the kiss, her body strangely unsteady as he kept his grip tight on her right hand and pulled her close. She'd kissed him with *enthusiasm* the first time, but it had been more to scare the idiot off, not egg him on.

But this...

She didn't want to scare him off from this. Not quite yet.

And Stefan seemed on board with that plan, evidently oblivious to the fact that they were on a public beach in front of God, the world, and everyone. Nicki fought for sanity, but all she wanted to do was keep going, keep pushing, to see how far they could take this moment, how far the very proper diplomat would be willing to go. Kristos and Emmaline had met on a beach, after all, but while they'd had to be circumspect because of his royal stature, Stefan didn't have those restrictions. He was a demigod, sure, but he wasn't...

"You're thinking too much," he murmured as Nicki caught her breath. One of Stefan's hands had snaked around her back, and he pressed against her. The heavy muscles of his chest against her breasts made her nipples go hard and alert despite the thick fabric of her jog bra. She'd dressed for running, not seduction, and the result was a curiously muted and wholly infuriating sensation, her body demanding more...more. Whatever Stefan would be willing to give. Which was impossible and stupid and pointless, and yet—

Screw it.

Angling her face toward him, Nicki surrendered.

Stefan met her more than halfway. His mouth was hard and firm against hers, his hands tightening to pull her close, despite the sand and sweat caking her skin, despite the tangle of nets around their feet. Her heart thudded heavily in her chest, but not too fast, not too hard, and she groaned with very real relief against his mouth. Stefan tasted of salt and heat, and she wanted to wrap herself in the moment and hold it tight, a barrier against the outside world.

Nicki lifted both hands to his shoulders, pulling herself closer to him. He was a fair amount bigger than she was, but their bodies fit together perfectly. His chest and abs were hard, the thin fabric of his running shirt pressed tightly against his skin and leaving nothing to the imagination. He arched her back and moved his mouth from her lips, to her cheek, to her chin, then pulled her over on top of him. Suddenly she was straddling his lap, his body rock hard, her knees sinking down into the sand alongside his hips as his hands locked into place. Stefan's eyes were dark and intent. They fixed on her with unmistakable need.

"Kiss me again," he rasped.

She leaned down into him, and for one precious moment she poured everything she had into that kiss. All her wants, needs, desires, fears—all the things Stefan knew nothing about, could never know anything about. For that beautiful second, suspended in time, she was as free as she'd ever been in her adult life, ever since she'd learned that life could be taken from her at any moment, ever since—

Stefan jerked himself away from her like a man who'd been ripped free of an oxygen tank, and she gamely tumbled to the side to give him space. Stefan's eyes were wide and startled as he re-focused on her.

"What?" Nicki blurted. "You didn't want to be kissed back?"

He stared at her, his expression becoming one of intrigue… and desire. "I think, Atalanta, you turn everything into a competition. It makes me wonder what else beyond kissing I should be training for."

Atalanta? Nicki wasn't wholly up on her Greek mythology, but she was pretty sure the name was a compliment. Beyond that, the unexpected heat in Stefan's words made her blink—but not as much as the shift of movement behind him. On the edge of the beach, wavering in the heat so as almost to seem a mirage, a man walked toward them. Not one man, either, but many of them. "Um, are you in trouble or something?"

Stefan stiffened without turning to look. "No," he said crisply. "There's nothing scheduled this morning, and my itinerary was logged."

She lifted her brows. "Your itinerary included making out with me on the beach?"

His smile was back for a moment. "It should have, but no. I advised that I was going to search for you. Clearly, I was successful." He'd moved back far enough that she could scoot completely off the netting, and she folded up the strands in as neat a packet as she could manage while he watched her.

"They could be coming for you," he said.

Nicki snorted. "Not hardly."

She said the words without heat, but she knew her place

among her friends. She was the fun adventure-girl sidekick, a little difficult for the rest of them to figure out, with their carefully laid plans for the future—never mind that for two of them so far, those careful plans were falling to pieces around them. But either way, she wasn't the one that people would be coming for, unless...

She glanced up with sudden interest. Just a few days earlier, she'd offered her services to the royal family in one highly specific way, a way that meant more to her than any of them realized. She'd never thought they'd take her seriously, but...

She cleared her throat, going for casual. "You don't suppose they found something new about Ari, do you? Maybe where his plane landed in Turkey?"

Predictably, all Stefan's good cheer fell away from him like an avalanche. Prince Aristotle Andris had crashed his small plane a year earlier, somewhere over the Aegean Sea. The family had been in mourning ever since—until recent new evidence pointed them toward a coastal town in Turkey...a coastal town that Nicki, of all people, knew well. Alaçati, Turkey, was host to an international windsurfing competition, and she'd competed there the previous summer. It was a thin connection, and in truth she didn't know how she could truly help—yet. But she *wanted* to help.

Needed to.

Stefan's face shuttered. He had no interest in accepting her aid, he'd made that abundantly clear. "Then they would definitely not be coming for you."

He rolled to his feet and held out a hand, which she ignored as she pulled herself to her feet as well, dusting off her legs. Somehow Stefan had managed to thrash around without marring a single hair on his head or dirtying his spandex with so much as a grain of sand. It almost made her want to push him down into the dune.

Instead, he turned smartly and began walking toward the

approaching men, and Nicki squinted into the sun, then followed behind him. She knew the tall, slender man in the center, his face impassive as he stopped, allowing them to come to him. Cyril Gerou was the royal family's chief advisor, with ties to the military, communications, and probably every other arm of royal rule in the tiny country. He was a good man, she supposed, but he suffered from a perennial case of the grumpies, which Stefan seemed to catch whenever he was within ten feet of the guy. Like now.

"Sir." Stefan nodded as Cyril bowed to Nicki. "Is anything wrong?"

Cyril shook his head. "We weren't sending a search party out, I assure you. The men are about to go on maneuvers, and I decided to accompany them. When you were spotted, I thought it would be a good time to discuss developments. My apologies," he turned to Nicki. "I didn't know you were with the ambassador."

Yeah, well, that's because the ambassador was mashed up against my face. "No worries. I was leaving for a jog anyway when Stefan and I ran into each other. I can let you guys talk?"

"Where are you going?" Stefan's words were too sharp, and she pivoted toward him, gratified to see the warring emotions flit across his face for a moment. He needed to get debriefed, or whatever the term was, but he also didn't want her out of his sight. His sight or his arms—though maybe, for him, they were both the same thing.

That thought made her stand a little straighter. Had his kiss been something more than simple lust? Maybe some sort of weird move to control her or keep her in place? It was exactly the kind of high-handed move Stefan would enjoy, and irritation riffled through her.

She hooked a thumb over her shoulder. "One of the hotels is

setting up their kayaks and boogie boards. I'm going to go work on that. You guys have a good time."

"Don't leave the beach," Stefan said, the words more an order than a suggestion.

"Sure thing," Nicki waved. *Not.* "I'll see you later."

She stamped off through the sand, aware that Stefan was watching her. Her heart had quieted finally, and she breathed a sigh of relief for that. The true condition of her heart was a complete unknown, though she definitely had dizzy spells and migraines, which were problematic enough. She'd been prescribed beta-blockers for the migraines, and despite her disdain for pills she'd continued taking them, hoping they'd keep any worse heart issues at bay.

Which was silly, really. Beta=blockers wouldn't fix her heart if what she really feared was true. Her brother and father had been diagnosed with familial hypertrophic cardiomyopathy... basically, their heart muscle was thick and inefficient, slowing down the flow of blood out of the heart. Her father had had a devastating heart attack five years earlier, and lived in fear of having another one. Her brother, once he'd been diagnosed, had lived in fear, too. Neither one of them had done anything active since.

Nicki had been tested...once. But she hadn't gone back. She couldn't live in constant fear. She wouldn't.

Still, any time her heart skittered out of control she knew she was facing a potentially deadly risk, and she needed to watch that. Plus, there was no denying that whenever Stefan got close her heart definitely did kick up a few notches, and not in a comfortable way. He made her feel out of sorts, defensive and aggressive at once, and she wasn't used to reacting to anyone that way, especially not a guy. Especially not a guy who people called "ambassador" with a straight face—let alone the whole demigod possibility. That wasn't the kind of man Nicki had ever attracted.

And what was Stefan's attraction to her about anyway? He had a way of seeming simultaneously interested and oppressive, and she thought more about that kiss. She hadn't been imagining his interest, had she? Again, was this all truly some weirdly obscure strategy to allow him to keep tabs on her?

Well, he could go spin in small circles if he thought she was going to put up with that. Regardless of what Emmaline and Kristos's upcoming wedding plans were, Nicki would need to come up with an excuse to get out of Oûros. Otherwise, she was going to go crazy.

Four

I f Nicki Clark didn't leave the peaceful kingdom of Oûros soon, Stefan vowed silently, he was going to go crazy.

He watched her jog across the sand as if she owned the entire beach, his attention fractured between her sun-browned legs and Cyril's preemptive throat clearing. "You're doing yourself no favors by displaying your interest in her," Cyril said, the words so blunt that Stefan swung his gaze back to him.

"My interest?" he scowled. "Since when do you care about any woman I speak to?"

"Since the queen has become fixated on the romantic lives of every one of the four young women presently under the royal roof. And don't think she hasn't noticed the way you and the American seek each other out. You would do well to be more circumspect if you don't want to find yourself in Queen Catherine's sights."

"Seek each—" he glanced toward Nicki then back toward Cyril. "Cyril, half the time I'm trying to track her down, not meet up for a chat."

"Half the time, yes," Cyril gestured to the dune where Stefan had most assuredly found Nicki...and for more than a chat. "The queen has eyes in the back of her head when it comes to ferreting out presumed romantic entanglements. Because you have not been careful, and given the woman's apparent connections in Alaçati, the queen is giving serious thought to assigning Miss Clark to you when you go to—"

"No," snapped Stefan, so sharply that Cyril frowned at him in surprise. It wasn't his place to rebuke the chief advisor, but he didn't care. Hermes had warned him about the queen's pastime, and he hadn't listened. Because of that, he might already be putting the American in danger.

Almost against his will, Stefan let his gaze return once more to where Nicki was haggling with a bodyboard vendor in front of one of the posh hotels along the beach. A small crowd had gathered around her, as small crowds tended to do. Again, not because she was classically beautiful...she was merely irresistible.

She was also a menace.

"Nicole Clark is untrained to go on any sort of mission, diplomatic or otherwise," Stefan said tersely, refocusing on Cyril. "She also has no sense of decorum, of her limits, or of—"

Cyril's lifted hand cut him off.

"I'm not the one you have to convince," he said. A cheerful horn beeped behind them, and they both turned. Stefan's eyes narrowed as Cyril merely sighed.

"As I said," Cyril murmured.

Rolling up to them in a golf cart was none other than Queen Catherine of Oûros, wife to King Jasen and mother to the crown prince, Kristos...and the missing former crown prince, Ari. She appeared thoroughly delighted to be out on the beach. It was early enough that there weren't enough tourists who understood the significance of a lead cart surrounded by three attendant carts, each with men holding guns below the sight line of the vehicles' dashboards.

For her part, Queen Catherine appeared to be unarmed, but Kristos rode with her. Dimitri Korba, demigod captain of the Oûros National Security Force and unofficial bodyguard to the royal family, rode in the closest cart to the queen's. Stefan grimaced. "What's happened?"

"The final interviews with the man found with Ari's watch were reported this morning," Cyril said quietly. "I'd hoped to work out a strategy with you before the queen was made aware of the information."

"It appears we're too late on that."

"It seems so." Cyril nodded. "And given her state of excitement, the news supports her desire to find Ari alive."

"And do you believe he is?" Stefan asked. "Still alive?" He knew Hermes' stance on the subject, but what a god knew and what a mortal could justify were often two different things. Even a mortal in Oûros.

Cyril managed a pleasant expression, but spoke through his teeth. "I don't know what to think any more. At this point, however, we have to find something other than a few bits of debris scavenged by fishermen in order to put the queen's mind to rest. Otherwise, I fear she'll never get past this."

Stefan schooled his expression into polite interest. He understood Cyril's concern. When Prince Ari had crashed his plane over a year ago, flying into a dangerous storm that he had no business trying to weather on his own, the entire royal family had been devastated. King Jasen had seemed to age a decade overnight, while the queen had held on to a fleeting hope that Ari was—somehow—still alive. A hope that was fanned with each new discovery of some missing piece of wreckage offered up by the Aegean Sea.

Now that hope had flared into a brilliant beacon of light.

"Stefan!" Queen Catherine said, jumping lightly out of the

cart as Kristos slowed the vehicle. "Tell me I've not come too late and that Cyril hasn't spoiled my update."

Cyril bowed. "Not at all, your majesty—"

"Oh, please." She waved off the honorific. "There's no one around. Dispense with the formality, I beg you." She turned to Stefan. "Our plans are moving forward. We have additional information about Ari's watch and where it was located."

"Near Alaçati." Stefan nodded. Dimitri and the American Lauren Grant had spotted Ari's custom flight and dive watch on the wrist of a random fisherman while traveling to a nearby island. The fisherman had insisted he'd gotten the watch from some scavenger—who claimed he'd plucked it out of the ocean. Dimitri had taken the discovery hard. Ari had been his best friend—and his responsibility.

"Yes, Alaçati, which is fully invested in its summer wind-surfing season," the queen beamed. "So there are tourists there, people, outsiders. It will be easier for you to blend."

Stefan didn't dispute her words. "What is the new information?" he asked.

Behind the queen, Kristos grimaced, his face unusually grim compared to his mother's excitement. The prince's eyes were fixed on the open water, however, not the queen, and Stefan angled himself carefully to allow a wider view as the queen spoke again.

"There's a whole network of scavengers along the Turkish coast. Small wonder, given the state of the economy and lack of military protections there outside the main cities," she sniffed.

"Your Highness," Cyril said mildly. "They are our neighbors and allies."

"And we are here, in Oûros, among friends," the queen shot back with an uncharacteristic snap to her tone. "Anyway, the fisherman who bought the watch told us there was other debris as well—a gold chain, journals, shoes—but that the watch hadn't come directly from the ocean, according to the man who sold it to him. It'd come from its owner."

"Its owner!" Stefan's exclamation had the queen straightening. "When was this?"

"He wasn't clear—months ago." Her mouth tightened but she pushed on. "But the man was alive, the scavenger had said. Disoriented, confused. The scavenger thought he'd sustained some sort of head injury."

"Possibly concussed," Kristos put in.

"Dressed in rags but he had the watch. He'd been exposed to the elements. Hadn't showered." The queen's lower lip began to tremble, and Kristos stepped forward.

"Mother—"

She ignored him. "Bottom line, we need to act. The fisherman had that watch since January—January! And here it is June, and Ari could have been wandering this whole time."

"You don't know that the man who sold the scavenger the watch in the first place was Ari."

"And you don't know that it wasn't!" she retorted. "There are windsurfers currently in the city of Alaçati for some exhibition, and we should be there too, finding out whatever we can."

A cheer went up from the crowd gathered at the edge of the beach. The queen glanced up—and her excited exclamation made Stefan turn as well. The reason behind that exclamation, however, made him groan.

Out on the open waters of the Aegean, Nicki Clark stood balanced on a thin board, her arms locked on the cross beams of a brightly colored sail. Flipping and twirling, she was doing an impressively acrobatic job of angling the sail to capture the most wind it could, resulting in her leaping over the small whitecaps offered up by the gusting winds over the azure water.

"Emmaline tells me that Nicki is a champion windsurfer, and her work as an adventure influencer makes it perfectly reasonable that she would take a side trip to Alaçati while she is so close," the queen said triumphantly. "And of course, we wouldn't want her to travel alone in a foreign country with such rapidly changing safety concerns. A small group of ONSF soldiers and you, Stefan, will go with her."

"We have already discussed this, Your Highness—" Stefan began, but the queen barreled on.

"Look at her! This is not an idle queen creating a fit where none exists. Nicki is clearly skilled, and if her reputation in the windsurfing community checks out as Emmaline indicates, she's the perfect choice to travel with you, and the perfect excuse for us to encroach on our neighbor despite the fact that we don't agree on much of anything these days."

"It's not safe, and she could be placed in danger. She isn't trained."

"No, but you are," the queen said. "And I would trust you with my life, Stefan. Can you really tell me that Nicki Clark couldn't?"

Stefan followed her gaze, tracking the tiny form of Nicki as she crested one wave and swooped into the curl of another, drawing more applause and cheers as a line of tourists formed at the vendor's stand to try the windsurfing boards for themselves. Nicki, oblivious to all of it, watched the wind and the water, her body taut, her energy focused. She was in her element, and she took his breath away.

There was no way he was going to endanger her life, however, no matter what the queen commanded.

But the queen wasn't finished.

"Give me one good reason—*one*—that she isn't the ideal cover for you, and I'll consider relenting," she said. "Otherwise, the royal yacht is already being prepared, Stefan. I expect you to be on it tomorrow. With Nicki Clark."

Five

"Nicki, I really don't know about this."

Nicki kept her head beneath an enormous bath towel for a second more, schooling her expression. By the time she emerged, she was ready to face the three scowling women who sat around her suite, all of them girded for battle.

Well, girded might be overstating it. Lauren, the one who spoke, was standing by a chair, as if sitting was out of the question during such an important conversation. Lauren Grant was the heiress to an international hotelier fortune, and had grown up used to running the show. She and Nicki got along because Nicki usually let her—or ignored her if her opinions were inconvenient.

But Lauren was serious this morning, and Nicki knew why. She'd confided in Lauren about her possible heart condition a week ago, when Lauren had questioned her usage of beta-blockers. It would have been foolish not to disclose the worst possible scenario—that Nicki might possibly have a slowly dying heart—but she'd told Lauren not to worry, that there'd be lots of notice if anything was truly wrong.

This wasn't exactly true of course, but Lauren hadn't pressed before. She did now.

She'd clearly told the others too.

Emmaline sat with her hands earnestly folded in her lap. Earnest was what Emmaline did best. Nicki couldn't help thawing a bit as she caught her best friend's eye and smiled, watching her brighten with the strength of the connection. Across the room, Fran also caught her attention. She tilted her head and Nicki held up a hand to forestall whatever she was going to say.

"No need to shrink me, Fran. I know what you're thinking— what you're all thinking. And you're right. This is a simple trip but it could turn crazy at any moment. And not even for any grand reason, but the simple reality of going to a foreign country and running into all the problems that could entail. But seriously, this is not that big of a deal. It's not like we're going to have people chasing us with guns."

"You could," interjected Lauren darkly.

"I won't," Nicki shook her head. "Have you seen the royal yacht? It's practically a cruise ship. We're going to sail down to Alaçati big as life, and give our validation to the windsurfing expo they've got going on. It's good PR for Oûros, a nice goodwill gesture for Turkey, and the guards they're sending along are going to ask all the questions they need to ask while Stefan squires me around as if I'm some sort of VIP. Which is hilarious, but that's beside the point."

Emmaline bit her lip. "He's not especially happy about you going, you should know."

Nicki snorted. "I think the 'No, absolutely not, she can't go,' to Jasen at lunch was a good indicator of that. But honestly, that's for them to figure out." She gave her best "I don't really care" shrug, honed to a fine point after years of being denied opportunities by her hypochondriac mother, who'd perfected the art of the flop sweat years before anyone in the family had actually fallen ill.

Once Nicki had reached her senior year in high school, she'd shed a lot of those restrictions, but then her father's heart attack and brother's later diagnosis had threatened to close her in once more. She couldn't live the way her brother and father did. Wouldn't. And she wouldn't back down from this opportunity.

Still, that didn't mean she couldn't throw her friends a bone. "If they decide it's too dangerous, then of course I'll abide by that. With Stefan out of the country and no longer up in my grill, I'll be able to explore some of the mountain trails he's constantly warning me about." She grinned. "So it's a win for me either way."

"You know, he could be warning you about those trails because of wild animals," Fran observed wryly. "Not simply because he wants to be a pain in the ass."

"Mostly, though, he wants to be a pain in the ass," Lauren said, and the tension in the room finally broke as everyone laughed. "I heard from Dimitri that you two were totally making out on the beach. Truth?"

"We were not making out." Nicki hesitated. "Well, okay. I was. But I honest to God think Stefan was trying to seduce me to keep from running down the beach. Like this was some sort of super new diplomacy technique he wanted to practice on me."

"And how did that practice go?" Emmaline asked. Her expression had also lightened, brimming with curiosity and the possibility of new romance. She among all of them was the most in love with being in love.

"For me—pretty damn well," Nicki said. "I think he might have been going through the motions, but trust me, it's been so long since I've been anywhere close to those kind of motions, I'll take it."

"I keep trying to fix you up, and you keep rejecting me." Lauren protested. "How are you supposed to date if you never go out?"

"I'm too busy to mess with all of that." Somewhat true, actually. She'd been a one-woman unstoppable force in college. Too small to play in most organized sports at any sort of elite level, and too worried about her possible heart condition, she'd known she'd needed to find something she could do solo.

To give herself a competitive chance, she'd set her heart on the outlier sports—windsurfing, adventure running, climbing. There she'd met an entirely new group of friends who knew nothing about her past, nothing about her possible heart disease. They only knew she sometimes got a little dizzy if she didn't stay hydrated...and that despite said dizziness, she was usually the first to jump off the cliff into the water below, no matter how deep that water was.

But though there were plenty of men in that group Nicki could have pursued—she hadn't. Because, despite the fact that she truly believed that she was okay, it was one thing to get your heart broken by a relationship...

It was something else to walk into a relationship with your heart already broken.

"Okay, well, let's be smart about this." Lauren recalled Nicki's thoughts to the present as she settled into a chair. "What are the risks here? Let's say you get stuck somewhere and you can't take your meds."

"What, my beta-blockers? Those aren't that critical, really." Nicki shook her head. "They're for my migraines, and there's some evidence they help with high blood pressure and all of that, so that's a bonus. But if my heart is really going to go..." she shrugged. "It's going to go."

"And you never got tested for this?" Fran's voice was incredulous. "That seems really reckless to me, I'm sorry."

"Oh, I did once—twice, even, I think," Nicki said, trying to keep her cool. She'd had this fight with her mother too many times. "The odds aren't in my favor, and I know that. But I... couldn't keep going back. Not in the end. I'd rather live with my heart condition as a maybe and actually live—than change my whole life because of some stupid test. I've seen what it's done to my brother. He's become as bad as my mom, sure that every cold is going to kill him. And my dad..." Nicki sighed. "I'm not going to get tested only to find out the worst. I'm not. As long as I don't put anyone else in danger..."

"But what about putting yourself in danger?" Emmaline's voice was soft. "We don't want anything to happen to you."

"It won't. Especially if Stefan is on the boat." She smiled. "If he had to rescue me, I'd never live it down."

Lauren snorted. "Okay, but let's say you have a dizzy spell or your heart starts to react to something scary or intense. Your pulse goes up, right? What happens then?"

"I faint," Nicki shrugged. "That's it, so far. If anything worse ever happened, I'd get tested—really, I would. But it's never gone beyond a momentary blackout, I swear. No one's even cracked out an AED around me."

"That might not work anyway," Fran put in. "A defibrillator is meant to restart a malfunctioning heart, not a dying one."

Nicki let the shiver roll through her at the idea that her heart muscle could possibly be dying, but kept her expression strong and steady—like she needed to be. "There you go. So there's no point in worrying about it. Besides, if Stefan gets a hint that I might not be a hundred percent physically fit, there's no way he'd let me go along on this mission. None."

Emmaline sighed. "And it's that important for you to go?" Her question once more was quiet, but it drew the attention of all the girls to her.

Nicki hesitated. They couldn't understand, she knew.

They'd never had a fear that they were...fundamentally different. Fundamentally unreliable. Nicki'd overcome that fear with a college life and new career filled with solo adventures and living on people's couches, never attaching, never committing. But this...

"It is," she finally said, and was surprised to find her words equally soft. "I just...I really want to be a part of this." To be a part of something that mattered. Something that her body couldn't hold her back from.

"Well, then you should go," Fran said, her calm voice easing the tension again. "You'll just have to be smart."

"They're meeting now, you know," Emmaline said, pursing her lips as she glanced at her phone. "I'm sure they'll be talking about you, Nicki. Making their final decisions."

Nicki stood, eager for any reason to move again. "Well, then maybe I should go listen in."

Six

"There is absolutely no chance I'm going to let her come with us." Stefan placed the dossier on the table in front of him. He didn't lean forward; he didn't lean back. This wasn't a negotiation; it was a simple point of fact. A point he'd made six times already, by his count.

Cyril turned from scanning the monitors. They were in the palace's main conference room. He addressed Dimitri, the last person to deal with an American targeted by outside forces. "Had you to do it over again, would you have taken Lauren to Miranos?"

"No," Dimitri rumbled. "We went there because we didn't understand the lengths to which her insane ex would go. Had I known he was so deadly, and deranged, we wouldn't have left the mainland. I would've put her in a safe house and sat on it." He grimaced. "I agree with Stefan. It's too dangerous to take an American into Turkey. Even one with a reason to be there."

"A very good reason," Cyril observed blandly. "Unlike any of us." He pointed to the screens. "Nicole Clark was actually bylined last year at the Alaçati competition. She competed deep into the tournament before falling out of the running, then continued on in her journalistic role."

"Adventure blogging is not journalism," Stefan countered. "She has none of the training of an international correspondent, she simply has a laptop and a Wi-Fi connection."

He scowled. "It is not her credentials, though they are nonexistent. I will grant you her experience in windsurfing and her presence at last year's tournament are worthwhile considerations. But she's an American, a guest in our country. She's also untrained. We'll be taking her into unmonitored territory, where the Turkish military will be the least of our concerns. She has already demonstrated that she does not follow orders well, and that is of paramount importance. Make no mistake—this is a military mission. I'm being asked to secure information or possibly recover Ari's remains from a potentially hostile environment, with nationals who may not be willing to give up those remains. It could get ugly very quickly, and an American would be, at minimum, a liability, and, at worst, collateral damage from which we wouldn't recover."

His statement caused everyone to pause, and he regarded them impassively. In his mind's eye, he saw Nicki's distant form windsurfing on the wide ocean, imagined her smile, her laugh, the sun warming her as the wind whipped the waves around her to a frenzy. He wondered if the sea nymphs were impressed with her, then pushed that thought from his mind. He could not —*would* not—be weighted down with someone who made him this protective. He couldn't put it quite that way to the others, of course, but—

"Stefan raises a good point," Jasen said. He seemed more tired suddenly, and something in Stefan's chest tightened. Ordinary mortals could be unexpectedly fragile, he'd learned over long years. Jasen worried him. "We need to weigh the costs against what we may or may not achieve."

"Ari is there, though. You know he's there." Kristos spoke up, his attention swinging from Dimitri to Jasen—neatly skipping over Stefan's icy glare. "And the location couldn't be better for a simple op."

The prince stood, moving quickly to one of the larger screens and with a few deft taps of the inset keyboard, pulled up a map of coastal Turkey.

Alaçati was nearly as far south as Athens, and perched on a strip of countryside that stuck out into the Aegean before the land broke away to form several small islands. "We're talking maybe two days by boat, going slowly—one long day if you're focused. Slow would probably be better for this mission, to convey the tourist nature of it. Then you stop here." He jabbed a thumb at a nondescript island. "That's where the scavenger gang dealt their goods."

"That's an unusual stop," Stefan put in. "Explain how we would make that a reasonable detour so close to the city."

Kristos shrugged. "Diving. Nicki dives, right?"

Stefan thinned his lips. "It wouldn't surprise me."

"So, do the research. I bet someone somewhere has written about the diving off that island. Have her post about the story—"

"You can't be serious—"

"Post about the story using Wi-Fi via a satellite uplink, take a vid showing how beautiful the scenery is, and done. Meanwhile, your men go ashore, maybe you go ashore and see what's what."

"We don't know if the encampment is still there."

Kristos shrugged. "Where would they go? The mainland is too crowded, and that place is desolate. Easy to get to by boat, but no reason anyone would be looking there. And it's an island."

He stared at the map a moment longer. When he spoke, his voice sounded strangled. "Ari could be there, Stefan. Dead or—

whatever. Eleven months is a long time, but not so long that he couldn't still be alive."

Stefan grimaced. If Ari was still on that island, he was dead. He'd been disoriented when he'd sold the watch to the scavenger—for food and a boat. But even the fisherman had shaken his head at that story, relayed to him by the scavenger leader himself. Ari had asked for a boat, but he'd accepted a leaky-hulled wreck. For a watch that fine on the open sea, he should have known its value. He should have asked for something more, perhaps safe passage aboard a commercial craft.

So what had happened to him?

Cyril grunted and began arguing with Kristos about the logistics of the trip—no matter who was on the boat. Stefan swung toward Jasen, then stopped for a moment as his gaze swept past the blank screens lining the opposite wall. There'd been a shift in the doorway, the barest of movements, but his hands instantly tensed on the table. Not very many people knew of his heightened senses, and he knew he was right. Someone was watching them.

Normally, it would be the queen listening in on their private conferences; that he had allowed more than once. This wasn't the queen, though her assistance was all over this intrusion, he had no doubt. This was Nicki. He knew it as sure as he was sitting there.

How much had she heard? He had to assume all of it—including his disavowal of her.

Well, too bad. It had only been the truth.

Stefan was about to end the conversation when another movement caught his eye—this one closer to him. King Jasen. The king was watching Cyril, but more importantly, he was watching Kristos with Cyril. Kristos, his younger son, who had wanted nothing more than to serve out his life in the military, protecting and defending the country of Oûros while Ari, the older son, took up the mantle of power. Those boys—both of them—were supposed to grow old as Jasen watched, maturing to the fullness of their abilities. Instead, one was tilting at windmills, hoping desperately to bring back the brother he could not let rest, and the other might be buried in a shallow grave in hostile territory—or worse.

Far worse.

Stefan scowled at the screen again. Alaçati was twelve hours away by boat, give or take. If they made the trip in one long day and a short couple of hops, it could work the way Kristos, Jasen and Cyril envisioned. Nicki with her...laptop, phone, or whatever she would use, would be surrounded by Oûros's guards, hand-picked by Stefan. He wouldn't let her out of his sight. Further, he wasn't unaware of the need for diplomatic overtures to the country. This sojourn would accomplish that and more.

And it would accomplish something else. Something the entire country needed: a king who could finally mourn the death of his first son and celebrate the life of his second.

His eyes trained on Jasen, Stefan drew in a breath.

"Very well," he said. "This is how this is going to work."

Seven

Nicki almost swallowed her tongue. Stefan had said, "Very well." Not another "no," not another sneer. She hadn't realized how much she'd been braced for more snubs when silence filled the room.

"We'll leave tomorrow morning. King Jasen, if you can personally reach out to the appropriate officials to communicate our intentions, that will help smooth the way. We'll dock off the coast of Turkey as Kristos suggests, if we can create a credible reason to do so."

"I'm on it," Kristos chimed in, and Nicki smiled. Once again, Stefan seemed so much older to her than Kristos, so much more reserved. Of course, the royal ambassador hadn't been reserved today on the beach, and as the conversation ranged on, she found her mind returning to that scene again. He'd wanted to kiss her, she was certain of it. It wasn't merely to keep her in place. He'd been genuinely startled at the arrival of Cyril and his men, and he wouldn't have been if he'd been running some sort of game.

Right?

The sound of her name brought her back to the conversation.

"Nicki will remain on the boat whenever it's expedient for her to do so. Obviously, in Alaçati that will prove difficult. We may need hotel rooms—adjoining. With her permission, I'll want a guard inside the doors, not out. No need to draw attention, but I don't trust a city we haven't had a chance to properly scout."

King Jasen spoke up. "With luck you won't have much to do in Alaçati proper. From what my understanding is, if Ari survived or didn't survive on the island, you'll be able to tell quickly enough. If he took a boat that was actually seaworthy—" a long pause, as if Jasen was trying to collect himself. "He could be anywhere."

"Agreed." Stefan's words were sharp, crisp, a reassuring counterpoint to the king's more hesitant tone. King Jasen had never struck her as weak, but perhaps his strength had been tested too much in the long year of steeling himself against the inevitability of his son's death being proven. Now, with that proof almost at hand, the cracks in his shield were beginning to show.

Stefan seemed to realize that too. With every statement, he grew in confidence, until the fate of the mission became a foregone conclusion. Nicki stole back from the door and retraced her steps to her chambers, her mind churning. What had made Stefan make such an abrupt turnaround regarding her involvement? And did he really mean those terrible things he'd said about her earlier?

Of course he had. She grimaced.

He'd decided she was brash and undisciplined, certainly not one to follow orders, but he was wrong. She'd prove him wrong. She was being given a chance here...and she meant to grab onto it with both hands.

Stefan was wrong about something else too. His comments about her work as an adventure blogger stung more than she'd ever admit. Yes, it was a job for the young and unattached, and yes, that's exactly what she was. But she was damned good at her work as a stringer for several adventure sites and blogs, and her work entertained people all over the world. She was also a good diver and a *great* windsurfer, and she could certainly be an asset on this journey, however she needed to be.

She could do it. She would do it.

The next day passed in a blur of packing and repacking, with more supplies than they'd ever need. By the time they set off for the open water, it was nearly noon. The sun was high in the sky, the whole world bright and full of promise.

Nicki held onto the railing, staring out to sea. This was happening. She was really going on a meaningful adventure, using her skills and talents for a purpose. No one was telling her no, no one was warning her off.

She was a part of the team!

Within a few minutes, Stefan joined her on the deck, appropriately casual in the same style of loose sweater and trousers she was wearing, suitable for deflecting the wind that picked up as the yacht gained speed.

"You have everything you need in your stateroom?" he asked as she turned toward him. At her nod, he kept going. "Good. We'll dock tonight near Alaçati, but not quite at our destination. There's a scavenger band we need to question on a nearby island. It shouldn't take long."

"That's where I'll be diving?" She'd overheard part of this plan already and waved off Stefan's lifted brows. "The queen gave me my instructions early. She wanted me to know so that I could get ready. So I wouldn't be caught by surprise."

"It's a popular diving location, yes. Whether you get in the water will depend on what we find and how long we stay there,"

Stefan said, giving Nicki the distinct impression that he didn't plan for her to get wet the entire boat ride. The sudden inappropriateness of that expression hit her exactly the wrong way, and she giggled.

"Sorry," she said, clearing her throat. "But that's, ah, fine. Whatever you think is best."

That response did make him focus on her, too closely. "Did the queen tell you to say that as well?" he asked, and though the gibe was teasing, she couldn't stop the blush from climbing her cheeks. Since when did she blush this much around...anyone?

"No she didn't." She'd practiced this part, and it was as good a time as any. He needed to know she was willing to follow orders. "But there *is* something I think you should—"

"Ambassador Mihal." A man in dress uniform strode up, breaking Nicki's concentration. She blinked as he dropped into rapid Oûrois, lulled by the melodic syllables of a language she had no hope of understanding. She'd barely made it through college French—which had the same melody, but that's as far as it went. Stefan started walking as they talked and she turned back to the railing, not wanting to tag along like a little sister. The boat picked up speed as it reached open water and she found her nerves unwinding a notch as the yacht crashed through the waves, her hair spilling loose from its short ponytail to fly in the wind.

"Nicki." Stefan's voice reached her despite the wind and the roar of the engines, and she turned to see him beckoning her closer. When she reached him, the ship's captain or whatever had disappeared. In the lee of the protected hallway, it seemed strangely intimate, and Nicki put her hands up to her hair self-consciously.

When had she started caring about her hair?

"We'll be sailing for several hours, and it occurred to me you probably haven't eaten."

"Oh—I...no." Nicki blinked in surprise. She hadn't thought about something so basic as food in the mad rush to get ready. "I'm sure I can find something."

"I've had something prepared for us. That way, we can continue our discussion." He turned and gestured her through the doorway. "Third door on the left."

Nicki moved down the narrow hallway past formal sitting rooms and paused at the door of a small dining room. Stefan brushed past her smoothly, pushing the door open for her. She entered the elegantly appointed space, feeling completely out of sorts. Her clothes were perfectly right, but she was the foreign object—awkward and at strange angles. A table laden with covered plates and a sparkling water waited for them, and they sat.

"A little quieter here, don't you think?" Stefan asked.

"What? Oh...yes. It is, thank you," Nicki said. She uncovered the plate, but the thought of food on her suddenly queasy stomach was unappealing. Her hands were starting to sweat, and her heart thudded oddly—too hard, too fast. *No*, she implored herself. *Not now.*

"I'm sorry, are you all right?"

"Of course," Nicki said quickly, giving him a wide smile. "I'm hungry, I guess. You were more right about that than I realized." She picked up her sparkling water and drank it down, then lifted her sandwich. Her hands were trembling. *Food, I need food, that's all.* Her nerves were simply jangled because she was suddenly alone with a man whom she'd kissed—twice— a man who currently was, in effect, her boss. A man who was also staring at her with inscrutable eyes, as if he could see into her mind.

Nicki swallowed a bite and stared back at him. "I *can* follow directions, you know," she blurted. "I'm not going to be a problem."

As soon as she said the words, she winced. He'd never said that to her in person—she'd overheard it.

Stefan knew it, too. His eyes lit with amusement.

"I thought that was you. And now you can tell me how annoyed you are with me."

Eight

Stefan was enjoying the sight of Nicki so flustered. He shouldn't be, but he was. Her awkwardness had started, he was certain, with the clothing. He got the feeling that Nicki didn't wear pants very often unless they were technical tights meant for scaling a mountain. But she looked exactly right, felt exactly right sitting across from him. He watched her over the rim of her glass, content to let her gather her thoughts.

It appeared to take her a moment to process his words. She frowned. "Why would I be angry?"

The question was genuine, and he answered it as forthrightly. "You heard me accuse you of being unable to follow orders, clearly. I'm sure there's more you overheard as well. My concerns about your fitness for this role, certainly."

"Well, you'd have no way of knowing what I was really like, based on the experience you've had so far," she said, shrugging. "I've done everything I can to annoy you. But this—" she waved her hand around the dining room. "This is different. This is a job. I'm on your team, and when you're my team leader, I follow your lead. To the letter."

He lifted his brows and noted the stain of another blush crawling up her cheeks at the unintentionally forceful words.

"You know what I mean," she mumbled, then she brought up her head, as if to be sure he understood. "You tell me to stay on this boat, I stay. I've got my laptop and Kristos showed me how to connect to the yacht's satellite Wi-Fi system. I'll post a couple of times today, and more tomorrow, with a few of my old stories from last year's tournament updated for filler so it appears I'm exactly what I'm supposed to be. I have a great underwater camera Kristos gave me for underwater photography if that works with your schedule, but if it doesn't, I'll stay put."

Stefan watched her soberly. "In other words, you'll follow my directives."

"Absolutely," she said. Then she sighed. "Look, I know you think I'm a liability on this trip. And I..." she appeared to rethink her statement, then pushed forward. "And I am, to some extent, because I'm new to all of this. I get that. But I'm your cover. Like this sweater." She tweaked the sleeve. "Here to put a good face on things. I'm not going to get in your way, and I'm not going to do anything to embarrass you. I'm not an idiot. I'll learn the ropes and keep quiet."

He snorted. "I should have assigned you on a mission when you first arrived at the palace."

Another woman would have winced with embarrassment, but Nicki simply shrugged. "You should have. I'm a lot more useful than you give me credit for."

He leaned forward. "I'm intrigued by the possibilities," he said, his words barely a murmur. A wild urge overtook him, so quickly that all rational thought flew out of his head. In front of him was no longer a team member, an American, a guest of the royal family. It was the woman he'd held on the beach. A woman who tasted of joy and sunshine, sea and life.

He spoke before he could restrain himself. "So if my instructions were for you to make love to me, would you do it?"

Once again, Nicki surprised him. She leaned forward with equal ease, giving him a broad wink. "If that would move the mission forward, absolutely."

His brows lifted. "And whose call would it be on what was required for the mission?"

"Ultimately yours." She grinned, ruining the seriousness of her tone. "But I get to be in the room when the king reads your debriefing report."

A broad smile creased his face as well—and Stefan considered that. He couldn't seem to stop smiling at this woman. Nicki sat back, far more relaxed than when she'd first sat down. She continued grinning as well, and she picked up her sandwich again and bit into it with more gusto.

She'd barely swallowed before she lobbed her next conversational bomb. "So, since you now know how much I'm willing to contribute to the mission, how about a little more information— about yourself, I mean." She waved her sandwich at him as he stiffened. "Relax. I get that you can't tell me all the super-secret details about what we're going to do, but surely I can know a little bit more about, you know...you."

He settled back in his chair. He'd been informed that Emmaline had advised all the Americans about the unusual natures of Dimitri Korba, chief of the ONSF, and himself. But he also knew from Dimitri that there was no depth to the information. Emmaline had shared that they were demigods, but Lauren hadn't known what that meant. Clearly, Nicki still didn't.

"I could tell you that the Crown has expressly forbidden me to share the details of myself," he pointed out.

She dropped what was left of her sandwich on the plate and leaned forward. "You could," she agreed. "But where's the fun in that? It's not like I'm going to tell anyone. If I did, you'd bounce me from the mission, and there's no way I'm letting that happen. Besides, it's your secret. I can keep secrets."

Her words struck him with unexpected force. She could keep secrets, he thought. He didn't know why she needed to, but that didn't matter. She could.

"Fair enough. What is it you want to know?"

"Well, gee." She propped her elbows on the table. "For starters, how about everything? Like, what does it even mean to be a demigod? Are you immortal? Are you like super strong, or can you fly or leap tall buildings in a single bound?" Her eyes rounded. "Is Superman a demigod?"

"Technically I think Superman's an alien."

"Totally not as sexy. But come on, come on, answer the question. Like, how old are you? Because you look about maybe 33 or so? Give or take?"

"Then I age well," he said. "I actually present as 35 years old, but you're right, demigods do age differently than ordinary mortals. We are not immortal. We can grow old and die, but it takes us a lot longer."

She narrowed her eyes at him. "How much longer?"

"Children who are born with the blood of gods in their veins, age normally until their 20th year. Then, if they commit to serving as a demigod, they go through a brief ritual that changes their bodies, and simply allows them to age more slowly and stay healthier, not as susceptible to all the damaging impacts of the environment and the aging process."

She stared. "You get healed? Like your bodies are healed of anything bad and you're given some magical mojo to slow down your biological clock?"

The question held an unusual urgency, but he'd experienced this before. He'd had a hard time wrapping his head around it himself when the option was first presented to him.

"Yes, in a manner of speaking. Now for every 10 human years, my body only ages one."

"One?" She scrunched her face. "Oh my god, you're going to make me do math. So that means—no way. You're actually 170 years old? No wonder I kicked your ass in swimming."

Stefan barked a laugh, but his heart thudded hard, his adrenaline spiking. He hadn't realized how much he'd been tensing himself against Nicki's reaction to his age. More than anything else, it proved difficult for people to handle, especially people he wanted to get naked with. But as always, she turned what should be a major revelation into a point of competition. And he was just fine with that.

"I seem to recall that wasn't exactly what happened."

"Yeah, well, clearly after 170 years, your brain's not as sharp as it used to be, even if your body is still pretty fine." She grinned. "So, okay, you're super old but don't look it. What else? Obviously Dmitri is pretty built, but are you both equally strong? And can you fly? And who...like, what god are you dedicated to or whatever? Lauren said that Dimitri was one of Zeus's offspring, but I'm not getting a Zeus vibe for you."

Once again, he couldn't help the smile. "Do I even want to know?"

"Well, let me think. You're smug, smart, cunning, and yeah, light on your feet. Super fit and good reflexes, always a plus. And you know a bunch of languages, I bet."

"All of them, to some degree."

"And so modest." She rolled her eyes. "Do you work for a male or female god?"

"Male. As demigods go, they tend to present in the same sex as their patron. It's not impossible for there to be crossover, but it's trended that way."

"And you would have had plenty of time to study those trends." She made a face. "Seriously—a hundred and seventy years? Like... that's straight up Industrial Revolution, Victorian England, colonization all over the place, wars...like, all the wars forever. And you were a *diplomat* through all that, for royal family after royal family, fading in and out like a freaking vampire."

He held up a hand. "Except I can function in daylight. And enjoy actual food."

"And you've got a way better tan," she agreed, tilting her head as her eyes unfocussed a little. "Still..."

Stefan watched her process it all, her mind rabbiting from detail to detail. She wasn't the first woman he'd shared this information with...but she was the first in a very long time. He was beginning to remember why discretion had always seemed the better approach.

Once again, though, Nicki surprised him, shrugging off the monumental realization as she snapped her fingers. "I mean, we gotta go with Hermes, right? Because no way Poseidon would put up with your slow-ass breaststroke, and you're too quick-silver for the rest of them. Am I right? I gotta be right."

"Got it in one," he acknowledged with a slight inclination of his head. "And before you ask again, no, I can't fly, not in the sense you're probably thinking. My affiliation with Hermes does help me travel quickly, but the only flight I can imagine is between realms."

She blinked at him. "Realms? Like, Earth and...what, Olympus?"

"Yes, as well as Earth and the Underworld."

Her eyes rounded. "Really? You can visit Hades whenever you want?"

"I can—though to be honest, Hades isn't the best company."

"You know, I think that's totally unfair. He's got access to all the world that ever lived, he is legit beneath the ground so he knows where everything is buried—including some kickass treasure, I gotta think—and he's like, all dark and mysterious and shit. He can't be all that bad." She grinned. "Could I meet him— him, or any of the gods?"

"You...could. Not Hades, perhaps. Mortals don't trespass easily into his realm unless and until their time on Earth is up. But the others, quite possibly."

"That's so *cool!*"

Despite himself, Stefan laughed. He decided not to share the other elements of Hermes's abilities that he could tap: the luck, the manipulation, the uncanny ability to pick up another person's thoughts and certainly their emotions. That last had only happened a few times early in his journey as a demigod, with women he had loved and then watched grow old. He'd learned to become more detached after that, but that wasn't anything he wanted to share with the effervescent Nicki Clark. Not yet—probably not ever. He didn't want any clouds to mar the sunshine in her eyes.

He jolted a little at the poetic thought, also very much unlike him. Clearly, it was time to refocus on the reason for this trip together.

"You do realize that I might have to ask you to remain behind, except when we are on PR stints in Alaçati proper. The Turkish Secretary of Ministry and Culture has agreed to meet us and—"

"Oh, him," Nicki said, wrinkling her nose. "I was hoping he'd gotten run over by a bus since last year's windsurfing competition." She grimaced. "I'm sorry, that wasn't very diplomatic of me. I promise I won't talk out of turn in Alaçati."

"You know him? Hasan Omir?"

"Well enough. He's kind of a pig, you ask me. Not too surprising, given his position and the kind of power he wields, and the fact that he was dealing with an international clientele of women in bathing suits. But yeah."

Stefan frowned. "He'll be our primary contact in Alaçati. The ministry has taken a heightened focus on tourism in the area. Will that pose any difficulty?"

"On the contrary," she said. "He's a fan—or he was. I met him last year at the competition. It's sponsored by the PWA. Professional Windsurfers Association," she explained as he quirked a brow at her. "That makes it a big deal, and there's something around ten thousand competitors there every year, not to mention spectators and tourists. So Omir was on hand, and because I both competed and put up stringer reports for various windsurfing and extreme sports blogs, he was all over me. I don't expect much has changed."

He didn't like the sound of that at all, but the secretary was a problem for another day. "We'll be arriving at our initial destination at night, a small island off the coast of Alaçati. Does your camera work for nighttime photography?"

"According to Kristos, it totally does. But he's never tested it, and I've found it's not always ideal to try out new tech in unfamiliar waters. I'm not sure how much attention we'll want to draw to ourselves, especially if people are expecting the videos to go live mere hours after I take them."

"You don't seem like you're one to avoid the limelight."

"The limelight, no. The light from crackling electrical fires —that's a little more worth missing out on."

"We'll have the men test it first. They're usually game for a light show."

She shrugged. "Your funeral."

Stefan's phone buzzed in his pocket, and Nicki pushed her seat back. "I need to catch up on my feeds, actually. Is one of the sitting rooms okay, or would you prefer me to stay in my cabin?"

The request was made completely without artifice, and Stefan experienced a surge of possessiveness, a need to not let Nicki out of his sight, or out of his reach. To see if she would bend in his hands, or break, or simply melt like burnished mercury, too quick and ephemeral for him to hold.

"A moment," he said.

Nicki stopped in place as he checked his phone. Cyril. They hadn't been gone but an hour and already he was getting tagged from the palace. But he didn't have to respond immediately to the chief advisor. Cyril could wait. For these few moments, he could imagine that there was no op that might open the door to an international incident or the crushing private loss of a family lived all over again.

He could simply imagine he was on a private yacht with a woman who confounded him at every turn, yet who he wanted...needed to touch again.

He stood and Nicki waited for him to reach her.

Looking down at her, his need to respond to Cyril faded further into the background. "I confess," he murmured. "I'd very much like to continue our conversation from the beach yesterday."

She wrinkled a brow at him. "That wasn't so much a conversation. Conversations generally require *words*."

He paused, waiting for her to catch on. "Perhaps you could show me."

Nicki's smile grew wider as realization dawned. "Is this one of those things that will move the mission forward?" she asked, her clear blue eyes warming with interest.

"It's a simple request." He kept his words bland. "If you find you're unable to complete it—"

"Oh no." Nicki continued grinning as she placed her hands on his chest, bracing herself against him as she lifted to her toes. The pressure was warm, and far more welcome than he'd expected. "Far be it from me to take issue with a command order. Especially from a demigod."

She brushed her soft lips against his once, twice, exploring his mouth with hers as he bent his head nearer, allowing her to move at her own pace, touching, tasting—searching. He felt more than heard her heart rate kick up, but it did so with a quickening rush as Nicki exhaled softly before following her breath with her lips and kissing him again.

He couldn't wait any longer. He put his arm around her waist and pulled her tight. He suddenly wanted more. Far more. As much as Nicki would give him, in fact, right here, right—

His phone buzzed again.

"You know, you should probably get that," Nicki murmured against his lips. "There could have been a bomb that went off or something in the capital city, forcing us to go back."

"Oûros has an entire security force to attend to such matters."

"Yeah, well, maybe the queen wants a particular souvenir from Alaçati. You'd hate to not get her the right snow globe."

"That would indeed be a travesty." Nevertheless, Stefan kept his arm around Nicki as he swiped for his phone. He connected on the third try.

"Sir," he said as Nicki went silent in his arms.

"How much of a briefing have you had on Nicki's physical capabilities?"

Clearly overhearing, Nicki sucked in a soft breath beneath him, and even Stefan blinked. Then his own adrenaline jacked as her hands slid down his waist, swirling to the front of his trousers to where his erection tented his trousers. "Extensive, sir. Everything is well in hand."

Whether it was something in his voice or Cyril understood that this wasn't an avenue to pursue, the advisor moved on. "Very well. Let her know there are both wet and dry suits in her size aboard, but the tanks aren't sized for someone of her frame. She'll need to stick to snorkeling. Also, there are several other issues to discuss in terms of what she should and should not do once you reach Alaçati—"

Nicki stood back with a forced smile on her face. He frowned at her, but she now regarded him far too seriously.

"Problem?" he mouthed, and she shook her head, leaning up to kiss him on the cheek.

Then she was gone.

Nine

Nicki rushed back to her stateroom, her heart squeezing in her chest.

Back off, back off, back off! she implored herself. Her deep breathing didn't help until she closed the door behind her.

Did Cyril know somehow about her dizzy spells? She put her hands to her face, willing herself to relax as she tried to recall exactly what she'd overheard. The girls wouldn't have said anything—she knew they wouldn't have. But if Cyril somehow had reached out to her parents...

No. No he couldn't have. There's no way he'd let her continue on the mission if he suspected her heart might go out on her. She was overreacting. Again.

"It's okay...it's okay." Nicki blew out a long breath, smoothing her hands over her head. Stefan hadn't pursued the question, so all she needed to do was stay out of his way. She'd tell him about her fears—eventually. There was no need to yet. Not so soon after Cyril's almost-bombshell. Especially since he'd just unloaded all the juicy details of his demigod status. He'd be uneasy around her, too, at least for a little while.

She had time.

Squaring her shoulders, she walked over to the small workstation in her stateroom and booted up her computer. As the screen lit up, she thought about what Stefan had said—and how she felt about it. She knew she should feel something beyond simply that it was super cool. The man could live for hundreds of years! Who did that? Nobody outside of Oûros, she was pretty sure. Hell, he'd outlive her by a *lot*—

Even as those words hit her brain, she rolled her eyes. Who cared how long he could live? She barely knew the man, and they weren't a thing. They weren't even a half-thing. Well, maybe a half-thing. Demi-thing? She grinned. Yeah, that.

With a final chuckle, she shook her head and bent to her work.

They reached the tiny island off the coast of Turkey close to midnight, but a storm had blown up late in the day from the southern Aegean, and the sea was too rough to allow for diving. After she'd finished her blogs for the day, Nicki used the time to go over the gear. She'd need a wetsuit, even for snorkeling. It was only June, and the Aegean would be too cold for comfort if she and whoever tag-teamed with her stayed in the water for any length of time.

Stefan remained tied up with Cyril for most of the night, as far as she could tell. Despite his dismissal of the idea, apparently he was a necessary component to the functioning of the Oûros government. Either way, the following morning Nicki marched resolutely up to the deck, carrying her underwater camera in its case. She wasn't going to be underfoot, she wasn't going to be in Stefan's way. That was her promise, and she was sticking to it.

Stefan hadn't, however, specifically forbidden her from exploring underwater. So at least this glorious morning wouldn't be a total loss.

After checking her own gear, Nicki rubbed her sternum absently as she once more studied the last and most important piece of equipment, the underwater camera. As Kristos had promised, it was state of the art, featuring all the bells and whistles for shooting high-definition action. So if there were any really fast fish out there, she was ready.

"Everything up to your standards?"

Nicki jumped, though she'd been half-expecting Stefan to check in before he and his team left the boat for the scavenger encampment. Now his presence filled the small deck as he strode toward her. He was dressed in loose pants and a microfiber shirt, as always cool and unflappable, while she could feel her skin begin to prickle beneath her swimsuit and water pants, heat flushing through her in waves.

"It's great!" she said, too loudly, then modified her tone. "It's great. I thought you were gone already."

"I have two teams out already," he said. "Depending on what they find, I'll go—or we'll go." He eyed her. "Cyril contacted me again an hour ago, saying that the viewership of your videos was at a clip large enough to appear legitimate, and the more we could feed of every stop, the better, as long as we didn't run into any problems."

He delivered this information neutrally, and Nicki frowned. "Is that a good thing or a bad thing, that the posts are working?"

Stefan's lips quirked up. "For your role as cover, I would say it's a good thing." He gestured to the equipment. "And for the moment, it affords us a few hours to try out all the toys Kristos sent along."

Us? Nicki stared as Stefan slicked out of his shirt. She'd seen the man in swim trunks before, but he'd already been in the water at the time. For some reason, having him standing right in front of her, dry and half-naked was kicking everything in her body up a few notches. He stopped, seemingly concerned by her staring. "You didn't think I'd let you go in alone, did you?"

"What? No," Nicki blurted. "I mean, I thought you were gone, that one of the crew members would go with me."

He shrugged and she watched as the muscles rippled across his sun-bronzed skin. She wouldn't have expected his tan to be so deep, given his role in the royal family. She pictured him wearing tuxedos and sipping martinis, not diving off the side of boats. Then again, demigod. Maybe gorgeously perma-tanned skin came with the package. "You, um, dive a lot?"

"Not diving, usually. But snorkeling, yes. It would be difficult to live someplace like Oûros and not take advantage of all the ocean had to offer." He picked up a snorkeling mask and proffered it to her. "Unless you think we'll need the tanks?"

"No—not for this first outing, and probably not at all. How deep is the water?"

The conversation steered easily onto safer topics, and Nicki followed Stefan across the deck, inhaling and exhaling slowly and carefully as she watched his muscles stretch and work beneath his skin. Even his trousers seemed tailor-made to make her stare, the fabric stretching over the thick muscles of his legs. She'd seen the guy practically naked already, but...

"One thing," Stefan turned to her, then waited as she jerked her eyes up from his ass to meet his gaze. His smirk told her that he knew exactly what she'd been staring at. "Tamas, one of the men, will be going with us as well. It should appear as if it's only the two of you down there. I should not be in any of the video feeds. You should be in the water with a single subject, not surrounded by guards. And I shouldn't be in the water at all, merely tapped for this assignment as a political representative of Oûros. You understand?"

Nicki nodded. "I'll keep you out of the frames, or we'll catch it in the editing pass before I push the videos live." Inside, however, her spirits deflated a little. Stefan's warnings reminded her that this wasn't the joy ride it was being touted as. More importantly, however, she'd thought she could capture some video of the man in the water. He truly had the most amazing body, and if she could have some souvenir video clips, it'd make all of this last a little while longer.

Oh well.

Within minutes, they were in the water, the sudden shock of it a balm to her senses and a needed distraction for both her body and mind. As promised, Tamas proved to be a willing subject, and they spent the morning coasting over an honest-to-God sunken ship that was clearly visible through the water, shallow caves filled with brilliantly colored fish, and rock forma-tions that glinted and burned with the reflection of the sun.

To the absolute shock of no one, Stefan's swimming abilities in the open sea were every bit as graceful as when he'd been in the palace lap pool, and she longed to capture him on video. With great effort she resisted—*Herculean* effort, she thought, which made her grin again. For his part, Stefan swam out and around, circling them in a wide arc, and some of the equipment he carried on his own weight belt looked suspiciously lethal. Another reminder that despite all appearances, this wasn't really a lazy afternoon in the Aegean.

Nicki was legitimately tired by the time they pulled them-selves out of the water, gratefully accepting Stefan's help as he took her equipment and stacked it on the deck.

"Stay here," he said when she cleared the ladder. He was already stripping out of his wet suit, and she followed his lead. "There's food, and we can see what you recorded. It'll save time."

She watched him as he took the camera and popped the drive, transferring it to a large-screened laptop that had been brought to a shaded alcove of the deck. She grabbed a handful of grapes and a towel, then flopped down on a teak bench to dry herself off as Stefan reviewed the footage.

It was as spectacular as she'd hoped it would be when viewing it under water. The fish were large and exotic. The centuries-old boat—while no bastion of lost treasure—was charmingly authentic, and the Oûrois guard Tamas was handsome and fit and truly at home in the water. There were shots of Nicki, too, taken by Tamas to continue the illusion that they were the only two down there, as she glided over a thick coral bed, then pointed the camera toward the glittering, glinting surface of the rocks.

Abruptly, Stefan's hand shot out and froze the screen. "What is that?" he asked, the impassive calm of his voice at odds with the urgency of his fingers on the trackpad.

Nicki stopped toweling her hair.

"That's great, isn't it?" she asked. "Something bright stuck into the coral. I assumed it was debris, but the way it's wedged in there is cool. It's obsidian, maybe—or some sort of thick glass. Something cut with facets to reflect all that sunlight." She pointed to two bright spots.

"Tamas." Stefan turned and spoke rapid Oûrois to the other man, who stared from him to the screen, then stood and crossed the deck to scoop up his discarded snorkeling mask.

Nicki frowned. "What?" she asked. "What do you see?"

"The chunk of glass you're pointing out could be simply glass, nothing more. Rock. Debris. But it also could be glass that has been shattered into specific facets, such as the glass monitors of aircraft tracking equipment."

Her eyes widened. "You don't think it's part of Ari's plane?"

"I don't." he shook his head definitively. "It could be anything. If it's debris, it could be from any plane that has flown over this space and crashed in the last five years. It's unreasonable that it belongs to Ari's craft. But it's at least evidence that planes have crashed here—potentially recent planes. And that's a start."

He stood abruptly. "Go get dressed. I want you to go with us ashore after Tamas recovers a chunk of that glass."

Ten

S tefan scowled as he faced into the wind, their small speedboat cutting across the water at a rapid clip, bisecting the azure waters as they approached the shoreline of the small island. His men had located the scavenger band's leader, who'd been more than willing to talk to them. The previous night's storm had yielded more gifts from the sea, and he had much to sell.

Stefan had much to sell, too. And now so did Nicki, unwittingly. The information she had on her video cam, if proven to be a connection to Prince Ari's airplane, was both good and bad news. Good, if Ari was found alive or dead, without foul play involved. Bad, if the king and queen had indisputable cause to do a full-scale search in this area—an area which wasn't Oûrois territory, but Turkish. The nightmare of navigating the politics of those permissions, and the inherent insinuation that the Turkish government hadn't done all they could to find Ari's plane or the remains of the son of one of its neighbors and supposed allies, wasn't a possibility he relished.

Worse, Nicki knew where that wreckage was. So if someone

wanted that information buried, she'd be the first person in line to be buried as well.

He grimaced. There were a lot of ifs in that statement, and he more than most knew the danger of getting too caught up in ifs. Part of what made him successful for the past century and a half was his ability to focus only on what mattered to the job at hand.

And what mattered at this moment was keeping Nicki out of access to anyone but him, until they returned her safely home to Oûros.

Home. His lips twisted at the word. The palace wasn't really his home, but it was the closest he'd probably get in all his long lifetime—an institution so entrenched in Oûros, it would outlive even him. His father had been a distant cousin to the king, but Stefan hadn't known the royal family well until after the accident that had taken his parents' lives. The reigning monarch at that time, King Orlof, had taken him in when he'd been barely fourteen years old, an idiot teen by any standard, and one who was perpetually angry at the world.

King Orlof and Queen Ida, King Jasen's great-great-great grandparents, had welcomed Stefan into the palace without question or conversation. They'd showered him with faith and understanding, and they'd asked for nothing in return but his unstinting service. He had given them that, and when his demigod nature had surfaced at age eighteen and he'd been given the opportunity to extend his service to god, Crown, and country at the age of twenty, he'd agreed to it with all his heart. He could do no less, and from generation to generation, monarch to monarch, he'd never regretted the decision. One of the high counselors to King Orlof had told him, sagely, that "after the first death, there is no other," and he'd found that to be true. He didn't consider himself heartless, but...witnessing the passage of time and even death *had* gotten easier, over time.

Beside him, Nicki sat forward on the edge of her seat with her lips pressed tightly together, clearly excited to be along for the op but trying hard not to show it. He tightened his jaw, thinking of what she'd heard in the conference room at the palace. He hadn't been wrong. She shouldn't have been asked to do this. But she wanted so badly to succeed...

He frowned, a new thought striking him. What was behind Nicki's urgency, exactly?

Stefan knew enough not to imagine it was solely because she was swept up in her attraction to him. So why? By all accounts, she was successful at her work. She was strong and fierce, and her friends and family adored her. Arguably, he hadn't read Nicki's dossier as closely as Emmaline's, after Prince Kristos had begun showering the girl with attention. Nicki had been a distant third in his concern behind the wide-eyed Emmaline and the shrewd-tongued Lauren. She was content to be in the background. Particularly if that background had a wall she could climb.

He pressed his lips together, considering. Despite Hermes's many gifts to his demigods, full-on mind reading wasn't one of Stefan's skillsets. He had a remarkable gift for reading emotions, though, especially for those he knew well. So what was Nicki's motivation?

She must have sensed his attention, because she turned at that moment, catching his expression. She grinned widely then, letting some of her excitement leach out before grabbing at the edge of the speedboat as the driver abruptly banked. They'd arrived.

Their trip had taken them around the southern tip of the island, facing out to sea. Stefan couldn't see any of the mainland from this vantage point, though it was only a few miles distant, and instead his attention focused on a small collection of huts that peeked out of the thick vegetation, virtually undetectable unless you were looking for them.

When they reached the sand, Stefan handed Nicki a broad scarf. "Hair and face," he instructed, and she complied without comment. Much of Turkey embraced Western ideas regarding a woman's need to cover herself in public, but Stefan wasn't taking any chances with these outliers. And Nicki didn't bat an eye—again, she was following orders, and delighted to do so. Her bright eyes took in everything, and her mouth stayed firmly shut.

They trooped up to the scavenger dealer and after quick orders delivered in Oûrois, Stefan and one man continued on while Nicki, flanked by guards who were trying to act like anything other than her protectors, stopped at a lean-to bristling with junk. She and the guards would pretend to paw through the offerings while Stefan met with the dealer. Without another word, he and his lone guard moved on.

The dealer sat outside his hut, beneath a large fabric shade. He was fat in the way once-strong men often were, layers of softness obscuring but not negating the tough core beneath. He nodded as Stefan walked up, then focused on his team.

"Who is the woman?"

"Guest. Didn't trust her alone on the boat."

The dealer smiled, displaying cracked teeth. "Always a good idea, that. Not worth being wrong." He spoke Turkish, and he gave his full attention to Stefan. "Big man, big boat. Your people clearly thought I had something of value to offer you. What do you need?" He didn't offer specifics, but Stefan suspected everything was on the table—guns, ammo, jewelry, drugs.

"Information." He pulled out a printed photo of Ari's wrist-watch adorning the wrist of the fisherman. They'd staged the photo to have the watch in close proximity to the man's face.

"Six months ago you sold this watch to that man," he said, stabbing his finger at the photo. "Do you remember?"

The older man squinted at the photo and appeared to consider his options. "I sell a great many things."

"And you sold this honorably," Stefan said. "The man said you'd received it in exchange for several items from a man. This man?"

He held out a picture of Ari and waited. The photo was of Ari working on his plane, dressed in what amounted to rags for him. But he was clean and healthy, obviously the son of a rich man. With luck the dealer didn't realize exactly who he was, but—

The man shook his head. "That man? No. That's not who sold it to me. He was a small man, not Greek. Maybe Egyptian. Crazy in the head." He touched his temple. "That man in the photo would not have traded the watch for a leaky boat and food. He is too smart for that, eh? Too smart to sell a watch at all, I'm thinking. There would be a story there."

Stefan pocketed the photo. "The Egyptian man, you ever see him again?"

The dealer shrugged. "No, but didn't expect to. He was drunk—gave me his flask too." He grinned. "Idiot. Didn't know what he had, either the booze or the watch. Maybe he got it from your friend, eh?"

Stefan smiled right along with him, but his heart knifed sideways. "Flask—you have it?"

"Yes, but it's not for sale." The man gestured to the table, his shrewd eyes missing nothing as Stefan turned. He didn't have to search hard. The flask had primacy of place on the man's side table, sticking out from the trash like a rose among thorns. It was six inches tall and three inches wide, a mixture of metal and waterproof leather.

And, in the bottom right corner, there was a defect. A part

of the leather had been burned away...where the flask had once been stamped with the symbol of Oûros.

Stefan's next move wasn't so much planned as instinctual. Rationally, he knew the man could be telling the truth. There could have been a mysterious Egyptian man, drunk from Ari's own flask. That man could have killed Ari, taken his valuables, and pawned them off. It was all totally reasonable.

He launched himself at the big man anyway.

The dealer shouted in alarm to alert his guards, and Stefan had the vaguest sense of guards rushing out of the next lean-to with semi-automatic rifles.

They were too late.

Hermes *had* gifted Stefan with lightning-quick reaction speeds. By the time the guards cleared the door, Stefan had knocked the dealer off his chair with a roundhouse punch and divested the dealer of his own gun. He pushed the weapon up against the man's temple before the dealer finished bouncing off the woven mat.

"First, call off your men," Stefan snapped. "Then, tell me the truth. I have money, friend. Money and nothing but good-will for you. I kill you, and your men won't mourn. They'll take all your money and goods and set up their own shop. I don't want that and neither do you. But I'm going to need the truth."

Eleven

⤳⤳

Nicki stood frozen inside the lean-to, the guards on either side of her aiming their pistols out at men who were now aiming back at them. Both sets of guns looked powerful enough to cause a lot of damage, but no one fired.

The big man in the hut—she assumed it was him—yelled something and all the men eased up slightly. Then the hut's guards stepped back and lowered their guns, backing away.

"What's going on?" she asked between her teeth.

"Let's get into the sightline of Ambassador Mihal. He'll want to see you're unharmed." Tamas's words were low and quiet. "Don't worry. This means the negotiation is going well."

She stared at him but did as he directed, moving into the doorway of the hut but no further. She was still protected by the flimsy frame of the hut and the less flimsy frames of her bodyguards. Stefan flicked his gaze toward her and then turned back to face the big man. They both stood close together. On the table between them sat a black neoprene bag—which contained money, she was nearly certain. The big man started gesticulating wildly and Stefan regarded him steadily, calm as always. She couldn't understand a word of what they were saying, and

Tamas remained silent. She didn't need to know, she reminded herself. She only needed to do what was required.

And what was required was apparently that she stay in Stefan's sightline.

While she stood, her eyes scanned the hunks of debris that counted as viable artifacts for sale. Clothing, oddly enough. Shoes. Some jewelry, but all cheap stuff. Radios and electronic components scavenged from God only knew where. Towels and soap. All the island luxuries, she supposed. There wasn't anything that appeared worth stealing, and even if she'd been so inclined, the presence of all the large men and large guns proved a significant deterrent.

She didn't have long to wait, fortunately. Within about five minutes, Stefan stood back from the man, gesturing to the moneybag. The man nodded and watched him with beady eyes as Stefan signaled to Tamas. The two guards moved out, with her in the middle, and they left the tiny collection of huts behind. Stefan joined them less than ten minutes later as they slowly made their way along the beach.

"We stop here," he said abruptly as they followed the shore-line. "Tamas, stand watch with the others. Nicki, get the blue camera out of the bag. The blue one, not the black."

She gaped at him as the men fanned out. Tamas handed her another black bag. "I don't know what this is," she said quietly as she pulled the blue camera out.

"Point and click like you're a tourist. We'll need proof you were on this island for a legitimate reason if our friend back there gets cute and tries to cause trouble. He won't betray his own hand, but he'll betray ours if there's money in it."

"Oh." She still didn't understand. The camera wasn't behaving like her normal one. It generated readings she couldn't decipher, but she willingly moved it around the gorgeous view, from the forest to the beach to the shoreline and open waters.

"Turn back toward me, click it off," Stefan said. "Now take this one."

He handed her the camera she'd been using on the yacht, a standard video cam. "Take a second sweep. Keep away from the direction of the scavenger camp."

She did as he asked, realizing suddenly that the first camera added to her purpose here. She was the cover, but she could do useful things as the cover. Even if she didn't understand them.

"We good?" Tamas asked the question after she finished the second sweep, and Stefan nodded.

"They would've attacked already if they were going to," he said. "We're in the clear. Debrief on the boat. At this point, we leisurely head back with Nicki snapping random photos, full view. No guns."

Nicki snorted. "Like they don't know you have guns under your tunics."

"We aren't the only ones snapping pictures," Stefan murmured. "Satellites and drone technology haven't reached much of Turkey, but we can't take that chance. To all the world, we visited a well-traveled scavenger hut, took lots of pretty pictures of birds and beach grass, then headed back to our boat."

"And what did we—" Nicki clamped her lips shut. She didn't need to know the information at this exact moment, she told herself. She could follow directions and be a good team member.

Beside her, Stefan chuckled.

They were back aboard the yacht within the hour, and Stefan dismissed the men, leading Nicki to a small cabin on the second level. The room bristled with communications equipment, and he flipped several units on. Within moments, Cyril was on the screen.

"Report," the chief advisor said, flicking his glance to Nicki. Then they both turned to Stefan, whose face had hardened.

"Who's with you?" Stefan asked.

Cyril didn't hesitate. "I'm alone. King Jasen is due here in ten minutes."

"You can speak to him, then, and decide what you need to share. The dealer saw Ari," Stefan said, his words clipped. "Timing was roughly a year, and from his description Ari was seriously injured, appearing concussed at a minimum, possibly brain-damaged. He was raving and disoriented. He didn't identify himself, and didn't mention that he'd crash-landed his plane."

"But he was alive." Cyril's eyes had widened. "He survived the initial crash."

"He was alive. He traded his watch and flask for a boat and food. The boat leaked, but he didn't seem to care, said he could fix it."

Cyril snorted. "Sounds like Ari."

"Agreed. He was sure he didn't need to go far, which points to some lucidity. The island isn't far from the mainland. He didn't appear to have money but the dealer couldn't swear to that. His clothes were ragged and torn and not of good quality."

Cyril frowned. "Not of good quality."

"Yes. Which means he'd encountered someone else first, before going to the dealer. Whether he did that intentionally to dress down for the sale of his goods or not, I don't know." Stefan paused. "According to his own testimony, the dealer suspected that something was wrong with the scenario, but took the deal. He sat on the watch for about six months before our fisherman visited him, saw the watch, and bought it from him. The dealer kept the flask. He gave it to me today."

Stefan reached into his bag and pulled the flask free, holding it up to the camera. "Seal was here." He said, pointing. "Looks maybe burned, then defaced. But it's Ari's."

"A year ago. Directly after he crashed." Cyril blew out a breath. "No sightings since?"

"None. The Turkish mainland is populated all along that coast, but there is a significant coastal park due east of here. If that was Ari's target, he could potentially survive there for a short time. That park is also known for smugglers and merchant bands, however, so it makes his whereabouts thereafter more problematic."

"You can go there?"

"We can. Nicki has taken enough footage to add veracity to her story of an adventure reporter. But the trail grows more complicated from here. We can dispatch the men to follow up on leads, but our time in Alaçati is short. We can't draw too much attention."

"Then we create a foothold and continue the search another way." Cyril nodded. "Go—go to where you most think Ari would have landed, if he wanted to avoid people. We'll send another team to follow up if you think there's a possibility."

"We'll be there in a few hours, and drop anchor overnight," Stefan said. "We'll enter the city tomorrow morning."

He and Cyril spoke on for a few more minutes, while Nicki's mind churned with possibilities. As usual, Stefan's report had been bland, matter of fact. But there'd been nothing ordinary about the information he'd dropped.

Prince Ari hadn't died in the fiery wreck as everyone had feared. He had—at least for a little while—survived and had had the wherewithal to get himself a boat and food. Where had he gone from there, though? Eventually, someone would have recognized him, or at least recognized his value. Why hadn't anyone notified the royal family? Whether for ransom or out of goodwill?

Nicki stared at the small, unassuming flask.

If Ari was alive...where was he?

Twelve

Stefan cut communications with Cyril, then swiveled toward Nicki. Her gaze lifted from the flask.

"Do you think it's possible he's out there, somewhere?" she asked. "Still alive after all this time?"

He realized with a start that he didn't have to lie to her or couch his words in any way, and the awareness was remarkably...refreshing. Nicki didn't want an answer she could use as a shield or a tool. She simply wanted information to act more intelligently. Information to her was power, but not for playing diplomatic games.

"No," he said, honestly. "It's most likely that he made it to the mainland and was ambushed in his weakened state, robbed and killed, his body dumped or buried. The fact that he survived the crash is a victory for the royal family. The fact that his mind was probably damaged will be a source of endless despair for Queen Catherine. So, it's a trade-off, and not necessarily a good trade-off."

Nicki nodded. "She'll want to know though."

"She'll want to know. And then she'll be furious that she knows and isn't doing more to get all the other answers she so desperately desires. So Cyril will hold off on telling King Jasen for as long as possible, at least that part of it. Once the king knows, it's inevitable that Catherine will find out."

Nicki's expression was wry, and he found himself wondering about her parents, back in the US. The dossier on them had been scant—they were both alive, and there was a brother, too, he was almost certain.

He decided to press the point. "You smile as if you know the type," he said. "Do your parents have a similar relationship?"

"My parents?" she blinked at him. "Ah—no. They're good people, but they're both a little too wrapped up in their own separate worlds to pay too much attention to each other's."

She spoke the words without heat, or even much sadness. When she noted his surprise, she shrugged. "That's probably unfair. I haven't been home for months, between work and the travel for work. But either way, for Mom to see through Dad would involve them talking, and they don't do a lot of that—or they didn't used to. With my brother out of the house finally, maybe they do."

So he'd been right about the brother. "He's graduated college?"

"Not yet, but he's at least in the dorm building there." She grimaced. "He couldn't imagine leaving home to go to school, while I couldn't wait to get out. I guess it's part of being a girl."

"A girl who likes to climb mountains and enter windsurfing competitions."

"A very specialized girl, then." Nicki laughed, and Stefan felt a surge of awareness shiver through him. He stood. Tomorrow they'd be in Alaçati, no matter what the stopover at the coastal park would net them. They'd be surrounded by people. Today remained bright and full, filled with possibility, and there was the smallest chance that a man the whole country had mourned was alive and healthy. For this moment, the entire ocean was at their feet.

"Come," he said. "We'll be setting off soon, but there's time for another swim."

"Can't," she said ruefully. She pointed to the camera. "I need to cut that video into some vlogs and prepare posts with the images from the camera." She hesitated. "You could—help, if you wanted?" she asked. "If you're not too busy?"

He let his own smile break open wide, the expression still foreign on his face. "I'd like that very much."

The video editing and social media posting process took longer than he anticipated they would. The yacht was prepared for departure and well underway to the parklands outside of Alaçati before Nicki finally sat back from her computer screen. They had half a dozen posts uploaded to what seemed an enthusiastic response, and more prepared for uploading overnight and the next day. Others were nearly finished should they have a need for more filler shots of a "generic deserted island getaway."

Now Nicki's stomach growled audibly, and she smacked her hand over her belly. "Sorry," she said, but he shook his head.

"You've more than earned a meal. While you were busy ensuring that we have done all that we need to shore up our bona fides, I've arranged to have dinner sent to my stateroom. There's a private deck there with an excellent view."

She lifted her brows. "You're inviting me back to your room? It's only six o'clock."

He smiled back, more than willing to put her at ease. "We do things differently in this part of the world."

Dinner was served less than an hour later, accompanied by white wine in sturdy glasses. The yacht had cut its speed to bare cruising level, and the wind curled deliciously over the deck as they neared the lush green coastline of Turkey. "How close can we get?" Nicki asked. "Are there laws for that I assume?"

"There are. The Turkish Coast Guard has been notified of our arrival and our guest manifest. We've provided links to your posts in the spirit of full cooperation. That and the fact that the online response has been positive has served us well."

"Yeah?" she brightened. "I haven't really been paying attention to the traffic. It's been good?"

"It's been good, and it's been expressive of the beauty of the Turkish seaside. The comments of surprise have been met with tourists speaking up, those who have visited before all the current unrest, sharing their travel stories about the country. Cyril has been in touch with the Turkish Ministry of Culture and Tourism, and they're taking note. It's an excellent way to strengthen our cover." He lifted his glass to her. "I was wrong to make light of your work," he said. "You're good at it, and it's proven very valuable."

"Oh," Nicki said. "Thanks." She smoothed her fingers over her napkin for about the fifteenth time, creating a crease in the perfectly folded fabric.

"What will you do next, when all this is done and you return home?" he asked, eyeing her. She seemed unreasonably nervous around him, more so than when they'd been on the mainland together.

"Yeah, well, I really don't know. I'm starting to see good money for my adventure articles and from advertising on my channel. Not change-your-life money, but at least something that makes me think it will be worthwhile to pursue for a little bit. My parents want me to come back to Indianapolis—" Her lip curled. "But that doesn't interest me at all. There's too much of the world left to see, you know?" As soon as she said the words, she looked like she wanted to take them back. "Well, of course you know. You may be living in the middle of a fairy tale kingdom, but I bet you travel all over the place—and probably have for over a hundred years. Jeez, the things you must have seen in all that time."

Stefan nodded, warmed despite himself at the admiration in her eyes. It had been a long time since he'd spoken so freely about his nature to anyone. "I frequently travel with the royal family, or serve as an envoy if they're not able to attend certain functions," he said. "And yes, I've traveled to just about every major nation in the world over the years. There's a certain luxury in having a place to call home, though."

"I guess so." Nicki shrugged, playing with the glass of wine. "Maybe if I travel around for a few more years, maybe I'll get tired of it. Then I'll think about settling down." She made a face. "As long as it's not Indianapolis. My mom's bad enough with asking me every other week if I've found someone nice. If I lived across the city from her, she'd be on my doorstep."

He considered her statement, and the opportunity it provided him. Had she deliberately opened that door? He couldn't help walking through it. "And you haven't found someone nice, I take it."

"Yeah, no. I don't really attract nice," Nicki said with a quick smile. She took another drink of her wine. "The men I tend to attract are hunting for a climbing buddy, not a girlfriend. And I can climb plenty of mountains with other people. Those who do say they want to settle down mean mainly that they want someone else to be the adult while they go off and still play." She shrugged. "And I'm every bit as bad. This job of travel blogger isn't exactly upwardly mobile. The moment I have an accident or get tired, there's someone else out there who can do it every bit as well, and at a lower price. So I think I'll find a real job before I worry too much about finding a real boyfriend, you know?"

Stefan watched her as she spoke, turning all the information around in his mind. She was single in every sense of the word, unmoored from either place or person. He already had the sense that she would rather fling herself off a cliff than build a house on one, and the image amused him. He suspected she wasn't telling him everything, but that was okay. First off, he didn't truly need to know. Secondly, they had time.

In fact, if he had any say in the matter, they would have lots of time during the remainder of this trip to get to know each other...starting now.

Thirteen

Nicki sat back in her chair and watched the sun sink lower over the horizon. She'd been to Turkey before, of course. This exact location, less than a year earlier. But she hadn't come here via private yacht, she'd come by economy plane, and she'd stayed in a quaint hotel that had shared bathrooms down the hallway.

Viewing the country from the deck of a freaking royal yacht was definitely a step up in the world.

She knew that Stefan was watching her, but for once, the prospect of his attention didn't fill her with nervousness or doubt—merely excitement. And not the excitement of cliff diving either. Or not exactly. The jump was the same, sure...but she knew she'd be totally safe at the bottom of the drop. Maybe she wouldn't be the second time she stepped into the open air, but this time...yes.

The thought made her twist her lips ruefully. Her one-time-only preference was really less of a rule than what had become the natural order of things, but it seriously worked for her. She scared off most men before they got to the first kiss, though that clearly hadn't been a problem with Stefan. The rest of the few guys she'd kissed she'd never really cared to see again, but those she did—after the second time, that was it.

Sometimes the decision was mutual, sometimes the guy simply drifted away. Most of the time she distanced herself— usually by heading off on a new adventure living halfway around the world. Her heart was unpredictable, and she would not—could not—endure the expression on someone's face when they learned that she had an off-the-charts risk factor that had nothing to do with her next snowboarding run.

But Stefan had several built-in failsafes against anything serious coming from a hookup between them. First off, he was a highly placed diplomat smack in the middle of a freaking royal family, which meant the guy stayed busy. Secondly, he was a flippin' *demigod* who was pushing 200 *years old*, which probably meant he wasn't exactly looking to hook up long-term with anyone. Thirdly, he—

His amused voice cut across her thoughts. "Do I want to know what you're thinking?"

"Hmm?" Nicki refocused, fast. "Nothing too deep, I promise. It's just so incredibly beautiful here—and so peaceful." She gestured to the coastline with her wine glass. "Which is amusing given what goes on in this country. It's not peaceful at all, I'm sure. But from out here..."

"Altering distance can provide an enhanced perspective." Stefan laid his napkin on the table, then stood. He reached out a hand and she put her fingers in his, feeling the zing of anticipation when he drew her to her feet. "For example, I find my perspective improves greatly when I'm closer to you."

He turned her in his arms until she was facing outward again, her back to his chest. She could feel the pulse of his heartbeat in this intimate embrace and the strength of it startled her. Forget the whole demigod thing. Stefan was alive, real, and more *vital* than any guy she'd ever met. He was capable, yes, but it went beyond that. She'd never once felt endangered today at the scavenger's encampment, when by all rights she should have. And the moment Tamas had urged her to move into Stefan's sight line, she'd experienced an almost surreal sense of calm—her heart steady, her mind certain.

She felt the same way now. Stefan covered her hands with his and brought them up, so that both his hands and hers were crossed over her heart. She closed her eyes and leaned back at him, willing the tears that sparked behind her eyes to go away. He didn't understand the significance of what he was doing. He didn't understand the symbolism of protecting her greatest weakness. And there was absolutely nothing sexy about a girl who cried the first time she had sex with a guy. Tears were so not going to happen.

"I suspect you're thinking too much again," Stefan said, leaning forward to brush his lips against her hair. "For a woman of action such as you, it's a surprising defense."

Nicki snorted, and her tension unraveled that much more, her back muscles easing until she leaned more heavily against Stefan's rock-hard chest. "I should be verifying whether this particular activity is moving our mission forward, shouldn't I?" she asked, smiling as he tightened his hold on her. She was surrounded by the strength of his body, its solidity. This may be ground that she hadn't covered in some time, but Stefan moved without hesitation.

He dropped his head down near her ear, his breath soft against her hair. "I assure you, this is absolutely essential to ensuring the mission goes off without a hitch. You trust me, don't you?"

With my life. The words were so forceful in her own mind it was a miracle she hadn't spoken them out loud. Instead, she managed a breathy, "Of course."

"Then I think it might be best if I tell you what to do at this point. So there's no confusion."

Nicki stiffened a little, and Stefan's chuckle was deep and rolling, filled with masculine certainty. "And here I thought you could take direction. Going back on your word, Nicki?"

The tension filled her to bursting then crested over again, and she sighed against him. "Not at all. You ask for it, you get it, though. So be prepared."

"Excellent. I think this will work out for us both." He loosened his hands on hers. "Turn around. I want to see you."

Obligingly, Nicki turned in Stefan's arms. No sooner had she done so than he lifted his hands to her face, drawing her closer to him. His lips brushed hers and she caught her breath as he nuzzled her mouth. "You taste like the sky," he murmured, and his voice held a note of wonder that made her stomach tighten and her limbs feel a little too loose, too unsteady.

She lifted a hand to his chest, feeling the steady beating of his heart. He leaned back from her and stared at her intently. "I want to make love to you underneath the open sky," he said, his lips quirking into a rueful grin. "Unfortunately, I can only trust my men so far."

Her eyes widened. She hadn't expected that. "Would they spy on you?"

"I would if I were them. So this is the better option." He held out a hand and pulled her back into the shadowy confines of the room, but he left the large French doors open to the deck, the brilliant sky beginning to turn a soft orange. In the shadows, Nicki almost felt self-conscious again, but Stefan didn't give her a chance to back down.

"Now where were we," he murmured, stepping close to her. "Oh yes." He dropped his head to hers as his hands came up to cradle her face in his palms. "Yes, much better."

This time, when he kissed her he didn't restrain himself to nuzzling her lips. He pressed firmly, insistently, and her lips opened naturally against his, the silky intrusion of his tongue foreign and right all at once. Her heart rate picked up then, but only in the best possible way, and she wrapped her fingers around his. He pulled away from her and his eyes glittered with intensity. "I think the next directive is definitely that you surrender your clothes."

A strange flare of power shivered through Nicki. Sex to her had always been merely recreational, but with Stefan, all of a sudden it felt momentous, like every second was something she wanted to preserve in her memory banks. She stepped back and grimaced down at her serviceable tank and cargo pants—perfect for a walk into a scavenger's den, but not for seduction. "I'm afraid there's no easy way to do a strip tease with these," she said.

"That's good," Stefan said. "Because I have no interest in waiting for one." He walked her backward until the back of her legs hit the bed. "If you're not out of those clothes in the next thirty seconds, however, I can't be responsible for what I do."

"Noted." She pulled off her tank with one tug, then dropped her pants to the floor, leaving her standing only in her underwear. She thought Stefan would stop her—after all, he'd seen her this naked already—but he didn't. So with a slight hesitation, she reached behind her back to unhook her bra, letting it fall forward.

If she had any doubts about how he would react to her body, his expression of profound pleasure resolved them.

"Perfect," he muttered.

Fourteen

Stefan was nearly out of his head with need as Nicki reached down to shimmy her panties down her legs, her body everything he knew it would be—and not simply because he'd seen her with a swimsuit plastered to it a few hours before. Her muscles moved sleekly beneath her skin and practically shouted of her strength and flexibility to take on any challenge.

He wasn't sure she was ready to take on him, but he was more than willing to find out.

"I'm kind of feeling under—hey!" Nicki gasped as he bent forward and flattened her on the mattress, half tossing her toward the head of the bed where a dozen pillows waited to cushion her fall. Then he climbed after her, his hands sliding up the outside of her legs as he rose to his knees.

"You're still dressed," she protested, giggling as he leaned into her. "And maybe you've never done this before, but you definitely don't want to be dressed for the next part."

"Maybe I'll kiss you for a while first," he murmured, deepening the kiss for a long, silken moment. Strangely, however, she didn't relax. He pulled away and met her searching gaze. "You don't like to be kissed?"

Her return smile was quick, but a touch of uncertainty remained. "I really, really want to see you without your clothes on. Any of them."

He recognized the overture for what it was, and rolled with it. "Perhaps you could help me out with that."

"I definitely can." She lifted her hands to the edge of his shirt and pushed it up, the heels of her hands pressing against his abs, then his pecs as she bunched the material up in her fingers. She pushed the shirt over his head then focused on his chest, the appreciation in her eyes sending a jolt of awareness straight through him, pooling in his groin. In fact, his cock was presently the most aware part of his body, by far.

Her gaze dropped to his waist, then further down, and her smile turned satisfied. "See? I told you clothes would quickly become a liability."

He sat up, but stayed on his knees and she unbuckled his cargo pants and pushed them down over his hips, dragging his boxer briefs with them. But while his legs were trapped with his pants around his thighs she shifted her hands, reaching forward to cup his balls in one palm while the other encircled his shaft.

"I see what you mean," Stefan said as she squeezed him, but Nicki wasn't paying any attention to him anymore. She moved with surprising speed to take him deeply into her mouth, the burst of sensation so immediate and shocking that he sucked in a breath in a startled gasp—then she slid away from him.

"Like that?"

"I—" before he could complete the thought, she leaned forward again. Stefan's sight dimmed as she sucked hard, her light grasp on his balls growing more insistent. This time when she broke free, she was more intent.

"You really need to lose the pants," she muttered, shimmying out from underneath him.

"I thought I was the one giving directives." Nevertheless, he let her push him to the side onto the wide mattress, and he rolled over onto his back as she yanked what remained of his clothes free of his legs.

"Trust me, this is for the good of the mission. You'll thank me later." She positioned herself between his legs and leaned down once more.

"I think I'll be thanking you right now," he said, his words ending on a moan as she nuzzled his stiff shaft.

"Mm," Nicki responded, the vibration of the word making him shudder in response. "I think I'm going to be taking over from here, if you don't mind?"

Stefan groaned. "I want you to do whatever you want," he said, and she glanced up at him, her eyes alight at the guttural rasp of his voice.

"Really?" she asked.

"Really."

"Then I want to do this." Nicki drew her face along the side of his engorged shaft as she watched him. "I want to take you in my mouth 'til you explode."

Stefan couldn't stop his eyes from flaring wide, but Nicki was staring at him, that curious mix of confidence and uncertainty there, hovering right below the surface. "Nicki," he warned as she dipped down between his legs again, her gaze tracking his the whole time. The sight of her burnished red hair spilling over her shoulders and onto his skin was driving him to distraction, and she hadn't put her mouth over him again. "That's not all that's happening here today."

She winked at him. "That's up to you, soldier," she said, and she sank over him again, her mouth moving slickly down his shaft.

Stefan fell back against the pillows. This absolutely wasn't how he envisioned the evening to start—or to finish. But all his plans were scrambled as Nicki tightened her hold on him as she pulled away again, her tongue flicking over his head once, twice, driving him almost mad with need before she took him deep into her mouth once more. The pressure inside him built and crested, and though he could resist the urge to finish, he definitely didn't want to resist.

He wasn't thinking especially clearly, but then Nicki watched him from between his legs, her mouth freeing him once more as she tilted her head up, her gaze pinned on his face, clearly trying to read every nuance of his expression. This mattered to her, somehow, being able to give him pleasure before she took any for herself. And while Stefan was used to running everything, from ops to diplomatic envoys to special intel missions for both gods and mortals, he got the unerring sense that this wasn't something he should run. This was something he should let go, something he wanted to let go, something his body very much was urging him to let go.

"Nicki," he growled as she dropped over him again, and the tight wet hold of her lips sank slickly down his length, then pulled up again, her fingers fanning out to flutter against the base of his ball sac. His eyes practically rolled back in his head. "Nicki, you should be very sure of what you want to have happen here."

She pulled free to speak against it, the words creating a new and opposite vibration as her breath hushed over him. "I'm sure," she murmured, circling the head of his shaft with her tongue. "I'm very sure."

She pushed down again, once, twice, and he surged up to meet her stroke for stroke, until the tide of need rose too high for him to call it back. Gasping out a warning, he grabbed the sheets into tight fistfuls as his back arched and his body surrendered to a release sharp and full enough to make him want to collapse. Nicki clamped her hands on either side of his hips, bracing herself, bracing him, as he gritted out her name in wonder and a little shock, the power of his release more than he ever expected, more than he'd experienced in longer than he could remember.

At length she pulled away and rolled off him, but when she would have left the bed, he snaked out an arm, yanking her back until she sprawled in the soft sheets.

"You stay right here," he said, with enough command in his voice that she blinked, startled. "It's time I took back control of this operation."

Fifteen

Nicki rolled to the side as Stefan left the bed. She pulled up the sheets to half cover her body, suddenly chilled with the absence of him. She watched him pad across the room to the bar, where a second bottle of wine sat in a large silver urn. He'd apparently planned on them being together long into the night, she realized with sudden clarity. The man wasn't anything if not confident.

Yet, he'd let her make the first move. Let her lead though his natural instinct had surely been to take control, to draw the lines firmly between pursuer and pursued and keep those lines intact between them. He'd brought her here, after all, clearly intending for her to stay. In his long life, he'd probably had hundreds of women more than willing to play whatever role he wanted—herself included, at least when it came to following his lead as a member of his team.

But she'd pushed to assert herself, to take charge, and he'd let her. Seamlessly and without question, without any apparent blow to his masculinity. She'd been half afraid that the skies would open up and god-like bolts of lightning would smite her when he'd climaxed—but then again, Stefan was a demigod of

Hermes, not Zeus or Poseidon. She probably should be glad he hadn't started spontaneously levitating or speaking in tongues.

She bit her lip to tame her grin as Stefan returned to the bed with two full glasses of wine on a tray, setting the latter down on the stand beside the bed before turning to her, his face so full of appreciation and open admiration for her that she wondered for a second if she'd somehow slipped into a dream world.

This guy wasn't just a demigod, he was a freaking unicorn.

"Here," the unicorn rumbled. Stefan lifted a glass to her, then picked up his own. "To your first command operation," he said. "May it not be your last." He touched his glass to hers, and the chime of the fine crystal echoed through the room. Nicki took a healthy gulp, feeling her nerves zing with anticipation.

Far from being ready for a break in the action, Stefan appeared...more than ready to continue.

She glanced hurriedly at his face after that distraction, a blush staining her cheeks, only to find him watching her, a decidedly smug grin tugging at the corner of his mouth. "You didn't think you could topple me that easily, I hope?" he asked.

"I—it's not a competition."

His smile deepened. "And yet I already feel at a decided disadvantage." He set his glass on the nightstand, taking hers from her unresisting fingers as well. Then he slid closer to her on the bed. "It's not a position I find I'm comfortable with, I have to tell you."

"Well what should we do about that?" Nicki blinked, surprised that the husky rasp that asked the question was her own voice—a voice that sounded nothing like her, and everything like the vamp she'd never been.

Stefan didn't seem surprised, but chuckled as he slid yet closer. "So many things," he murmured. And he leaned in to kiss her softly on the lips.

No sooner had Nicki sighed against him than he shifted—

quickly, grabbing her hands out from their stabilizing position beneath her body and dropping her flat to the bed on her back. His body levered over hers and he stretched her arms out high against the pillows, his legs anchoring her thighs as she arched beneath his hold.

"So many things," he said again, "But first, I want to taste every inch of you."

"I—"

"Like here." Stefan dropped his head to Nicki's lips and kissed her soundly, his grip loosening on her hands so that he could reposition palms to either side of her face, framing her as if she were a cup that he was drinking from. He deepened the kiss, his tongue dipping into her mouth in a sensual assault, then shifted to her cheek, her brow, her temple. When he drifted his mouth along the curve of her ear, he murmured words too low for her to hear. But the tone of his voice warmed her to her toes, making her feel safe, protected, secure in his arms.

Then he angled down, his mouth tracing a fiery line along the curve of her neck to her collarbone, while his questing fingers found her breasts. He cupped them, his thumbs tweaking the already erect nipples, and lifted his face to stare into hers.

He could have any woman, she thought. Did he find her small breasts wanting?

As she frowned, he seemed to read her mind. "You're perfect. You have to know that."

"Well, I—ohh," Nicki was spared the embarrassment of a response as Stefan returned his mouth to her skin, only to place his lips where his hand had so recently been. The soft touch of his lips on her nipple made her back arch, and he rolled his tongue over her breast, teasing the nipple into a tight peak. All the while, this left hand fondled her other breast, the double play of attention splitting her focus and most of her brain cells.

Then he moved further down her body, over her softly rounded abs, and his hands dropped to anchor her hips. Nicki couldn't stop the shiver of expectation, a tight frisson of worry and need that caused Stefan to growl deep in his throat. "Perfect," he muttered again, only there was such a note of irritation in his voice that she stiffened.

"What?" she asked. "What's wrong?"

"Nothing," he sighed, and the touch of his breath against her most sensitive skin made any coherent thought flee. "Nothing at all." He leaned forward and touched his lips to her, his tongue snaking out to find her clit, teasing and exploring in the same way he had her breast, mapping her body with his mouth. She gave up trying to pick apart the specific sensations, and let herself slide into a sensual puddle as he laved her folds slick then blew a wisp of cool breath over her, making her gasp.

"Stefan," she moaned as he ducked toward her again. She held her breath as he traced a new pattern against her skin, shifting, adjusting, learning every curve. She would burst if he kept this up, and she dropped her hands to his shoulders, unsure of whether she wanted to egg him on or warn him off.

"My directions," he reminded, and his words were spoken against her clit, making her jump. He turned his face into her thigh and kissed a trail up to her hipbone, nipping it until she stopped squirming. "And I direct you to tell me this: are you enjoying what I'm doing?" His teeth came down on her hipbone, pressing in, and Nicki squeaked again.

"Yes!" she said. "Yes."

"And you'll tell me if I do something you don't enjoy?" he pressed.

That seemed more problematic, as she was barely able to breathe at this point, but she managed another shaky "yes."

"Good. Then otherwise, roll with it. I'll stop when I'm ready to stop."

Nicki's half laugh ended on a choke as Stefan's tongue snaked out to the key points on the map of her body that he'd clearly already learned by heart. He stroked her long and deep and then flicked her tight nub, alternating between the sensations until she couldn't tell where one ended and the other began. Another, different pressure began building—but this time, it was in her mind. First a rush of wind—then voices, they had to be voices—barged through her brain, chattering and laughing, sighing and murmuring. She could...it was almost like she could understand them, then another new wave would tumble through her, then another. The more Stefan wound her closer and closer to her own release, the louder the voices got... only to ebb away again, finally.

Nicki drew in a long, shaky breath, regaining a fragile sense of control. The second she got her bearings however, Stefan moved one millimeter to the right, and a new blast of sensation crashed over her.

"Stefan!" she gasped, and something in her voice must have tipped him off that she wasn't about to tell him to stop. His entire body stilled except his head, his mouth, the effect of him focusing so intently on her pleasure starting her down the long, delirious, inevitable slide toward orgasm.

Her legs seized first, spasming quickly together but blocked by the obstruction of his body. Nevertheless, she locked down against him, his grunt of surprise lost as the maelstrom built within her. He didn't move from his focused position, didn't give her any relief. Instead, he redoubled his efforts, apparently unaware of her growing tide of urgency as she whimpered inarticulate instructions, words that made no sense to her own ears, unwilling to tell him to stop but unable to keep herself from catapulting into the churning roil of sensations.

And then she was over the edge and her body fairly jack-knifed in the bed, the violence of her orgasm bouncing her up and back again as her hands sought Stefan's shoulders and she tried to push him away and pull him close simultaneously, her fingers so weak that she could gain no purchase to do anything. She gasped his name again as her entire body went rigid, before one final, explosive convulsion made her sight go bright white for one heartbeat—then two.

The best climax of her life, bar none.

"*Fovero*," she moaned as her legs fell open, leaving Stefan to trail a swirling line of kisses toward her knee.

He finally lifted his face to regard her with eyes so intent, they practically gleamed gold, and she blinked at him dazedly.

"Nicki," he asked, making the word almost a drawl, "why are you speaking Greek?"

Sixteen

$\sim$

"What?" Nicki blinked back at Stefan in total confusion, clearly not tracking the question. It didn't matter. He already had his answer...because this time, she'd used Egyptian.

Unexpected satisfaction, pride, and something more rocketed through him—*possessiveness*, he realized with a jolt. She was his. She *had* to be his, and his alone. This crackling live wire of a woman had given herself over so fully to him, so completely that she'd pulled one of his most treasured gifts over herself like a well-worn sweater. In all his long years of giving and taking pleasure, that had *never* happened before, and the very idea of it made his nerves sing, his heart thump so hard it nearly hurt. He wasn't sure if Nicki would maintain his ability to speak any language in the world when the haze of her own pleasure wore off, but it didn't matter. She was *his*.

Even if she didn't know it yet.

Stefan reveled in Nicki's contented sigh as he moved back up her body, retracing his path with his hands and his mouth until he was once more face-to-face with her. Her lips were full and open, her eyes nearly glazed. And when he pushed at her gently, urging her legs open once more, she complied with another deeply happy sigh.

He took that as a resounding yes to his next stage of the operation.

Leaning forward, his questing fingers found the other item he'd carried over on the tray. He slid the foil packet off the nightstand and sat back on his heels as Nicki watched, her eyes now wide and fascinated. He knew she'd watched a man sheathe himself before, so her interest wasn't in the generic act—but the fact that it was *his* cock being readied to enter her, *his* shaft accepting the tight constriction of protection. She watched as he leaned back over her, caging her in, but her expression held a curious mix of delight and excitement—the best combination he'd ever seen on any woman, ever.

Mentally berating himself to maintain control, he nudged between Nicki's legs with unerring precision. Her deep moan of approval did nothing to help his iron lock on his own reactions, and as he found her center and pushed in, he gritted his teeth against the sudden shock of wet heat surrounding him.

"Oh...my," Nicki muttered, this time in Hindi, and he blinked his eyes open, unaware that he'd closed them. Nicki apparently had been suffering the same level of eyestrain, because her lids remained resolutely shut, her mouth opening a tiny "o" of pleasure as he pushed in another quarter inch, allowing her body to get used to his sensual intrusion. He could feel the moment she relaxed, welcoming him in deeper. He pressed into her in one long slide, watching as her eyelids fluttered open, her unfocused eyes a mixture of pleasure, satisfaction and new, deeper need.

His favorite combination.

"Ah," she sighed, no translation required, as he slid home, her body moving with his as he rocked into her, finding the pace that fit her natural rhythm beat for beat. She shifted with him, angling her knees up so he could sink even more deeply inside her, reveling in the new sensations that shuddered through him at the intimate access to her body. She was unbelievably tight, surrounding him with wet heat, and every muscle in her upper body was pulled taut as she stretched up to meet his. Sex with Nicki Clark clearly wasn't going to be a relaxing activity—ever. At least not until after they'd both reached orgasm more than once.

Stefan could practically feel his eyes dilate at the thought of bringing Nicki to the brink again. And again.

He plunged deeper into her and something in her manner gave way, her body suddenly going nearly limp beneath him as she breathed out a long, gratified moan. Her surrender pushed him inexorably closer to that goal. She stretched out beneath him languorously, allowing him to sink further still, and her eyes fluttered open.

In that moment, he realized he had never known anyone like this woman. Her masks—and there were multiple ones he realized in a flash of clarity—had fallen away, and there wasn't anything left in her expression but an aching, raw need.

His heart beat harder again, heavier, with an urgency that made his chest tight, but he ignored it. In this moment, he wanted to ignore everything but Nicki Clark.

"Kiss me," he whispered, and Nicki's lips twitched into a smile, her neck arching to meet him as he bent toward her. She offered up her kiss as a benediction, and he drank in her absolution, unsure of why she was blessing him, but knowing that he craved it more than air. At the touch of her lips, a renewed strength poured through him, lighting his blood on fire. Then one of her hands came up and slid behind his neck, another over her shoulders, and she broke his braced-arm position and dragged him down to her body, so they were fused together, inch by perfect inch.

Nicki ran her hands down his back, pressing the heels of her hands into his muscles until her fingers reached the curve of his ass. She panned her hands wide and pulled him in as she surged forward, actively stroking him with her body, her hand, and her mouth all at once. The combination of pressures built within him an impossible force, and he grit his teeth to maintain his concentration. He wasn't going to give up this sensual assault anytime soon, not even for the unbearable pleasure he knew that release would afford him.

Then Nicki was pushing against him, her leg lifting to brace against the bed. "Roll over, you big ox," she muttered. She was back to speaking English again, and he followed her direction willingly, their bodies separating for a head-clearing moment until she was on top of him again, her legs straddling his hips, her hands on his chest as her breasts swayed forward, tantalizingly out of reach. She didn't give him much chance to recover as she positioned herself over him, her toned legs taut as she took him into her body again, only a bare inch, then slid free.

"Nicki," Stefan growled.

"What, you don't like to play?" she teased. "All that racing we've done, the swim competition, the climbing—you can't tell me that's true."

As she spoke she dropped down further over him, her abs knotting to hold her position for a bare moment before she slid up to the tip of his shaft again.

Stefan glared at her as she continued the sensual assault, sliding up and down with a disruptive rhythm, clearly enjoying herself as she teased him. All the while her efforts had the exact opposite of what he was sure she intended. She wasn't slowing him down, not at all. She was driving him to a fevered pitch.

"*Nicki,*" he managed and she finally sank home, clenching around him as she swayed forward.

"Better?" she asked, and he grimaced, but his gaze was filled with her. Her beautiful red-gold hair cascaded around her shoulders. Her hands were positioned on his chest to frame her small, rounded breasts. Her face now angled down as well, her green eyes lidded, her mouth slightly open as she rocked into him, focusing intently on his face.

Stefan pulsed up to meet her. Her breasts swayed into reach, and he leaned up, drifting his mouth across one soft globe as Nicki sighed. His hand came up and around her back, anchoring her to him, giving him greater access to one, then the other breast. He leaned back and drew her down closer, drawing her face to his as he settled back on the pillows.

"Kiss me," he whispered again, and she smiled, the pressure of her driving down on his cock an intense counterpoint to her soft expression.

"Okay," she said quietly. The touch of her on his lips sent him spiraling upward faster than he would have expected, and though Nicki pulled away, he found himself already at the brink. She seemed to realize it too, because her movements became steadier, more urgent, and her eyes were bright as she focused on his face.

A tide surged within Stefan, and he fixed on her face as well, wanting to memorize every detail, every nuance, as if all of this might be a dream that he was on the verge of waking up from, and he couldn't bear to let it end.

When he reached his climax he nearly shouted, an almost soundless battle cry, but it reverberated through Nicki and into the air around them, joining them together note for note, pulse for pulse. The room was suddenly thrust into a brilliant golden light, everything sharper, more focused—gilded. Nicki rode out his orgasm, her hands tight on his chest, her gaze intent, appearing to completely ignore the transformation around them. But there was no denying the smile that spread across her face as she watched him lose control. Then she was the one rolling off him. Grabbing the towel from the nightstand she tossed it his way before wheeling away.

"Hey—"

"You about broke me. Quiet," she snapped, the laughter in her voice lightening his mood further as she retreated to the bathroom. He sank back into the bed, his hand lifting to massage his jaw. He'd never smiled more in his life than in the days since he'd met Nicki.

She was back moments later, piling into bed with him, her gaze searching his face as she forgot her hesitation for a moment. He didn't let her recover it, instead reaching out and pulling her against him.

"That was extraordinary—and you are extraordinary," he said, his chest quaking as she laughed against his body.

"I think you've shunted off a ton of adrenaline. A good thing for the mission." Her English was easy and confident. Had she even realized she'd spoken fully a half-dozen other languages with him? Would she be able to do it again?

He was more than willing to try, but for now, he simply chuckled. "I'm grateful for your efforts to ensure our success. I'll note it in the report."

She burrowed a little more closely in his arms, as if she was born for his embrace. "Appreciated, sir," she said.

He leaned close to brush his lips against her hair and held her tight.

Seventeen

〜❧〜

Nicki woke with a start, her body dwarfed by the enormous bed. She blinked, but she knew where she was. It wasn't a dream, despite the fact that she hadn't woken up in a room as tidy as this since she'd shared college dorm rooms with Emmaline.

In fact—the room looked too clean. Almost swept.

She moved up against the pillows. The bed was cool beside her. Stefan had fallen asleep with his arms wrapped around her, but he clearly hadn't been there for the whole night. The dinner dishes on the table outside were gone, the wine taken away and the glasses removed. The glasses on the nightstand had vanished as well. There was no evidence that Stefan had remained there, she realized. No visible clothing, no drawers left askew, nothing out of place on the tables. Even the remote for the TV was in its holder.

Had he abandoned the room in the middle of the night, a wolf gnawing off its own leg to get out of a trap?

"You slept well?"

"Oh!" Nicki's pulse jacked as she turned to see Stefan leaning against the doorframe to the bathroom. He was freshly showered, his hair slicked back carefully over his brow, his body draped in a low-slung towel. Nicki's gaze dropped to his damp chest with its scatter of fine hair—and then it dropped further, following the trail as it pointed down his abs to his groin.

As she watched, the towel dropped to the floor.

Stefan didn't give her a chance to react as he strode quickly across the room, climbing up on the bed until his shower-damp body flattened her to the sheets. His head dipped toward her and she squirmed to the side. "No!" she laughed. "Stop it, I need to fix my—"

"You don't," Stefan murmured, following the angle of her head until she surrendered and allowed him to kiss her. He kissed her mouth, her brow, and followed the line of her head and neck until he reached her outer shoulder. "You're as perfect this morning as you were last night."

She turned beneath him, staring up at his impossibly chiseled face. "You can cut that out, you know. We've already had sex."

It was his turn to frown. "Cut what out?"

"The chivalry thing. I mean—it's nice, don't get me wrong. But it's totally unnecessary. And it's got to be exhausting." Despite her best intention to stay focused, she was distracted by the curve of Stefan's hard pecs and the tension in his biceps as he held himself above her, giving her space. Whatever, it allowed her to focus on his chest, not his face.

"I've broken my right leg and my left arm—here—" she pointed out the scars, clearly visible in the morning light, no matter how filtered it was through the French doors. "I cracked myself in the head when I was twenty falling off a monument and they glued my eyebrow back together—here." She traced the line along her right eyebrow. I have a high hamstring tear that kicks up when I sprint if I don't stretch out, and when I don't have my nails manicured, I have a tendency to rip them down to the quick."

She stared back at Stefan's face, resolution firming her words as a smile played about his lips. "All I'm saying is, I'm not perfect. I know I'm not perfect. You don't have to use that word."

"Noted." Slowly, tenderly, he dipped his head—not to her mouth, but to the hairline scar she'd pointed out on her brow. "But this—this scar you received while being careless on a monument. You were careless, I suspect?"

"I was the worst. I didn't know my limits."

"Ah." He drifted his mouth along her brow, the movement sending a thrill down her spine. "This scar is perfect, because it's yours. Because you received it doing something that only you would have done."

"Mm." Nicki fought to follow his words as his mouth drifted down to her shoulder, her arm. "I wasn't the only idiot up there that day."

"And this—your arm was reset after—what?"

"Snowboarding accident, spring break in the Rockies," she said automatically, sucking in a breath as he traced the old scar with his tongue. "I was totally not being an idiot then. The course was well marked, but there was a snow ghost—tree buried under a drift—they hadn't gotten to. I veered too high in a turn, got incredible air—but when I came down I was right on top of the thing." Her eyes drifted shut. "I didn't stop though. No one knew how bad I was injured until we got to the bottom of the mountain. Not even me."

"I'm not surprised." Stefan transferred his attention to her thigh, where the angry whorls of her pin scars stood white against the dark tan of her skin. "The leg, was it also snow-boarding?"

"Bike—hit by a car on campus, old lady visiting her...ohh..."

Stefan put his hands on either side of her thigh, the pressure of his palms steady as he massaged the muscles around the long-ago injury with a sure, strong touch. His fingers dug into the knots of her thighs, knots she didn't know she had, and Nicki flopped back, suddenly feeling oxygen-deprived.

"My God. You should take that act on tour," she groaned. Was this also a demigod thing? Was Hermes the god of massage? If not, he should be.

"I suspect this is the same leg with the hamstring tear?"

She could barely make out his words as pleasure crested within her. She'd known she'd needed a massage, but she'd never imagined it could be so electrifying. She didn't complain as his hands firmed on her body, easing her first to her side, then her stomach, his large hands transferring their pressure to her back. He stroked long and firm, and when he got to the curve of her ass, she belatedly realized she was still naked, and he was—

"Hey—" she spluttered, half rising from the bed.

"Humor me," he said, pushing her back down with the flat of his hand. Then both hands returned to her glutes. "Your left leg, right?"

"Yes but—ow!" she went rigid again as he pressed two fingers in a sharp, deep line down the curve of her upper thigh, the muscle spasming beneath his touch for a harrowing moment, driving all thoughts of pleasure from her mind. "That hurts!"

"It won't in a moment. Endure it," he said, his voice low but absolute. He stroked again, more deeply, and Nicki ground her hands into the sheets, tightening them into fists around the luxurious fabric. She tried to scoot away, but he restrained her, talking low as she gasped and panted.

"Relax," Stefan growled. "You're doing yourself no favors fighting me."

She snorted. "Spoken as someone who always wins—ouch! Enough!"

"For the moment," he said, the pressure of his hand changing to the broad flat of his palm as he pressed up with more general force into the intersection of her hamstring and glute. The warmed muscle tightened then gave way, and a spiral of pleasure radiated outward as Stefan continued the deep massage. He chuckled as Nicki groaned into the sheets once more.

"That's so much better," she managed on a sigh.

"It wouldn't be so, without the pain. As you more than most should know."

She was too aroused to be completely wary, but fear pricked in the back of her mind. *What did he mean by that? What did he know?*

"You think so?" she managed.

"Don't tense up." He brought his hands down both legs, and shifted them slightly wider. When his long, brushing strokes moved back up, they fluttered between her legs.

Despite his admonition, tensing is exactly what Nicki did.

"Hey—" she managed, but the combination of the deep tissue massage and this new, arousing pressure was too much for her brain to process. She let her legs fall naturally wider, accepting more of his touch as his laughter rumbled low in his throat.

"You're so wet," he murmured, dipping his fingers into her to verify. The touch of him woke up nerve endings that had barely recovered from the night before, but the endorphins from the massage overrode any complaint, and need erupted within her with each of his lazy strokes. He dipped into her again, pressing up against the slick skin, and she moaned into the sheets.

"Stop teasing me," she breathed out. "I want you inside me."
Stefan proved he was also excellent at taking direction.

Eighteen

Gritting his teeth at the delay, Stefan sheathed himself, then returned to the bed and covered Nicki's body with his, sliding smoothly up her curves until he was positioned tightly against her. She sighed with satisfaction as he seated himself inside her, the purely feminine sound winding him tighter.

Nicki did him one better, as he was already getting used to her doing. Bracing her arms beneath her, she lifted her body until she was on her knees, providing him more leverage as she leaned back against him. He groaned and she turned her head, her hair spilling over her shoulders as she smiled back.

Her change of position afforded him his own freedom too, however. Bracing one hand on her hip, he curled his body over hers, his hand snaking around as she stiffened in surprise to feel the touch of his fingers against her clit. Then it was her turn to sigh, pulling her breath back in with a short hiss as his fingers moved gently against the tight nub of nerves. She was slick with need and desire, and she opened more to him as he traced intricate patterns against her clit, the clenching of her channel exquisitely tight.

"I'm—I'm not going to last, Stefan."

He stifled the urge to laugh as she echoed the same thoughts rocketing through his mind. "It's not a competition," he said, a reminder more to himself than to her, but her laughter was cut off short as he teased her into another shiver of reaction. Then her body went taut for one long, perfect second, her breath catching as she suddenly convulsed against him, the heat and the energy of her release setting off a similar explosion inside him. He bucked forward and she met him with equal force, the twin intensity of their releases providing equal, violent reactions that devolved into Nicki shivering uncontrollably, sliding forward as he moved back and rolled free from the bed, landing on unsteady legs.

Nicki, for her part, flopped to the side, tangling in the sheets as she gasped and flung herself over onto her back. "I think you broke me," she moaned...only, she spoke in ancient Sumerian.

"You said that already," he answered her in English. "I can't break you twice."

That seemed to reset her language filter, and she responded in English as well. "I'm pretty sure you can."

Stefan continued laughing as he moved into the bathroom, knowing he needed another shower and not minding a bit.

By the time they made it to the deck, it was nearly ten a.m., and the intense Mediterranean sun was high in the sky. Nicki had retreated to her own room and showered, and was now dressed perfectly for her role. She wore a pair of long, feminine linen pants, a light, nearly sheer blouse that covered her neck and arms, with a matching camisole top underneath, making her appear fresh and cool and respectably conservative at once. A large hat shaded her face, also part of the artifice of her as a demure female photographer, but the ensemble would get her easily through the streets of the resort town. Her camera was slung over her arm, and she turned and smiled as he strode toward their small group, all of them waiting for his orders.

"Hasan Omir has graciously agreed to meet us at the beach to tour the local events. There are currently teaching clinics and windsurfing expositions, which Nicki, we'll need you to video and upload later today. You'll be watched, I'm certain, but the man remembers you and appears completely comfortable with your work with a camera." Stefan slanted her a glance. "He asked if you would be doing any surfing demonstrations."

She shrugged. "I could, if that's helpful. Or if we need a distraction."

It would certainly be that. His gaze raked over her, remembering her tousled in the sheets hours before. His vantage point of her back had revealed more scars—scars he was sure she would have been happy to explain had he asked. A scrape on her shoulder that had turned into a fine web-like tracing of white, a bruise along her triceps, probably picked up clambering into the yacht yesterday after their snorkeling adventure.

Somehow, rather than detracting from his fascination with her, they made her more irresistible. Nicki was so breathlessly, vitally alive—and he couldn't wait to get her back in bed again.

Ruthlessly, he forced his mind back to the conversation at hand.

"The men we dropped at the park have reported no word of Ari, though their search is only beginning. We'll need to move quickly—the chances of us finding anything are low, but we'll be noticed if we stay too long."

"A disoriented homeless man," Nicki said, squinting at the quaint seaside town. "He'd have been noticed here. If he's not in that park, you have to try the countryside near the ruins. They're pretty amazing. Ephesus, old churches..." She grimaced. "Never mind, those are tourist meccas. Once again, he'd be seen."

"Not all of Alaçati's ruins are picturesque, though," Stefan said. "We'll be focusing on anything that is out of the public eye. If Ari somehow scrabbled together a living, perhaps injured, perhaps mentally unstable, he would be holed up there, not in the middle of a horde of tourists."

She turned toward the low mountains ringing the seaside village. There were squat buildings in the distance, their features virtually identical. "It's too much," she said.

Stefan shrugged. "It's a start. The scavenger dealer didn't merely provide direction, he provided contacts." He turned to the men to his right, switching to Oûrois as he relayed additional orders. He half expected Nicki to react to the language with an unexpected familiarity, but she didn't. To Nicki, once more speaking English, he said. "If anyone knows of a mentally unstable stranger in Alaçati—we'll find him."

His men departed. The yacht was moving at a slower pace, and they soon docked near the city amid a cluster of workers processing the bustling tourism crowd. It took them another hour to weave their way through the town of cobblestoned streets, charming villas and shops, but they finally reached the main bay of Alaçati.

A light breeze was blowing, and Nicki lifted her head to the sky, appearing to let the sun warm her face. "This place truly deserves all the accolades it gets from the windsurfing community," she said. "It's also the perfect place to learn. The water is super clear and shallow, and there's a constant stiff breeze—breeze, not gale-force wind. The city is darling—I barely got out to do any sightseeing last year, but the year before I hiked all over, and everyone knows that tourism is their primary industry here. So they actually welcome visitors, unlike a lot of places."

Stefan eyed her. "Spoken like a true entitled American."

"Hey, Americans have lots of locations we can spend our

money. All we ask is to not get crap for it when we do. Sure, some of us can be obnoxious, but most of us mean well."

He lifted his brows at her unexpected vehemence. Nicki had probably endured her share of rebuke for her behavior, no matter how well-intentioned. Perhaps that explained her sensitivity. Perhaps it was something else. He wanted to find out more about her, but his exploration would have to wait.

As they stood on the boardwalk, Nicki stiffened. "That's our man. Hasan Omir, the local secretary or whatever of the Turkish Tourist Ministry. That group runs everything in Alaçati they can—which is a lot," she said. "He's kind of an officious prick, but he's efficient."

Stefan braced himself as the Turkish official and his entourage of well-dressed attendants reached them. "Welcome!" the man said, eyeing Nicki briefly before turning to Stefan with unexpected cheer, given Nicki's warning. "Your royal family is most gracious."

Beside him, Nicki blinked, but Stefan responded smoothly. "We're grateful for your hospitality," he said. "We promise not to take too much of your time."

"Nonsense. We'll show you what Alaçati has done to transform itself into this beautiful resort city you see." The pomposity of his words was earnestly delivered, and he swept his arms wide. "Perhaps one day your capital city can rival us, eh? But you will not be blessed with our winds and our sea. For that, others must always come to Alaçati."

"As you say," Stefan said, and Nicki's eyes rounded with understanding. King Jasen hadn't simply called to put in a good word for their visit, he'd sent money as well. Money in the form of a donation directly into the coffers of this pompous official, under the pretext of him providing Stefan with information about Turkish tourism practices. Not exactly in keeping with the way things were done under the current administration, Stefan was sure, but it would get the job done.

And, if they were lucky, it would buy them the time they needed to learn something about the fallen crown prince.

Nineteen

Nicki finished her video feed and swung back to regard Stefan and Omir, their heads together as they talked beneath a shaded portico right off the beach. They'd been at it for hours, after the official tour of the surf schools and the requisite oohing and ahhing of all the people taking part in the sport.

She wasn't going to lie, she wished she could be out there too. Surfing always beat taking videos of other people having fun.

But, as good as she was at the activity side of the equation, it didn't pay the bills. Her work as a blogger did—and that only barely. Stefan's ever-so-slightly sneering commentary on her "profession" wasn't that far off the mark. The low pay for this job was only worth it because of the adventure. But in another five, ten years, who knew what her interest would be in trekking around the world?

She smiled wryly, turning again to stroll along the boardwalk. Granted, trekking around the world in a luxury yacht wouldn't be a hardship. But she wasn't Emmaline, and she certainly wasn't Lauren. Both of her friends ending up entangled with handsome men connected to the royal family made sense. Nicki's life didn't work that way, though. She was the utility player of the team—the girl you wanted with you in the foxhole, but not necessarily the one you'd race across enemy lines to save. More likely, you were convinced she'd figure out how to save herself in the end.

And Nicki had no problem with that, not really. She was used to pulling her own weight, but also used to having no one else rely on her. With her heart possibly a time bomb, it was safer that way all around.

Stefan was relying on her, sure. But so far, this "mission" had proven more than manageable. Especially with him stretched out over her body.

"Oh—sorry," she said as she drifted into a table of laughing tourists. She righted her direction as she scanned the mountains surrounding Alaçati. They were as picturesque as the city, and she might as well get images of them too, while she had her equipment.

She set up her camera and spoke into the mic, doing a slow sweep of the city in long view. In her finder she picked out the remarkable diversity of homes—from abandoned hulks to adorable cottages to freshly painted townhomes. As she panned, she thought of Ari, stumbling ashore in one of the region's vast parks. Where had he gone from there? If it had been her, what would she have done? He had food and water, and he'd made it to a mainland. Even if he'd been disoriented, he would have wanted to find home. Would he have trusted the first people he met?

She grimaced. Probably. Ari had grown up in a loving family, with all the advantages of belonging to the royal ruling class. He would have an innate trust of others. And if he was already concussed, injured...

Her heart sank as she fixed on the cheerful homes high

above the city, then swung the camera out to the beach again filled with laughing, happy windsurfers.

There was simply no way he was alive.

"Nicki." Stefan's voice cut across her gloomy thoughts and she jerked her head back from the camera, surprised to see him so close.

"Oh, sorry—I didn't hear you come up."

"Clearly," he said, with a twist of his lips. "You were fixated on the homes overlooking the bay. Did you find anything interesting there?"

"No, not really." She lifted one shoulder. "Unless you count amazing places where I'll never live."

His brows lifted, and he shifted his gaze upward as well. "Too close together," he said, with a certainty that surprised her. "And too far from the water."

"Ha! Don't tell me you're house hunting. I gotta assume you picked up some amazing oceanfront villa sometime around 1900 and have been letting it appreciate since then."

It was his turn to shrug, but his expression grew thoughtful for a moment as he stared at the homes. Then it cleared as he glanced back at her. "Do you have enough footage for your posts?"

"I have enough for a week's worth." She peered down the beach. "Where's Omir?"

"Attending to other business. We'll be dining with him tonight at his hotel—both of us. I told him we would be honored."

She grinned. "I'm sure you did."

"To maintain the illusion that we're here on holiday, I've also booked us into a private hotel. If you'll pack your bag when we get back to the yacht, we'll have it transferred later today."

"Oh—of course," Nicki said. They turned and walked back up the boardwalk, and when Stefan suggested they stop at a beachside café for lunch, she accepted, blinking in surprise as he rattled off an order in perfect Turkish as they were led to a tiny table. He lifted her camera equipment from her shoulder and slid it over his chair before settling in.

Something about this...felt a little off, Nicki realized suddenly. Her heart kicked up with an ominous flutter. Had she done something inappropriate? Slipped up in some way?

"What's wrong?" Stefan's gaze pinned her to her chair, and she offered him a weak smile.

"Nothing—nothing at all. I'm a little shaky for some reason. Too long out in the sun, I suspect."

"I should have broken away sooner," he said as a waiter deposited water, bread, and dates on the table. "Eat, please. Our orders will be here shortly."

She didn't argue with him. She was hungry, to be sure, and her skin was running hot and cold. *No, no, no.* This wasn't the time for her to be weak. She needed to take better care of herself, or all of this would be pointless.

"I've heard from the guards," Stefan said, interrupting her self-recriminations. "They report that despite what the scavenger dealer reported, there are far fewer squatters in the park than we'd hoped. The ones they'd found were cagey enough to stay out of sight, for the most part, until it became clear that the men were offering money. That isn't totally reassuring, as people lie for money, but there was some useful information."

Nicki perked up. "There was?"

"Not specific, but interesting." Stefan nodded. "These men hadn't heard of Ari, nor had they seen anyone matching his description. But when the talk turned to homeless wanderers and drunkards, they all said the same thing. Those people were locked up, kept out of the public eye. Alaçati thrives on tourism and on putting up a good face for the well-heeled aristos of the big cities. They suffer no drunks on their watch."

She made a face. "I guess I can see their point, but what do they do with them? Shoot them at dawn?"

"They put them to work in some sort of local mental asylum. Guarded, they say, by *monsters*."

She almost dropped her fork. "*Monster*, monsters? Or, like, vicious animals who seem monstrous?"

"That we don't know. I'd received some...previous intelligence that there might be some animal trafficking going on in Alaçati, but I don't trust the source, here. The locals spoke of this asylum with certainty, and also with fear. Apparently, the threat is real enough to them. We haven't been able to get any corroboration from external sources, however. Not yet."

Nicki nodded, considering the quaint city around them. "I can't imagine this place having a mental asylum. Let alone one guarded by monsters."

"It doesn't, not officially." Stefan sat back in his chair, rolling his glass in his hands. "But there are several facilities that could be used in that role—abandoned warehouses, industrial buildings. The particular warehouse the squatters were warned to stay away from was on the southern range," he gestured, and Nicki turned in that direction. She couldn't make out anything on the ridge with the midday haze. "It's next to a recently excavated ruin of an old temple that's started to cause some buzz for the city, but isn't open to the public yet. It will be soon, by all accounts. The squatters are hoping the site's opening might force the Alaçati police to come up with a different policy on drunkards, not simply a different holding cell."

"And you think Ari could be in this—in an asylum, um, guarded by monsters?"

"I don't think anything at this point. But if he was clearly disoriented and a vagabond, he'd fit the description of the men they were rounding up. And if they use them for unpaid manual labor, essentially, Ari was tall and strong. He'd be a good candidate for a work detail if he didn't know any better. If he thought he was some kind of criminal, he would do the time. That was how he was brought up."

Nicki tilted her head. "How well did you know him?"

"Ari?" Stefan's lips twisted. "In some ways, not well, for all that we've been forced together for most of his life. My father and the king of Oûros were brothers, all those years ago, so I'm still considered something of a royal cousin. My aunt and uncle took me in when my parents died—though not as an adopted son, by my request. More as a lodger, for lack of a better word. Nevertheless, they ensured my schooling was top-notch, and when I showed an interest in politics, they moved me into the domain of their royal advisor—a man similar to Cyril in temperament. He mentored me from age fourteen on, even after my connection to Hermes became apparent and I pledged myself to him at age twenty."

Nicki stared at him. "I—" she managed. There was so much in that brief statement she wanted to unpack, but she started with the most personal. "I didn't know your parents died when you were young. I thought you..." she waved a hand, clearly at a loss. "I didn't know."

He frowned. "There was no reason for you to know. It was a long time ago. I was eight. They were on a yacht and got caught in a storm."

"And you're still willing to *sail*?" she protested. "You didn't even blink at taking a yacht here."

Now it was Stefan's turn to stare. "Why would I hold the sea at fault for doing what the sea does? My parents took a chance being out on the sea that night, much as Ari did when he flew off in his plane. It wasn't the fault of all yachts, everywhere, that their boat was unable to withstand the pounding it took. It wasn't the crew's fault that they did not survive despite their best efforts."

He delivered this with an icy calm, but not a robotic one. Nicki got the impression he really did believe what he was saying.

"Do you miss them?" she asked, her voice small.

Then a soft, sad smile creased his lips. "Every day. But the pain has changed, over time. It doesn't go away. But it becomes... different."

Twenty

Stefan kept his manner relaxed, but inside he was berating himself. There was no purpose in confiding in Nicki, no matter how easy it was to say what he honestly felt. She would be leaving shortly after their return to Oûros, and he knew that information shared was power lost. Somehow, he had lost power with Nicki, in telling her about his past. He should probably care more about that than he did, but in this case, he didn't mind so much. Empowering Nicki Clark had its advantages.

Not that Nicki realized it yet. She chattered on as their food arrived and turned the talk quickly to the images she'd captured on her video blog. In fact, her manner was overly lively, almost agitated, and he glanced at her hands as she reached for her sparkling water.

They trembled. Was she really that nervous around him?

His own heart gave a strange, sideways thud—then Nicki's bright words pulled him out of his reverie. "Out of curiosity, what happens if we do find Ari and he's legitimately some sort of criminal?"

"What do you mean?"

"Well, let's face it. He showed up on a foreign shore with no passport, no identity, possibly out of his mind. He got arrested, let's say, and put in this work camp place, with or without monster guards. The crown prince of Oûros, mind you, cooped up by Turkish officials like a common vagrant, despite a countries-wide search for any scrap of information about him…"

Stefan quirked a smile. "It would pose an interesting political challenge."

"Beyond that," she waved her spoon. "What do we do, point and shout, 'Oh, by Zeus's lightning bolt, it's the prince!'? I don't think so."

"If we have positive visual identification, we'll try to extract him immediately. If that task is beyond the abilities of the men we've brought, then it will become an escalated effort. Obviously, if we can avoid such an escalation, that would be ideal."

"Obviously," Nicki said wryly.

"If we don't have positive visual identification, or if the identification isn't of Ari proper, but his remains, or more fragments of his clothing or the airplane, then it becomes more difficult. The burden of proof will be on us, and we can't act with speed or any sort of stealth. The Turkish government will be made aware of our efforts, and it could become an international incident."

"None of that sounds ideal, either."

He grimaced. "It most definitely does not."

"So, let's consider it from the other direction. Ari is alive and relatively healthy, simply imprisoned. Maybe he knows who he is, maybe he's afraid of sharing that information, for fear he'll be killed. After all, he's been rotting in there a long time."

Stefan pursed his lips. "You might want to avoid the term 'rotting' as you consider relaying this story to the queen."

Nicki winced. "Fair enough," she said. "He's been a guest of the Turkish officials in Alaçati for nearly a year. He's been biding his time, hoping for an out, and if he sees any friendly faces from Oûros, he can shout out, draw attention somehow. Then it could all be explained away as a misunderstanding."

"True, if he's lucid enough to engage in such a subterfuge. But it still relies on us getting close enough for him to see us. Which is a more challenging issue."

"Not so challenging." Nicki swiveled her head to peer at the mountainside. "There are new ruins up there, and ruins mean dollars, once they're cleared enough for tourists to pay to go gawk at them. You can bet they're moving heaven and more importantly, earth to get that to happen, especially with the windsurfing competition coming up. We're in high season, and that's potentially thousands of tourist dollars a week that could be going to the city's coffers. If the thing isn't open already, it will be soon. And that's exactly where you'd think they might be keeping the imprisoned vagrants."

"So?"

"So, what better way to promote the new archaeological wonder of Alaçati than to have it as part of my video blog tour of the expo? It's the latest and greatest development for the city, it's got the wow factor with those vistas from the mountainside, and it's being overseen, I'm sure, by Omir. So, he'll get all the acclaim his heart desires if we promote it. As long as it's anywhere close to being ready, it's a no-lose situation for him. And once we're there, maybe we can see how we can break into the asylum-prison place, or whatever it is. Easy peasy."

"I suspect it will be anything but." Nevertheless, Stefan couldn't discount her words entirely. He needed more information—and he needed his men to gather it. He signaled to the server for their check and considered Nicki anew. "These are good ideas. Logical. It's helpful."

The smile she flashed him confirmed his earlier concern. It wasn't that Nicki was starved for attention. She was brash and active, always ready for the next challenge. She sought attention and she got it. But she didn't get attention for certain things—her mind, her logic, her discernment. Maybe that bothered her more than she realized.

They walked leisurely back to the boat, the camera over Stefan's shoulder. As he'd expected, his men were waiting for him when he returned—all of them.

Even better, the two he'd assigned to the park had more information.

"Possibly a sighting. It was too long ago to be certain," Tamas said, in English for Nicki's benefit. "A full year."

"So quite close to the crash event."

"Very close," Tamas said. "But he was here, closer to the city than we'd expected. And the woman who spoke with us knew it was June, because it was the beginning of the tourist season. She said his manner was definitely that of a falling-down drunk man. He'd been beaten up pretty badly, but though he staggered around, he didn't have any broken bones that she recalled. He was big and strong, and she and her children stayed away from him. The next morning, the trucks came, and everyone hid—but not this man. He simply watched them pull up. When they approached him, guns drawn, he cowered down, covering his head with his hands." Tamas grimaced. "He seemed crazy to this woman. And the account fits what we've heard elsewhere."

Stefan said nothing for a long minute. "This was June," he commented finally. "He'd been missing for maybe two weeks then, nothing more. How had he not been found by a search team? Was he disfigured?"

"We don't think so," Tamas shook his head. "The woman recognized him from the picture. Said his nose was out of joint and there was old, dried blood in his hair, but the eyes were right, the hair and the height and weight."

"It's enough to go on," Stefan said. To think that Ari could have been here all this time, as Nicki had put it well—rotting in a Turkish detainment center, forced to work by hauling rocks and dirt away from a monument while his own family lived in luxury not a half-day away.

The queen wouldn't be the only one who'd have difficulty accepting that reality.

"We need to get into that asylum," he said. He turned to Tamas. "Find out everything you can about it. Who owns it, what it's officially being used for. Ask our contacts if there are any known unofficial uses for it we should be aware of. The squatters know it as a work camp, but what other theories are out there? We need to be prepared for them all."

Tamas nodded. "We'll have satellite imagery of the site and the adjacent ruins later tonight, as close as we can get to it. We'll also scout out methods of ingress and egress, who visits and for how long, what deliveries, etc. There will be a way in."

"There will." Stefan turned to Nicki. "And now, we have to get ready for a party. Be sure to pack whatever you need into an overnight bag as well. As tourists go, we're giving Alaçati the full treatment."

Twenty-One

Nicki straightened her dress down her legs, unusually awkward with the thigh-high length. The racy dress would be frowned on in central Turkey, she thought—but in the coastal resort towns, attire was much like that in any European city. And normally she had no problem showing off her legs. She'd earned them the hard way, and she strode with strength and confidence. But the vivid blue dress had been chosen by Lauren, along with the strappy sandals, and the silky, swishy style felt foreign against Nicki's skin.

"Nerves," she muttered. She hadn't been paying attention to eating regularly and staying hydrated, so that wasn't helping either. But her videos were all queued and ready for release, and she'd scheduled them to drop over the next twelve hours. No one could accuse her of not doing her job.

Now she stood in the lobby of the most prestigious hotel in Alaçati waiting for Stefan, who'd sent her on ahead while he cobbled together all the information he could about the new attraction on the southern ridge of the city. There was little officially said about the ruins, but that hadn't stopped him from leaning on his unofficial sources. From those accounts, it was an early Christian-era church, made yet more interesting by the clearly pagan temple remnants beneath it. The combination, though common enough, would add an intriguing twist for tourists to the resort town. There was definitely money to be made.

A flutter of activity made her glance up, and sure enough, it was Stefan causing the commotion, crossing the open lobby as if he owned the place. He was perfect in his suit, somehow seeming formal though the jacket was casually cut, and his soft buttery trousers were summer weight perfection. He wore no tie and his white shirt was open at the collar, but that didn't take away from the aristocratic figure he cut as his long strides ate up the distance between them.

"Nicki," he said as he reached her, his gaze sweeping over her. He offered no further comment, though as he took her arm and curled it into his.

"Is it too short?" she murmured as they moved to the elevator bay. "It's too short, isn't it?"

"There's no such thing as too short on your legs," Stefan said, his impossibly polite accent at odds with the roughness of his voice. "I suppose I have Lauren to thank for it."

Nicki grinned, and the tension eased between them, allowing her to catch her breath. "She thought you'd approve."

"She's a woman of unparalleled discernment. Here we are."

They stepped into the elevator and rode the full distance to Omir's penthouse suite. When the doors opened, the party was in full swing, and Nicki relaxed a notch further. She was used to navigating the noise and bustle of a large group of people.

And she had plenty to work with, here. Easily a hundred people crowded the network of connected rooms, and all the rooms spilled out onto a wide, equally populated veranda. The hotel, one of the tallest in the city, had a commanding view of both the mountains and the sea, and Nicki gravitated toward the outdoors even as Stefan's hand pressed on her arm.

"We had another separate verification of a man matching Ari's description being taken by city police," he said quietly. "With the promise of money, the squatters yielded the few trinkets they'd taken from his stash in the woods. One of them was an altimeter component."

"Oh," Nicki said, her eyes wide. "He made it this far. If he... maybe..."

He squeezed her arm. "We're offered an unparalleled view of the city tonight, and the sun has not yet set. Perhaps we'll be able to glean something new about the asylum or the ruins."

"Ambassador Mihal, Miss Clark." The booming voice of the Turkish tourism secretary interrupted them, and Stefan turned. "Thank you for gracing my humble party this evening." He and Stefan shook hands, then he turned to Nicki. "As enchanting as I remember you," he said, lifting her hand to his lips.

"You're too kind." True to her role despite the odious man, Nicki's smile was genuine and her words warm. Nevertheless, a part of her couldn't deny a thrill of vindication as Stefan stiffened beside her. He suffered the Turkish man's embrace of Nicki's hand a moment longer, then spoke up, drawing the man's attention.

"We had the opportunity to tour the city a bit today after you left us. It is every bit as idyllic as you described it. You're right, you've done much to enhance its natural beauty with the development of its buildings and lands."

"You see? I wasn't boasting when I said that Oûros would do well to learn from its neighbors," Omir said, too loudly. Stefan looked pained and Nicki disengaged herself from his arm and pointed to the buffet table. He nodded, a bit too relieved. As she moved across the room, she wasn't sure if he simply wanted her to eat, or if he worried about her virtue at the hands of Omir. Either way, his concern touched her in a way that most men's wouldn't. It didn't irritate her—it was simply...nice.

"Snap out of it," she muttered, pausing at the buffet table. In truth she wasn't hungry, but having food in her hand would provide her with the needed business for her to blend in with the crowd. She chose fruits and cheese and bits of spiced bread, then headed to the veranda, pausing only to pick up a glass of champagne from a passing server.

The evening was already turning cool, but her excitement and the crush of people made her impervious to temperature as she moved toward the southerly facing veranda.

"Bless all that's holy—Nicki Clark! That is you."

She wheeled around and a bear of a man broke free of the crowd. His grin was wide as he strode up to her, and he was only held off from picking her up bodily because her hands were full of food and drink.

"Josef!" Nicki said. "I didn't think you'd be here until August." She had competed with Josef and against him in mixed competitions, and he was one of her favorite windsurfers on the circuit. At forty-five, he was old enough to be her father, but he was everything her father wasn't—active, happy, filled with boundless energy and an optimism that never wavered.

"All the to-do, how could I stay away—especially because we're getting into training, did you know that? Beginners and improvers up through intermediates. It's a great setup. You should come and do a story on it—hell, you should come and be a trainer! South Padre Island is a sweet location—never gets cold."

"Josef, you don't change," Nicki laughed. "You in Alaçati long?"

"Here for the week. We've got a full slate of students who flew in to experience the best windsurfing in the world. Hey!" His eyes lit up. "One of them said something about video blogs on the place. That's you, isn't it? You're doing your whole adventure reporter thing. It'd be a good time to do a report on us, I'm just saying..."

"I'll think about it—I'll think about it!" Nicki laughed, edging toward the low wall of the penthouse veranda when it was vacated by some of the guests. Josef followed her. From here, it was a clear shot over to the southern ridge, and she could easily see the clear-cut trees and construction vehicles, next to a large, ugly cinderblock structure, appearing to be hunched over the mountain.

"What's that, do you know?" she asked, as casually as she could.

Josef tracked her sight line. "Nothing yet," he said. "One of my students is a total archaeology freak, went up there the other day. They're nowhere near opening, but he says it'll be pretty cool when it's done. Despite the fact they're moving too fast to really preserve any of the more delicate artifacts that might be there, according to him." He shrugged. "That's what happens when you're tripping over ruins everywhere you turn around, I guess."

"I guess so."

"Hey, you should come out tomorrow!" Josef said, refocusing on her. "They're doing an expo of trainers, and you could show off your stuff."

"Except I'm not a trainer."

"Yet," he teased. He glanced over her shoulder and grinned. "There's the maestro himself. I'll ask him. You got your board with you?"

She stared at him. "Of course I don't, Josef. I'm here to video the expo, not participate in it."

"Not a problem, I've got plenty! Wait here." He bounded off with his good cheer, hailing Omir. Nicki winced. So much for keeping a low profile.

"You've made a friend."

Stefan had materialized in front of her.

Twenty-Two

Watching Nicki across the room with the much older man had set off a riot of reactions within Stefan, none of them worth paying attention to but all of them impossible to ignore. Clearly, the two were familiar, and clearly they were not inappropriately entangled. He could tell that by their body language. Yet he'd found a reason to break off his conversation with Omir to come striding over like a jealous boyfriend, and now that he was in front of Nicki, he didn't have anything specific to say.

What was wrong with him?

"Josef is a well-known windsurfer—a former champion, though he'd never admit it. He's running a training school." Nicki's eyes were alight with interest. "More importantly, he had information about the ruins. Says a student of his went up there, and they're nowhere near finished, and that the place is closer to a construction zone than an archaeological site. Chances are someone's cutting corners to get the excavation done before heritage sites learn about it. Which would be a really good reason to use workers who can't gossip."

He nodded. "Was he able to get inside?"

"Nope, only check it out from over a fence. But how difficult would it be to get in for someone who probably has his *own* ruins to exploit in Oûros, the Alaçati of the North?"

Stefan blinked at her, startled, then realized she was joking. "I've tried suggesting it already to Omir," he said. "He wasn't interested in talking about anything but the surfing expo."

"Oh, give me a break." Nicki rolled her eyes. "If you really want to get his attention, I can do that." At his skeptical glance she handed over her plate. "Why do you think Lauren really chose this dress? She wasn't expecting you to jump my bones, I can tell you that."

She turned on her heel and sashayed across the room to where Josef and Omir were huddled. Predictably, Omir's face brightened as Nicki stepped up to him, and Stefan dumped her plate in irritation onto the nearest passing server's tray. He moved through the crowd, nearing the trio, until he could hear Nicki plainly.

She actually cooed.

Stefan grimaced and forced himself to extract the details of the conversation. Yes, yes, Omir was familiar with the site. It would be a future pride of Alaçati. No, it wasn't ready—there were no tourists allowed. Yes, it would be beneficial to have video shot of the work in progress...

At that point, Stefan knew they had him. There was no need for Nicki to continue to flirt with the official, but she didn't seem to realize that. She pressed up against him as if he were the most interesting man in the southern hemisphere. She wasn't merely dangerous in that dress, she was a lethal weapon, and one he was more than willing to disarm. If only he could—

"Sir."

Stefan looked up, surprised to see Tamas. They'd made arrangements for updates to be relayed during the party by person, not by electronics, in case Omir was scanning anything.

Sometimes the simplest solution was the best. But Tamas had chosen his moment well. Stefan remained on the open veranda, and the wind had picked up, swirling around the conversations and serving as an effective scrambler to everyone's words.

"How has your tour of the city been?" Stefan asked easily.

"Perfection." Tamas grinned. "The weather, the restaurants, everything in its place. And the residents are so trusting and welcoming. You can walk in almost anywhere and feel at home." He shrugged. "There are exceptions, of course, but until you get up into the mountains, you will never exhaust the goodwill this city has."

Stefan nodded. The security was lax throughout much of the old town, from what Tamas was saying. But up on the ridges surrounding the city, the story was different.

"I haven't been exploring much. I have heard Ephesus is remarkable."

"Eh, why bury yourself *outside* the city when there is so much more here to see? Everything you want is right here."

"You've heard that story enough times that you're starting to believe it?" Stefan asked good-naturedly, clapping Tamas on the shoulder. This time, however, Tamas's expression lost its good humor. Turned as he was away from the crowded veranda, he was only visible to Stefan. But now his face appeared almost ashen, his eyes stark and cold.

"I have heard it often enough to know it is true," he said. "All roads lead to the same walls. There's no way to tell what those walls are hiding, though."

"Such is the nature of walls," Stefan said. "What about anything locked inside that isn't human?"

"Heard that too." Tamas shrugged. "That I believe less, but it's still unsettling. Still, you should be prepared for dogs at the very least."

"Agreed. You've been at it long enough, and tomorrow will be another long day. You should get some rest."

Tamas ducked his head, firmly back in his role of earnest tourist. "I couldn't agree more," he said brightly. The two of them exchanged another round of pleasantries, then the Oûrois special forces operative slipped back into the crowd, drawing appreciative glances but little true attention as he made his way back out.

For his part, Stefan couldn't shake the expression that had transfixed the young man's face. Whatever Tamas had heard had convinced him that Ari was, in fact, a prisoner inside the asylum they'd been targeting—a hulking warehouse on the southern ridgeline above Alaçati. Whether he was alive or not, there was no way to guess. Security was also tight around the asylum, which would surprise no one. If people knew there were inmates in the building, they'd want to be sure they were kept inside—and even if not, asylums were the type of buildings that invited extra security.

Even with the tour that Nicki was in the process of adroitly arranging, getting into the asylum wouldn't be as easy as asking Omir if they could pop in next door for an extended visit. But seeing the building close up from the vantage point of the ruins might prove useful. So would seeing exactly who was working on the excavation teams.

He had a feeling there were very few actual drunkards that had been roped into service. Chances were good they were all squatters, the poor, the mentally ill, or small-degree felons, offered a chance to work off their debt to society. If so, and if Ari had eventually stopped acting erratically, there was a good chance he had survived. As Stefan had told Nicki, Ari was tall and strong, and was no stranger to hard work. He could— possibly—have survived this long.

"Hey!" Stefan turned as Nicki bounded up to him. "I spoke to Omir, and guess what?"

"He agreed to give us a tour—tomorrow, under the pretext that you'll be shooting video footage of the ruins to aid him in his promotion of the city's project."

"That's right! He didn't completely skeeve me out either, which I was expecting. I mean, there was low-level skeeve, but totally manageable. I can't believe that was so easy!"

"And your friend Josef? Will he be joining us too?" Stefan eased his expression as he spoke the words to lessen their sharpness, and Nicki squinted at him.

She laughed. "Seriously? Is this jealousy? He's twice my age and has five kids. Um, no."

He lifted his brows, unable to keep from asking the question. "You don't care for children?"

"Not when they're other people's, and not for myself until I have oh, I don't know, a roof I can put over their heads. Somewhere that's not in Indiana, preferably."

"I'm not so certain. Indiana sounds like a very wholesome place to raise children. Although unless I miss my guess, it's not a place famed for its windsurfing opportunities.

"You would be correct."

Nicki laughed then, single-handedly dragged him out of the dark waters of his own thoughts. He couldn't—wouldn't—wait another moment to touch her again.

"Stefan?" Nicki finally caught his mood and misread it, her face shuttering into a mask of concern. "Is everything all right?"

"It isn't. I need to speak with you a moment."

Nicki peered around the room. They were an island among a hundred or so milling guests, and no one was paying attention to them.

"You can't talk to me here?" she asked.

He shook his head, unable to keep the harshness out of his voice. "Not for what I need to say."

Twenty-Three

Be *chill,* Nicki admonished herself as she and Stefan moved easily back through the crowd. But how had she so totally misread Stefan's response to her? How had he slid from interested to infuriated?

She went over her actions in her mind. Yes, perhaps it was impetuous for her to suggest that she could simply ask Omir to show them the ruins and assume he'd pander to her... but it'd worked. They had a tour scheduled for the next morning, and all because she'd been willing to lean over and show a little cleavage. Granted, she'd also gotten roped into surfing at the expo tomorrow afternoon, but that was a price she was willing to pay. And besides, she hadn't gotten in any serious exercise since they'd left on this jaunt. The sex, though remarkable, didn't count.

Her cheeks flamed thinking about the previous night in Stefan's stateroom. He'd so completely exceeded her expectations that she'd now set a completely unfair and unrealistic bar...a bar none of the ordinary men back in her ordinary world would be able to clear. Sleeping with Stefan had been the equivalent of standing too close to the sun, and her retinas were permanently singed.

She giggled, then stifled herself at Stefan's black look. They were moving out of the main party area into an antechamber where a few small groups chatted while more of the servers weaved in and out with drinks and hors d'oeuvres. Private conversation was completely possible here, but Stefan angled off into another hallway, past the kitchen and another sitting room—this one dark.

He stopped and moved back, glancing up the hallway. Then he pushed her into the room.

"What are you doin—" Nicki's hiss was cut off mid-sentence as Stefan pressed her up against the wall, his hand over her mouth.

"Shh," he said and her eyes went wide, only in part because of the utter gloom in the room, its shades drawn against the fading sky outside. "Can you be quiet?"

She blinked, nodding. Of all the secret agent things she'd been expecting to see from Stefan, this wasn't it. But it felt exactly like something out of a movie, and when he pulled his hand away from her mouth it was all she could do not to burst with the questions piling up in her mind.

"Good," he said tightly.

Then he kissed her.

It wasn't an ordinary kiss, either. Stefan put both hands on either side of Nicki's face and tilted her up to him, as if he was a starving man offered his first meal in days. The moment their lips touched he reached around her body and hauled her close, cradling her backside with his hand as he lifted her higher against the wall.

Nicki could barely draw in a second breath when he kissed her again, hungrily, deeply, his mouth leaving hers to ravage across her face, her ear, and down into the hollow of her neck.

The short length and flirty swing of the dress were uniquely suited for backroom trysts, and for a moment Nicki thought about protesting—but only for a moment. Instead, she flexed and lifted her legs, locking her ankles around Stefan's back and pulling herself tighter against him. He growled against her neck then moved to her mouth again.

"Sunshine," he practically moaned, and a nervous thrill zipped through her. She didn't know what to say, what to do. She didn't want to break the spell that Stefan was weaving around her, around them both—but her heart was already beginning to race.

At that moment, he dragged himself away from her mouth. She smiled up at his dazed face, her hands gripping his shoulders. "So...it was a good thing that I talked to Omir? Because this feels a whole lot like a reward."

Stefan barked with laughter and swung her around, the movement causing her to unlock her legs. She slid down until the heels of her strappy sandals hit the floor, but Stefan held her close until she steadied herself.

"I'm sorry," he said, shaking his head. "That was unnecessary of me."

"Well, I'm not sure about the necessary thing, but I didn't really need it to be necessary. It was all good." Nicki spoke the words slowly and carefully, as if Stefan was a colt about to shy away. The impetuous move of feeling her up in a back room seemed totally unlike him, but he was the one leaning back from her, studying her as if she were a different species.

"You do the most incredible things to me," he said, shaking his head. "I don't know if you're doing it on purpose, or if you were simply brought to me by the gods to teach me a lesson."

Nicki lifted a brow. "Well, that depends. Am I a path not taken or a horrible mistake so far?" she grinned, softening her words. "Or both?"

"Definitely not a horrible mistake," Stefan murmured, drawing her close again. "And as to paths not taken, the night is young, and we have many paths before us."

He dipped his head and kissed her again, but lightly this time, gently, as if she were made of fine bone china. Rather than feeling left out in the cold with the softness of his touch, Nicki's heart turned inside out, thumping out of time despite her silent pleas for it to relax. She forced herself to remain still for as long as she could, but when Stefan shifted, she slithered out of his embrace, putting a few feet between them as she made a business out of smoothing her dress.

"Do I look okay?" she asked as he watched her, for once completely fine with the blush that stained her cheeks. Let him think she was flustered—she was. As long as he didn't think she was going to faint, she was safe.

"You do. But I took you rather precipitously from the room. Getting back might be a trick."

She shook her head. "You go first. No one notices me the way they notice you, and if you're in the room for a few minutes, me slipping back in won't cause a stir. If the reverse happens, they'll start thinking about it," she said. "It's never good when people start thinking."

He scowled. "I don't want to leave you alone in this room."

"Okay, don't—we'll go back partway, then split up."

A strange expression flickered over his face, but he nodded. He took her hand and led her back to the door, then smoothly moved out with her arm curled over his, as if they'd just returned from an evening stroll. There was no one in the corridor, but his steps were so sedate and measured, they served to slow down Nicki's heart rate by the time they reached the first sparsely populated sitting room. He glanced down at her and she shrugged.

"You know, as long as I'm not wrecked, I don't think anyone will notice if we walk in together."

"You don't look wrecked," he said, his gaze roaming over her face, her hair. "Clearly, I'm losing my touch."

"That's the benefit of not wearing much makeup," Nicki said with a wink. "I always look like me. Even if I've been up to no good."

He laughed, which lightened her mood further as they headed back to the party. She was right again, too: no one noticed them slip back in, precisely because it seemed like Stefan was moving in slow motion, as if by his own hand he could slow down the turning hands of time and preserve this moment.

They parted ways shortly after entering the room—him to mingle with the Turkish officials, her to meet and re-meet the remarkable number of the windsurfing community that knew or remembered her from past years.

It always surprised her, the sense of community that these athletes had. They were ferocious competitors, but for the most part, they were the glue that made everything work in between the competitions. Josef had clearly made the rounds before her, because she had no fewer than three job offers before she'd returned to the food table.

With another glass of champagne to steady her fingers, she gazed out over the sparkling town of Alaçati and into the cold gray building at the top of the southern ridgeline. She wondered about the inhabitants of that building, if the stories were to be believed. Was there a lost prince out there under all that gray? And how would life change if they found him—either dead or alive?

Twenty-Four

Stefan watched Nicki mingle across the room as he made his own rounds. With everyone she met, she was bright, vivacious, engaged—and authentic, despite her almost relentless cheer. Was that due to the people who connected with her, all of them athletes or former athletes? Or would she be that way to everyone who approached her, from toddler to grandmother?

He frowned, shaking his head at the unexpected thought. Nicki Clark had so far performed exactly as he needed her to. She'd shown up and done the work, logging the video blogs, going where he told her to go, doing whatever he'd asked. She hadn't lost her nerve on the island—and she should have. She hadn't balked at working long days doing articles purely for cover, not for pay—and she should have, given that she was a professional journalist. She'd endured his sarcasm and his judgment and taken it as her due.

That last continued to bother him, and he lifted his hand idly to rub his chest as he studied her. There was something about Nicki that was almost fatalistic, as if she was always waiting for the other shoe to drop. She was only twenty-three...too young to have come by that belief the usual way. She didn't appear to be crushed by life's experiences, but instead was someone who took them on full force, learning and adapting to each new challenge.

So why was she so hesitant? Timid wasn't the right word— no one would ever accuse her of timidity. But there was almost an expectation that she would somehow do the wrong thing, say the wrong words, react the wrong way. It didn't make sense.

At that moment, Nicki caught him staring at her across the room. Another woman would have acted coy, or pretended she didn't notice. Nicki merely grinned and raised her champagne flute, appearing for all the world like she was exactly who she was pretending to be: an adventure blogger thrilled to be rubbing elbows with the glitterati and her home crowd alike.

Only this *was* who Nicki could be, if she truly wanted to be. He wasn't unaware of the attention she was receiving. He overheard or intuited the job offers. That Nicki responded to each with gracious, non-committal answers once again left him wondering why. She was here as cover, yes, but these offers were for the life she would lead after the need for cover was through. This little jaunt to Turkey was three inconsequential days out of her life. Would she follow up on those opportunities later, if one truly caught her interest?

He shouldn't care. He knew he shouldn't care. Nicki Clark wasn't his mission here, Aristotle Andris was. And Nicki was doing everything she could to ease their way so they could find Ari sooner—whether it was the prince himself, or simply his remains. She was working hard, sacrificing. The least he could do was the same.

If only every time she glanced over at him, his resolve to treat her with polite indifference didn't shatter into a million pieces.

That...was an issue.

By the time they left the party, Nicki glowed like an incandescent bulb, attracting a stream of admiring glances—none more so than from Omir. She knew it too.

"Is he still watching?" she asked with a sunny smile, her words unusually biting despite her carefree expression.

"I think he might well stare a hole in the elevator door."

"Then let's take the stairs," she said. "Anything to move us more quickly out of here is all right by me."

The stairs didn't take them down to the front of the lobby, however, but to the sitting room in the back—a sitting room that opened onto another wide veranda that led down to the water. They exited the hotel that way.

"Our hotel is on the waterfront. We might as well walk," he said, and Nicki nodded.

"It couldn't be a more beautiful night."

Within minutes they were walking down the paved sidewalk to the waterside, Stefan with his jacket slung over his shoulder, the sleeves of his shirt rolled up to his elbows. They looked like what they supposedly were—two visitors to the resort city with nothing on their mind but surf and sun and whatever the next day's adventure would bring.

Except the next day's adventure would probably bring challenges that would, at a minimum, darken the mood between them. The prince could be behind those walls at the asylum. He could be dead, injured, or damaged beyond recognition. It was unlikely that even if he was alive, he would be the same man who had taken off in that plane nearly a year ago. He might have survived the accident, but he would be irrevocably changed.

"So Omir is warming to the idea of a tour, aided in no small part by Josef's glowing accounts of his student's recon trip up there, despite the fact the kid was peeking over the walls." Nicki said the words casually, gently easing Stefan out of his dark thoughts, as she always did. "He's thinking about ten a.m. That to me is interesting. If the workers up there are truly scrubs from the asylum next door, I'd think that would be high work time for them."

Stefan considered that. "It's possible he doesn't know the details of the work camp, not intimately," he said. "He may know that work is getting completed, but not how, specifically."

She blew out a breath. "Yeah, agreed. The more I think about it, the less realistic I think it would be that he'd be talking about the site at all if there was something hinky going on. Speed is fine. But using prisoners and drunks to build walls and pathways for a tourist destination seems like something that *someone* would oppose, no matter what country you're in."

Without thinking, Stefan reached for her hand, smoothing over the action by helping her up onto a flight of stairs that led to their hotel. But he didn't let go when he could have—when he should have, for anyone watching. He didn't want to let go.

Nicki, being Nicki, rolled with it. "Josef has wrangled me into the expo tomorrow, you should know," she said, keeping her words light. "It won't be a big deal, a few runs demonstrating more advanced moves. The wind is always perfect here, and the water shallow, so if I wipe out, I won't ding myself up too much."

Her phrasing struck him as odd, and then he remembered— she didn't want to be a liability. He smiled, shaking his head.

"That's no problem. If it strengthens your cover—and our purpose here—for you to show off your windsurfing skills, then that's only to the good. You can't derail the mission."

Her hand stiffened a little in his grasp, and she pulled herself free, moving ahead to the railing of the hotel's wide landing. She rapped on the sturdy wooden crossbar. "Don't jinx us, not when this is all going so well," she said, offering him a lopsided grin.

He stared down at her for a moment, half-caught between light and shadows. He didn't plan to kiss her, not in the open. It wasn't part of his cover, or hers. It didn't move the mission forward.

And, strangely, he didn't give a damn about any of that.

She seemed to know it too, opening her mouth to warn him away and then her face was transfixed, her eyes blinking rapidly as he leaned down. He slid one arm around her, his hand finding her warm skin beneath the silky folds of her dress, and his body responded immediately to the intimate touch. When his lips met hers, the kiss galvanized him, sending all his nerves alight with need—the need to draw her closer, the need to touch every inch of her body, the need to make her his.

Something else overtook him as well. A sudden knowing, a searing awareness that went far deeper than any ordinary connection between a man and a woman. In his arms, Nicki suddenly felt like a spark lit too brightly, flaring bold and fierce in the darkness—and then winking out.

He gasped in real pain, but the devastating vision was gone almost as quickly as it appeared. Nicki swayed in his grasp and pressed closer, her back arching so she could deepen the kiss, her arms up and around his shoulders cradling his head. He bent toward her hungrily and she gave as good as she got, straining toward him on her toes as if she could add another few inches to her already ridiculous shoes.

Stefan's hands dropped, skimming her waist before curving to her backside. Without thinking, he dragged her against his groin until he could feel his shaft stiffen unbearably. Nicki gave a small, feminine moan and wriggled closer still.

"I suppose it wouldn't be a good idea for us to have sex on a public staircase in Turkey?" she whispered.

Stefan barked a laugh, the sudden impossibility of her words combined with her teasing tone striking him exactly the right way. He pulled away quickly, smoothing Nicki's hair, shaking his head in surprise at his own actions.

"I shouldn't have done that. I...I shouldn't."

"It's okay," she grinned, giving him a broad wink. "I have demigods falling all over me all the time. It happens."

Their laughter threaded around them, a comforting balm, all the way to the doors of their hotel.

Twenty-Five

They parted at their rooms to complete their separate work, and Nicki fell asleep at her table instead of in Stefan's bed. This was less than ideal, but when she'd woken she'd at least gotten through the rest of the blogs and videos she wanted to post for the next twenty-four hours. She'd be in the clear to do whatever Stefan needed. And Stefan hadn't come for her either, which had kind of surprised her. Then again, she supposed he was busy too.

And of course, there was the guard stationed in her sitting room. That sort of put a damper on things as well.

The next morning she learned that Stefan received notice during the night that the tour wouldn't be possible due to a work conflict—construction involving heavy equipment would be all over the site. Visitors would be strictly forbidden to ensure the high safety standards of the construction company.

Nicki frowned as Stefan relayed the news to her over breakfast. "You think he's clearing out evidence of undocumented workers?"

"He's clearing out evidence of something, without question," Stefan said. "He believes the tour is possible, but only if we go tomorrow, not today. Clearly, he doesn't think anything is seriously amiss, or he wouldn't be letting us get anywhere near the site."

"Fair enough," Nicki said. "Is it private property though, around it? Josef's student was able to get pretty close without issue."

"I suspect there's probably some security within the site. As to around it, I'd doubt it." Stefan eyed her over the table. "Why?"

"Well, I have this windsurfing thing later in the day, but I haven't worked out in an age. Might be nice to, I don't know, hike around the city?"

His smile was all the reward she could have asked for. "You have climbing equipment?"

"Packed it in case. I assume you have what you need here as well."

He nodded. "Packed it in case."

Within the hour they were decked out like any of a thousand Alaçati tourists that morning—hiking shoes, tee shirts and cargo pants, packs slung over their back that could carry anything from sandwiches to maps. In their case, it carried rope and carabiners and soft-soled shoes. They didn't expect to run into any cliffs, but it was always good to be prepared.

The walk to the edge of the city was short, and mostly uphill. It was good to get out, to feel the sun on her face while she was moving, Nicki thought. She'd let Stefan set the pace, but he hadn't slowed appreciably for her, she was certain. Her energy was high, and she'd eaten and consumed enough water. She'd be fine today.

"According to the squatters, that's the asylum, directly behind me," Stefan said. He had a tourist map and was facing the city, while the thick, ugly building rose up from the cliff. "On the map it's indicated as a warehouse. Possibly was at one time. Not too difficult to convert that into a makeshift hospital or holding tank, particularly if it's broken up into small rooms."

"Not too easy for anyone to get out of either," Nicki said. She squinted up as if trying to gauge how much higher they would climb the ridge. "No windows at all on this side—which is odd, since it's the side with the view. Holds with the warehouse idea."

"Agreed. I think we're looking at a usage of convenience, not intended as a long-term solution. Then again, they've been using it for a year."

"Must have proven very convenient," Nicki said. "Either way, we're not getting in on this side. Let's move around and see how protected it is."

They continued up the street. At this height, in this particular section of the city, the quaintness of Alaçati was less in evidence. They appeared to be in an industrial area that hadn't quite been reached by the touch of gentrification. That development was coming though—there were indications all around. Most of the houses were empty and bore official placards indicating likely demolition. Construction equipment grew more prevalent the further up they went, and workers too in patches. No one seemed to care they were there, however. At the top of the ridgeline, the countryside spilled into more parklands. So, they could easily be heading in that direction.

The warehouse loomed to their right as they continued mounting the hill, separated from the street by a thick patch of vegetation and a relatively new fence that abutted the asphalt.

"Electrified?" Stefan wondered aloud.

"Nope," Niki said.

"You sure?"

"Hey, I grew up in Indiana. I know things." She reached down and ripped off a blade of grass. She laid the strand against the wire, and touched the tip of the grass section. "See?" She grinned. "Also, this is a new fence. Way newer than the build-ing. Maybe see if there's a tag on it from the builder, if we need to get in legitimately?"

"Agreed."

They walked up the street a further distance, then an inter-section opened in front of them. Up was definitely the direction of the park, but the ruins were helpfully on the other side of the warehouse, and a huge swath of trees and vegetation had been cleared out, revealing a hint of the excavation beyond. More of the same fence that circled the warehouse snaked in front of the excavation site, but there was still plenty to see. It was easy to justify them altering course to check out the site. If they got caught, even by Omir, it wouldn't be a big deal—Nicki didn't have her camera.

"No name on the fence," she said as they walked along the perimeter. "And the warehouse isn't exactly in good shape."

"They could say they're fencing it for public protection until it can be torn down or renovated in connection with the site. Or they could say nothing at all." Stefan's tone was distracted as he surveyed the building, scanning its roofline as they walked. "This isn't America."

"Thanks for the update. At least they have a truck intake. So someone's going in and out."

The fence broke into a wide gate. They paused to peer in, not stopping long enough to draw attention. The sound of construction at the ruins site was clearly audible, but the ware-house was silent, the huge truck bays shut. The doors on the bays were newer, however, and the locks were as well.

"These guys are up on their security."

"No cameras though." Stefan moved past the opening, his attention squarely on the excavation site. "Fence isn't wired, no closed-circuit monitoring. This isn't meant to be a permanent holding cell. Probably squalid inside—I'd be surprised if the plumbing or the electricity worked. Couldn't afford anyone to see the lights. Windows are only on the upper floors, and then not many."

Nicki made a face. "No plumbing? And they have a bunch of workers stashed in there, and maybe animals too? No way someone wouldn't eventually notice that."

"Fair point," Stefan said. "There'd have to be a waste dump close by." He glanced over her shoulder. Between the warehouse and the excavation site there was another thick knot of foliage, bristling with jungle-level brush and trees and vines. A ditch that looked to be cut by natural forces a long time ago, snaked from the road through the trees, heading downslope. "Can you remember what was on the other side of this ridge? To the right of the warehouse as we faced it from below?"

Nicki tilted her head. "Trees, I think. There was a sheer wall directly beneath the warehouse, but the ridge sort of ducked in at that point and it was all vegetation. No houses beneath the jungle growth for another hundred yards, maybe, and then those started up again."

She nodded, thinking it through. "Plenty of land to dump or bury waste, if needed. Trash anyway. Let's say there are plumbing facilities—that's one thing. But it's not as if they can truck out typical garbage without someone noticing. And again, definitely not animal waste."

She peered back up the street. There were workers in hard hats at the excavation site, but the fence angled in enough that they weren't directly in their sightline. If anyone happened to turn the corner, though...

Meh. That wasn't likely. "Up and over," she announced and as Stefan turned to her, she hit the fence. It was a standard interlocking wire fence with a metal crossbeam at the top—no razor wire, importantly—and she was over it in less than thirty seconds, Stefan right behind her.

"Ditch," he directed and she headed that way. It'd be the least clogged with vegetation, and chances were good that it'd find its way down.

They were under the cover of trees almost instantly, slowing to a crouched walk. The ditch was narrow, allowing only one of them to go through first, and Nicki stood back to let Stefan take the lead. His op meant his ass sliding down the mountain if the dirt gave way unexpectedly.

It was preternaturally quiet as they crawled through the underbrush—no birds up here, probably scared away by the loud machines and people. It didn't take them long to get to their destination.

"Hold up," Stefan said, raising a hand. "This is it."

Twenty-Six

Stefan surveyed the ditch as it cascaded down the mountain. Piles of organic material that wasn't natural to the forest—the rotting rinds of fruits and vegetables, disintegrating paper and grease—littered the area, but the tree cover was less intense, allowing bugs and animals and rain to pound down on the detritus, returning it to the earth. There were other more permanent junk items as well. Utensils and clothing mostly, nothing of value.

"No way are we going to find something legit here," Nicki said, coming up beside him. "They're not stupid. This could be anyone's junk."

"Agreed. The fact that it's here, though, lends credence to someone living in the warehouse. Not that anyone would necessarily listen to that proof unless we were in the midst of an international incident."

"Still." Nicki peered off into the trees. "If this is where they're dumping stuff, it has to be the shortest distance to the warehouse, right? I mean, wouldn't they cut a path of literal least resistance?"

"They would." Stefan stood and bent into the foliage. "They wouldn't be dumping anything in broad daylight, either."

Silently, they moved out of the ditch and into the thick underbrush, following a trail beaten down by what appeared to be months of travel back and forth. The warehouse was only a hundred feet into the brush, the fence not gated but bent back and secured with thick twine, making a makeshift opening.

"Not very secure."

"It is if no one knows it's here." Stefan pointed past the opening. More foliage loomed beyond the fence, the jungle ever encroaching, and then a flat asphalt drive and an equally blank wall. "If the workers never saw anyone dumping the trash, they wouldn't have any reason to suspect this is here. And no gate saves the need to either explain why there's a gate here in the first place, or to entrust your guards with keys that they'll inevitably lose. With this setup, they can rescue the fencing as necessary, no one the wiser. The entire building and fence line will be torn down soon enough, I suspect, as construction ramps up on the ruins."

Nicki poked at the fence. "Should we go in?"

"I don't think so," Stefan said. "Still not enough proof that there's anything on the other side, and we'd be seen if that court-yard is open to the sky. But..." he smiled. "This definitely argues for no dogs. They'd never leave this open if losing dogs were a concern."

Ari was close. Stefan knew it. Still, he forced himself to remain calm as he and Nicki traced their way back to the main ditch, then kicked at a few more mounds of trash. Bugs skittered away, but nothing more useful revealed itself.

"I say we go down," she said, scanning the trail. "We need to know where this ends up, and what kind of climbing we'd need to do." She flashed him a quick smile. "You know, hypothetically."

The ditch went on for another few hundred feet before the cliff wall that had been evident below the warehouse showed its face. The ground dropped off precipitously into maybe a thirty-foot drop. Nicki peered over the edge, but there was no denying the delight on her face.

"Not really worth ropes," she shrugged. "How're your free climbing skills?"

"Adequate," Stefan said. "A descent isn't necessary, though. We don't know where that bottoms out."

"True." She picked up a good-sized rock, leaned further over the edge and dropped it. They heard the crashing of tree branches, then a distant splash. "Water," she said. "Not deep. Probably where the ditch drains. Maybe houses beyond it, but I bet it's a shared ravine system, probably more trash in it—yard waste, scraps, that kind of thing."

"Snakes, bugs," he said. "Rodents."

"Excellent." She squatted down and surveyed the rocky outcropping. "Seriously, they might as well have cut stairs into this thing. Totally no big deal." She rolled back up to her feet and turned to him. "You up for it?"

They went over the side minutes later, their feet clad in climbing shoes, and ropes attached to their belts in case they were needed.

As Nicki had predicted, the ridge was thick with crags and handholds, and the cliff face angled out slightly, offering a gentler grade than straight down. Gravity was also on their side, allowing them to scramble more quickly than an upward climb would allow. As he'd seen before, Nicki proved to be a fast and nimble climber—better than him at discerning footholds and ledges. She went first and proved her value by calling out the path in a low, clipped voice. It took the guesswork out of the descent, and within a few minutes, they were hovering over a small stream.

"Not deep," she said. "But the rocks could be slippery."

Stefan peered down as well. "To the right?"

She nodded, and he noted the leaves and dirt tangled in her hair. She seemed completely oblivious to them as she glanced back at him and grinned. Then she was off the wall, dropping in a crouch with a small splash, making sure her feet were steady before she moved out of the small stream.

"That hurt like a bitch." She laughed. "Hang down closer to the ground, and bend your knees more. There's not enough water to give you any sort of cushion."

He moved down quickly, following her direction. "You're injured?"

"Eh, not really." She was sitting on the grass, working off her shoes. She rotated her ankles and gave him the thumbs up. "Jarred me, that's all. And thank God we've got dry socks and shoes. Because it'd be a long soggy walk back to the street otherwise.

They changed and headed out of the woods, but there was no denying that Nicki wasn't moving as fast. "You *are* injured," Stefan said as they cleared another stand of underbrush. They were in a shallow ravine behind a row of brightly painted cottages, but they could see a cobblestoned street above. "I should call a car."

"You should shut up and let me get out of the forest. I'm fine," Nicki said, her tone unusually tight. "Quit lagging. I need you to stamp down the brush or I'd set the pace."

He turned back, not fooled by her vocal bravado. Her stride appeared steady, though, and they made it to the street quickly enough. From there, they hiked toward the center of town, and the moment Stefan saw a cab, he hailed it despite Nicki's protests. She wasn't limping, but she was...off.

In the cab, she leaned back against the seat, rolling her eyes as they set off. "I'm fine," she said. "You worry too much."

"It's an occupational habit."

She snorted. "One you've honed over a long, long time."

"So, you should trust my instincts."

"Yeah, yeah."

When they reached the hotel, she exited the vehicle with surprising speed and Stefan quirked a glance at her. "You're better. That was fast."

"I told you I was okay." She grimaced down at herself as they stood on the front steps of their hotel. "But I'm not gonna lie. I'm a little gross. We totally just climbed through a garbage dump. You know that, right? Even if it was a really nice one."

He laughed, gesturing her up the stairs. "I need a shower as well. And I can arrange for our medic to see you."

"Oh for God's sake, Stefan!" Nicki stamped ahead of him, clearly recovered, but with a speed that didn't make sense to him. "I'm fine. I would tell you if I was hurt, and I'm not hurt. I'm good. I stink, but I'm good."

"Perhaps." Smiling at her groan, he watched her as she crossed the lobby and punched the elevator button.

When they reached their rooms, he addressed the neatly outfitted guard who stood at attention inside Nicki's room. "Any issues? Visitors?"

"No sir," the operative said. "A sleepy day in Alaçati."

"Good," Stefan nodded as Nicki moved out of earshot, and focused on his man. The operative's face had changed subtly.

"Everyone's back aboard the yacht, sir, and ready for your orders. Tonight?"

"No," Stefan said. "The official tour isn't until tomorrow, and if we find anything in our recon, we'll need to leave quickly. But unless I miss my guess, we're stable until tomorrow. You find out anything else?"

"We've pulled out of the parks and surveyed from a distance. The squatters keep to themselves. They took the money and blankets and supplies, then vanished back wherever they came. I don't think we'll have any trouble there."

"Good." Stefan glanced back to the door that led to Nicki's sleeping area. Nicki had already turned the shower on. "I need eyes on the excavation site, as much information as we can get. Security should be light—no more than three men, standard weaponry. If you see anything more involved, notify me immediately."

The man stepped away and Stefan secured the hotel door, then considered the second closed door between him and Nicki. Something was definitely unsettled about her, and he was determined to find out what.

Twenty-Seven

Nicki closed the door of her bedroom and darted across the room, kicking off her shoes as she went. Two water bottles sat on the dresser, and she grabbed one and tilted it into her mouth. She was being silly. She was drinking enough, she knew she was. Her nerves were on overdrive, was all. She simply needed to relax and stay hydrated.

A short knock sounded at the door. She froze.

"Nicki?" Stefan's voice was cultured and aristocratic, and currently overlaid with a distinct tone of concern. And she didn't want him concerned—not about her. Not when they were so close to doing something so cool.

"Yes! Yes, hang on." She moved quickly over to the doorway. Today's walk in the woods had been exactly as she'd imagined working with Stefan would be. They were partners, equals, since there weren't any sophisticates standing around and no one was firing guns. She knew how to hike, and how to read terrain. She knew how to climb, too. He might be a demigod, but she didn't suck.

The fall into the water had jarred her ankles, but it hadn't hurt her. Not really. It simply had jammed the leg she'd broken in the damned bike accident four years back, and she'd had visions of traction in her head violent enough to make her dizzy. Once the dizziness had started, all the usual freak-out followed —*Was she having an incident? Would she be okay? Was this a heart attack of any sort?* And of course that kind of thinking invariably kicked up her heart rate. A vicious stupid cycle that she knew better than to—

She opened the door.

"Hi!" she said brightly. "Sorry, I was getting ready to take a shower."

Stefan's expression was solemn. "One of the finest features of this hotel is its suite's primary bathrooms. They're four times larger than typical Turkish hotel suites, did you know that?"

Nicki blinked. "I—I didn't know that," she said, taking a step back though she hadn't expected, hadn't planned for him to follow her into her hotel room. But she could definitely roll with it. "I'm not sure my hotel room is as well-equipped as yours is, though. Maybe you should double-check."

Stefan took another step forward, shutting the door behind him. "I think that's an excellent idea," he said. "You can never be too careful with quality control."

"I've heard that."

He lifted his hand, smoothly pulling off his shirt, and she marveled once again at the perfection of his abs and pecs. He wasn't muscle-bound from a gym, and he wasn't corded the way athletes were, but he was somewhere deliciously in between.

He kicked off his shoes, then reached for his pants. "Showers are usually improved if you take off your clothes," he said. "You might want to catch up."

"I—" Nicki reached for her shirt, but she stopped when he undid the clasp of his trousers, allowing them to fall to the ground. They didn't get stuck on his smooth hips or muscled thighs, but fell in an expensive whoosh. He stepped out of them, and padded toward her, working out of his boxer briefs as well.

"Now you're really behind," he said. "Maybe I should help you out."

Nicki couldn't move if she tried. Stefan stepped closer and pulled her shirt up over her head, then hooked his fingers underneath her sports bra. "How can you breathe in this thing?" he muttered. Nicki laughed and kept her arms raised, but as he lifted the bra to her biceps, trapping her arms, he left it there.

Instead, he leaned forward and nuzzled her breasts with his face, holding her close when she would have flinched away. "I really need a shower, Stefan—"

"We're getting there." Leaving her to finish pulling off her bra, he sank to his knees, trailing his hands down her now-quivering abs. He flipped the tab loose on her pants and pulled them down along with her underwear, but when he would have leaned in for a kiss she stepped back.

"Race you," she said, kicking off her pants and heading for the bathroom. Stefan gave her a head start, but there was only so much space in a hotel room, even one on the celebrated coast of Alaçati. Nicki squealed as he caught her one step shy of the shower, and he reached over her head, turning the spigots on full blast.

"You should never try to race me to water," he warned. "I will always win."

He crowded her into the shower as it heated up and she clung to him while he adjusted the temperature to something shy of boiling. The water pounded onto her back as his arms went around her, and she groaned at the competing sensations of man and hot water, surrounding her in a cocoon of comfort.

"Better?" he murmured, angling her head under the water enough to drench her hair.

"So much better," she said. And it was. Her dizziness was

gone, her heart rate was steady, and she felt rejuvenated despite the fact that she wasn't precisely clean yet. Stefan laughed and turned into the stream of water as well, soaking himself as she reached for the shampoo—which he took out of her hands.

"Let me?" He asked the question as if she might say no, and she coughed a laugh.

"A hot naked demigod wants to wash my hair, you think I'm going to say no to that?"

"Any hot naked demigod?"

"Anyone I allow into my shower. And believe me, you... qualify." She let her words trail off as Stefan massaged thick, luxurious shampoo into her hair, his fingers massaging her scalp then down her neck and over her shoulders.

"You're hired," she moaned. "For whatever cost you want. Please don't stop doing that."

His laughter rumbled behind her, and he slicked the soap through her hair—and his own, she vaguely realized. That done, he turned her in his arms and pulled her to him, the water cascading around them in a warm, sensuous haze.

"Better yet?" he asked.

"Infinitely, impossibly better yet." Nicki was plastered against Stefan's chest, the tilt of his shoulders protecting her from a direct hit of the blasting water, and his heat expanded around her, making everything safe. She sighed, and to her own ears it sounded a bit more intense than she intended.

Stefan apparently agreed. He shifted to look down at her, but she kept her head tucked against him a moment longer, until his hand touched her chin, lifting it up.

"You were injured in that ditch," he said. "But you walked steadily after, no limp."

Nicki nodded. Her heart didn't skip a beat, though, and her adrenaline didn't fire up. Something about the lulling patter of the shower and the feel of Stefan's arms around her made his questions concerned, but not intrusive, not dangerous. She knew what she needed to say to soothe his worries. To soothe her own. And she said it.

"I thought I tweaked my old leg injury. The biking one. That one had been super painful to come back from, and every time I stick a landing I react all out of proportion to the actual impact. It's ridiculous. I know it's ridiculous, but I can't help myself." She grimaced, knowing the words sounded accurate—because they were true. She was also being ridiculous about her possibly-maybe-never manifesting heart condition.

But that she couldn't share with him. Not yet.

"And did you disturb the leg?" he asked. "Is it weaker?"

She shook her head, feeling safe enough to meet his gaze. "Not that I can tell. It may hurt tomorrow, but not much."

He frowned. "You shouldn't participate in the expo today."

"Oh, that's not going to be a problem," Nicki said. "It's on water, and I won't be going at the speed of say, water skiing. Windsurfing can get dangerous, sure, but not here. The water is shallow and the winds aren't crazy."

"Would you know you were overdoing it before you actually injured yourself?"

She considered that. It was a good question, both for her heart and her leg. "I would," she said honestly. "I'd feel the pain start up—if for some reason the wind is unusually bad or the currents tricky or whatever, I'd know I was heading into danger."

He appeared to accept her response and dropped a kiss on her forehead. The movement was so gentle that something quivered in Nicki's chest. Something good this time.

Stefan reached out to the wall, turning off the faucets. "I think we should be doubly sure," he murmured.

Twenty-Eight

~∾~

Stefan stepped out of the shower first, pulling a towel off the granite counter and shaking it out. He wrapped Nicki in it as she watched him, her entire body quivering with the need to dry herself off on her own, without his help. "This would be one of the times you need to follow my directions," he said, softening his words with a smile. "Are you willing to give that a try?"

"Sure," she said, drawing out the syllable as she tilted her head. "You're not going to tie me to the bed or anything are you?"

He lifted his brows. "Would you like that?"

To his surprise, she winked. "No. Not until I've saved your life and you owed me big. I have a feeling you can tie a hell of a square knot, and I'd need to make sure you'd let me go."

"Mmm." The thought of Nicki tied to the bed was more arousing than he would have expected. Not because he wanted to dominate her, either. Even locked in chains, he suspected that Nicki wouldn't be easily dominated.

No, this had more to do with giving her the attention and care he was sure she'd never claim for herself. For having the leisure to treat her the way he wanted to treat her. If he needed

172

to tie her up to make that happen, then he would, eventually. But he wondered if he didn't need to...if all he needed to do was ask.

His body responded with swift and insistent urgency, and he tightened his jaw against its intensity. He tousled Nicki's hair with a second towel, then threw it aside. Then he pulled her to the door.

"What about you?" she asked.

"I'll dry." Turning swiftly, he caught her up in his arms, her natural athleticism making the move easier as she anticipated his movement and braced herself on his shoulders.

"Should it bother me that you've been carried before?"

She grinned. "Team adventure races. Sometimes it's just easier to throw me."

Before she finished the words he tested the theory out, tossing her toward the bed as she burst into startled laughter. He followed as quickly, climbing onto the bed and tangling them both in the sheets.

"See? I told you I would dry off."

"Not by using me as a towel!" she protested, but she wrapped her arms around him anyway. "Now I'm all wet again."

"I was counting on it," Stefan said, and he lowered his mouth to hers to give her a searching kiss before breaking away again. "You're right, though. You're definitely good at being thrown." He nuzzled her lips. "How good are you at lying still?"

"That depends." She scooted up onto the pillows, smiling as he propped himself on one arm. "Am I lying in a shallow ditch while a fire is racing over me, or lying in a sleeping bag with a bug crawling over me?"

"Nothing so nerve-wracking, I assure you," Stefan said. "You won't have to leave the comfort of this bed. And I assure you, I would gladly defend you from any attacking bugs."

"Then what are you..." her voice trailed off as he slid off the bed.

"We'll start with something easy. Stay there," he said, then he moved swiftly back into the bathroom. This hotel was usually occupied by celebrities and the glitterati, and management had spared no expense to ensure they were properly taken care of. In one of the cabinets there was a complete supply of sun care and beach recovery supplies, including a myriad of suntan lotions and exotic oils. He picked up one of the bottles and read the label. Close enough.

He padded back into the room, and Nicki's gaze drifted decidedly south as he approached the bed. Then she spied the oil. "I don't think that's going to at all be necessary—"

"I do," he said as he knelt again on the bed.

"Seriously, Stefan you don't need to massage me every time we get naked. Which is not to say I mind it, in the slightest. But it's not necessary. I'm not that broken."

Her words made his heart thump in a strange, discordant cadence, but he set the bottle down on the bed, then reached behind her to shove the pillows to the side. "I'm not trying to fix you, Nicki," he said, his voice rough. "I promise."

He put his hands on either of her shoulders, pressing her down flat. Then he picked up the oil again. "I'd like to tell you that this is for your pleasure, but it's not," he murmured as he flipped the lid of the oil bottle open. "It's solely for mine." He shook the bottle, catching her attention. "And it's water-based, happily enough."

Nicki watched, mesmerized, as he tipped the bottle over, at an angle that ensured that only the thinnest trail of oil drizzled out from the tip. The oil slid in a long, sensual line through the quiet air until it landed, pooling over the pebbled nipple of first her right breast, then her left as he shifted the position of the bottle.

Nicki released a guttural sigh as she sank more deeply into the only remaining pillow on the bed, offering no protest as Stefan continued the thin trail of oil down her quivering abs and over her belly. Fierce satisfaction rose within him as she arched beneath the sensual assault, her mouth falling open as the cool slide of oil spilled down her skin.

"You're going to have to replace these sheets," she managed as he tossed the oil aside.

"They can put it on my bill." He leaned forward and slid his fingers over her breasts, slick with oil, taking her nipples between his fingers and squeezing enough to make her focus back on his face. She was flushed, her breathing more of a pant, but there was no hesitation, no doubt in her gaze.

He spread his fingers over her breasts, palming them as she arched beneath him. "I'll give you exactly three hours to quit that," she half-moaned, and her face was a wonder to behold. Nicki was always in motion, ready to dash to the next adventure or take on the newest challenge. She never slowed down. But now she had stilled, now she was solely focused on the present. Her mouth was slack, her lips softly parted, her breathing low and deep as he kneaded her breasts with a slow, sensual movement. Her brow was untroubled, and her eyes had drifted closed, giving her the aspect of a woman asleep, lost in dreamless relaxation.

You're beautiful, Stefan thought, and grimaced as Nicki's eyelids fluttered. He hadn't realized he'd spoken aloud.

"You don't have to say things like that," she murmured, though her smile was dreamy as her eyes fixed on him. "I mean, they're lovely, but again, they're not necessary."

"It's only the truth," Stefan said. "You appreciate the truth."

Her lips twitched. He hadn't changed the rhythm of his hands, his movement, and he could almost see her sinking further and further into deep bliss as he lavished attention on her. When he dropped his mouth to the stiffened peaks of her breasts, she hissed another sigh, muttering something far too incoherent to make out. With the focus of her attention, though, he dropped his hands away, sliding down to smooth the oil and warmth further down her waist and belly. His touch was gentler here, though her abs knotted briefly, resisting his touch. But he didn't take long to get to his destination.

The oil shimmered on Nicki's thighs as she tensed again, but he whispered reassurance while his fingers dragged along the outside of her lean hips and strong legs before curving in again. "Have I done anything you haven't enjoyed so far?" he asked.

"No...oh, God no," she said, her heavy-lidded eyes watching him as she struggled up onto her elbows. "But you're going above and beyond the call of duty here—seriously."

"And you're not following directions," he smiled. "You're supposed to be relaxing." His hands shifted, his fingers dipping down into the vee between her legs, running along the outer-most edge of her most sensitive skin.

Nicki's gasp was tight. "You seriously expect me to relax while you're doing that?"

"I expect you to try." Stefan held her gaze, drinking in the sheer vitality of the woman who lay open before him, his to cherish and hold...and to thoroughly, completely enjoy. "I don't think you're trying hard enough."

Twenty-Nine

Nicki flopped back down on the bed as Stefan pulled her legs wider, her mind lost in a riot of sensation. The midday sun streamed through the windows, leaving nothing to shadows or gloom, but she didn't feel self-conscious about her body being fully revealed to him. If anything, her body was something she could count on, at least the outside of it. She knew she was fit, knew she looked as good as her genetics would allow. She wasn't embarrassed, despite Stefan's intimate gaze.

But she *was* close to toppling over the edge, before the man had even laid a finger on her where it mattered most.

Stefan solved that problem as she thought it, dragging a soft finger against the tiny nub of nerves that made up the pinnacle point of sensation for her, the exact nexus of need and want that had her clenching the sheets with her fists as he zeroed in. Then he moved off it as quickly, and it was all she could do not to reach up and guide him back, give him a map, read off GPS coordinates if it would get him back to where she needed him to be.

"Patience," Stefan breathed and Nicki's eyes shot open, only to see him watching her face as he brushed his fingers against her once again. "I want to explore your body, to touch and taste you. That will take time."

"Not too much time, I hope," she gritted out. He swirled his fingers closer to where she most wanted him. He grazed her clit and she sucked in a breath, her legs locking down to stay still, and he rumbled a soft laugh.

"So sensitive," he murmured. And he spread his fingers over the skin of her inner thighs, kneading the oil in more deeply. He lowered his mouth to her hipbone and touched his teeth against the skin that rested above the bony knob, the shock and pleasure of the nip startling her. She jumped beneath his touch and his laughter sounded again, but his mouth traced a scorching trail over her leg and down the curve of her inner thigh, not stopping until his tongue had replaced his fingers over the sensitive folds of skin. He suckled her clit, and Nicki felt the pull of need more strongly than ever, the urge to burst getting inexorably closer.

"Yes, yes," she muttered as if it were some kind of incantation to bring what she most wanted into reality.

Stefan was happy to comply. His right hand shifted to grip her outer hip, and he flicked his tongue over her in a rapid staccato of movement that made her breath catch in her throat, her heat beginning to stutter-step but only for the best of reasons as he twisted her higher and higher, seeming to know instinctively when she would crest, when she would break, and easing back from that brink in time—only to start the progression all over again, each rushing tide faster and faster as she built toward her release.

"I think, perhaps, this—"

Nicki's brain melted as the unmistakable pressure of Stefan's fingers slipped fully inside her channel, pausing momentarily before dipping deep inside her. As he filled her, he pressed more insistently against her clit, this time with his mouth, his tongue, the slight scrape of his teeth. The rushing tide became a waterfall and a strangled cry escaped Nicki's mouth before she clamped her teeth shut, half lifting out of the bed as the orgasm shook her entire body. She bucked hard, but Stefan only let up a little, allowing her to settle back into the sheets only a half breath before his tongue skated again over the over-sensitized skin, his pressure both within and without driving her toward another impossible release before the first one was complete.

"Stefan—I can't—" was all that Nicki could manage before she tumbled over the edge a second time, and then he did withdraw, but only briefly until he returned to her body, holding her against him, her back to his chest as she half-curled into a quivering mass of convulsions.

"Shhh," he said, again and again as she trembled in his arms. Surprisingly, she felt the sudden need to cry, and she blinked her eyes hard against the sensation. Stefan merely tightened his hold around her, his murmurs sliding between English to what had to be Oûrois, then something else, and then back to English again. Except it all seemed the same—the words sounding different but her understanding of each new whisper crystal clear, as if she knew what he was saying in a zillion different languages. That couldn't be right—wasn't right, she was sure—but she didn't stop him from his quiet endearments. Her mind twisted and turned, doubling back on itself, and if he knew she was enduring a cacophony of reactions, he gave no indication. He merely held her, as if they had all the time in the world.

He did, of course. She didn't, but he did.

Nicki blinked out toward the windows of the hotel room, where light poured in past the sheer curtains. From this angle, she couldn't see the ocean or the city, or the boats clogging the bay. She could only see the crystal blue sky, staggering in its beauty, with only a few clouds chasing across. How many times had she laughed up into that sky, whether she was clinging to a mountain or toeing the edge of a cliff or standing at the top of a summit? That same exultation swamped her, the sense of it dizzying her almost—but not the dizzy of danger, of her heart beating too fast and her blood coursing too slow. It was the dizzy of magic, the dizzy of possibility.

She blinked. It was the dizzy of falling in love.

Oh, no you don't, she willed herself as Stefan leaned forward to nuzzle her shoulder. No, no, no. This wasn't real, what she had with Stefan. This wasn't long term. It couldn't be. Stefan wasn't lovestruck. She'd caught his fancy and she was certain he was earnest in all of his compliments, but she was a moment's fascination with him. The same way he was a moment's fascination for her.

Yeah. Exactly like that.

She schooled her breath to slow, her legs to unkink, and reaching her point of relaxation was easier than she thought it would be.

When she unbent enough for his satisfaction, Stefan spoke again.

"Had enough? Or would you—" His thick shaft nudged against her back, and she turned more fully to him, pulling him over onto her as she lay back on the bed again.

"Please," she said, surprised at the brokenness of her voice as she realized he was already sheathed. "I want—yes."

Fortunately, Stefan had apparently added "satisfied garble" to his list of foreign languages, and understood what she wanted perfectly. Slowly, with infinite gentleness, he leaned forward and nudged against her center, waiting until the next paroxysm of tremors subsided to ease himself into her. She sucked in a breath as he stretched her, but his gaze was locked on her face and when she met his stare, her body relaxed all at once, allowing him to slide into her with greater ease. He pressed forward, filling her, and her legs fell loosely to the side, her back arching. She savored the pure sensual pleasure of the two of them so intimately connected.

"Good?" Stefan asked, and she sensed the intensity of his stare—she'd closed her eyes again, and now she fluttered her lids open to meet his beautiful blue-gray eyes. He watched her with such infinite tenderness and unmistakable desire that her heart swelled with joy—it was so much—too much—yet she wouldn't trade this moment for the world.

"Good," she managed, her mouth wobbling into a smile. "So, so good."

Thirty

A surge of triumph surged through Stefan's blood, quick and hot, thickening his shaft further and causing the muscles in his back to knot up, if only to keep his position steady over Nicki's sweat and oil-slicked body. She surrounded him with heat and need, and he pulsed inside her, glorying in the wonder of her strength, her intensity, her passion.

Her lids drifted shut again, but he knew she was struggling to focus, to store up every touch, every twitch, every pressure of his body against hers. She was no stranger to sex—no stranger to him anymore—but with her headlong race through life, he suspected she didn't often take the time to truly indulge herself. He would give her that time, though he could almost hear the crash and clank of her thoughts banging around in her head. She couldn't rest for thirty seconds before her mind started up all the fervor usually reserved for her body.

He wasn't unfamiliar with the condition.

Now he rocked into her with gradually increasing speed. He could afford to let the pressure build within him, secure that Nicki was beneath him, surrounding him, willing to ride this tide of pleasure for as long as it might last. He watched as her body relaxed further, the reaction allowing him to bury himself further with each thrust. At some point the tide of his urgency woke an echoing response within her, and her lids fluttered open again, her sex-glazed stare meeting his, flickering with renewed desire. Her mouth curved into a grin as her hands came up, curling around his forearms.

"You're the one who's perfect," she said, her words a purely feminine purr. "You're built exactly—right. You are."

The words seemed oddly truncated to him, like half of what she'd meant to say, but at that moment Nicki tightened around him, and Stefan's brain short-circuited briefly before coming back online. She continued to roll her muscles along the straining length of his cock, and she smiled up with him with clear knowledge of what she was doing.

"Showing off?" he murmured, dipping down to kiss her.

"It's important to exercise your muscles whenever you can," she said. "Especially your core."

"My compliments to your physical trainer. On second thought, he's a dead man. I'll happily cart him to Hades myself."

As Nicki laughed, Stefan lifted himself to his knees, bracing her hips on his thighs as her legs stretched to accommodate the movement. He went further still, though, bringing her ankles up until her legs formed a vee in front of his face, her ankles bracketing his jaw.

"What are you doing—" Nicki gasped as he bent into her, and her thighs tensed even as they accepted the gentle pressure he was applying.

"Every complete workout demands stretching as well," he said, sinking into her as her body accepted the different pose.

"You're so good to me," Nicki said wryly, but her head tilted back and she sighed, her legs lengthening into the stretch. "That feels...unreasonably awesome."

It was the expression on her face that did him in. She

watched him with pure, unfiltered pleasure lighting her features, her eyes half-lidded, her face creased with a slight smile, and that was all it took. The need built up within him, quick and hot, and his grip firmed on her ankles, urging her knees to bend and allow her legs to relax as he rocked into her.

"Ohhh—" Nicki's gaze was fixed on his face, her eyes alert, searching, and once again he sensed she was tracking his movements, his reactions, cataloging his every shift to play it back later. He didn't plan on letting the experience fade into memory, and the thought of that ratcheted him up further, until he hissed her name through his teeth. She grabbed his forearms, moving with him, rocking with him, experiencing the explosion that jolted through him as he felt it shatter him completely, everything he wanted, yearned for, needed suddenly releasing in a swift and fiery rush.

A blast of awareness punched through him, another flash of understanding of that light, that too-bright light, bursting into a supernova and then winking out into nothing. All the breath rushed out of him, and he felt suddenly—strangely—impossibly bereft. As if the long, cold fingers of the Underworld had reached out to drift along his skin.

Then it was gone again, so quickly he couldn't quite recall what he'd seen. His mind a jumble, Stefan collapsed to the side, rolling away from Nicki briefly as she moved as well—then froze. "I'm covered in oil," she announced, staring down at herself. "I think if I move I'm going to destroy these sheets."

"You worry too much."

She snorted. "You're the absolute first person to ever accuse me of that." But she remained on the bed as he fetched towels, and the cleanup of her body required another shower, and then an extensive drying-off period that filled the room with laughter and teasing and the kind of kisses that alternated between long and slow and fast and hard. And Stefan watched the hours slip by too quickly, until suddenly it was three p.m.—which he knew only by Nicki's reaction.

"Is that right?" she squeaked. "That can't be right—is that really right?"

"What?" He glanced up from where he was pulling on his boxers—and Nicki pointed to the clock.

"I have to be at the beach in an *hour*—an hour! Ready to give a demonstration. That means I need to be there in a half hour, which means we should already be on our way!"

She flew to the dresser, pulling out clothes and throwing things on the floor until she found what she needed. Then, as if suddenly realizing what she'd done, she picked up the discards and shoved them back in the drawer—all more quickly than Stefan could draw breath to protest.

She was wriggling into a sport suit when he finally got words out. "We're only a few minutes away from the beach by speedboat. We'll go that way."

"Great!" she said, diving for another drawer. He had a feeling he'd see a second avalanche of clothing. "Go get ready—and hurry! I don't want to give Omir a reason to cancel the tour again tomorrow. Go!"

Stefan went, not even trying to stay his laughter. Nicki had transformed from languorous to hyper alert in the blink of an eye, all over a demo that she was doing not for love, not for money—but simply because it was the newest thing required of her to get the mission to the next step. As ridiculous as that sounded, it was enough motivation for her.

He was still laughing as he emerged from his own room a few minutes later to find Nicki already at his door, wearing a sundress over her bathing suit. "The concierge said you're right, said you'd called for a boat. We're only a few minutes away," she blurted. "But we've got to go!"

They made it to the marina in less than ten minutes, Nicki

chattering the whole way, mapping out her planned moves for the demonstration.

"It'll be quick, I'm thinking, maybe only twenty minutes, though could be up to an hour," she said, shouting over at him as they streaked across the bay toward the open beach. "I have no idea if I'll like their equipment, but I'm sure they've got top of the line stuff. It depends on how its rigged."

The wind whipped around them, forcing her to stand close to him in order to be heard. He didn't mind. While he refrained from wrapping an arm around her, he leaned in close ostensibly to hear her chatter about the demo. In truth, however, he simply wanted to be nearer to her, as near as he could manage in the public eye. She was a live wire once more, all the fogginess of her mood directly after the short fall at the cliff gone, and her breathless excitement was intoxicating.

She pounded his arm. "Are you listening to me?"

"Every word," he shouted back, transferring his gaze to the beach as they neared it. "Who'll be out there with you?"

She turned and squinted, then nodded briskly, up on her toes, as if she was going to hop overboard and swim if that would get her there to shore quicker. The boat banked and cut speed, heading through the no wake zone.

"Josef—that's half his staff right there, on the beach talking to the crowd. Oh good, they have kids. They're the best with wind surfing, it's so much like play they pick it up quickly, not as intimidating as surfboarding or as boring as bodyboarding. That'll be—" she flashed a glance at him, coloring visibly despite the glare. "Sorry," she said. "I chatter when I get nervous."

He lifted his brows. "This demonstration makes you nervous?"

"Any performance does. It's part of what makes it good, I guess, but I'm always keyed up, even for something simple, at least until I get rolling on it." She blew out a breath. "Once I get rolling I'm fine, usually. I simply have to get started."

The boat swung in close to shore, and the gathering of men and women on the beach turned, one of the men raising a hand. Josef.

"Go ahead," Stefan said. "It's quicker from here if you swim. I'll be along before you get started."

"Good. Right." Without further word Nicki stepped up on the ridge of the boat and jumped into the water, dry-tech dress and all. Her beach shoes were meant for exactly that, and she stroked briefly through the water before hitting a section of the beach where she could stand, then she moved swiftly out of the water, her arms pumping, her skin shining bright in the full sun.

Stefan couldn't stop watching her as the boat whirled around, putting distance between them once again. Nicki had everything she needed—but he didn't. He wanted to capture her demonstration on video.

He wanted to hold all that sunshine in his grasp, before it slipped away again for good.

Thirty-One

N icki blew out a long breath as she reached the knot of people gathered at the shoreline. Her usual pre-performance nerves were fully in evidence, despite the very thorough, *very* relaxing time she'd spent with Stefan. She'd hoped that languor would endure for a little while longer.

"Miss Clark! Excellent, you're here." Omir came forward first, her efforts last night clearly paying dividends. She didn't mind flirting with the Turkish official as a concept, but the reality was proving a little more tedious. She only had one more day, though. In twenty-four hours or so, they'd take their tour of the excavation site and get the information they needed—she hoped. Either way, she would forever be done with Omir and his musky cologne after that. She doubted she'd participate in another windsurfing competition in Alaçati until he left his position. There were hundreds of other places to windsurf in the world.

Of course, none of them were as close to Stefan as Alaçati was. He was here, and she doubted he'd ever consistently live anywhere else in the world but here. If she ever wanted to see him again, she'd need to drum up some reason to come to this side of Europe...and the most obvious would be windsurfing. Otherwise, she'd look pathetic.

That thought struck her with unexpected force as she and Omir were joined by Josef and his crew, all of them buzzing happily about the moves they were going to show the beginners—and the ones they had saved to impress the intermediates as well. Unlike the international competition in August, not too many world-class windsurfers were in town for the exposition, given the focus on the newer adherents to the sport. Still, there were a few, and Josef fully planned to strut his stuff.

"You good, Nicki? We found a board we think you'll like." Josef waved his hand in front of her face, snapping her focus forward.

"I'm good—but don't stick me out there first round, at least not doing anything interesting," she warned. "I haven't had much time in the water so far this year." She cracked a smile, trying to quiet her own nerves. "Not all of us live on the beach, you know."

"Not yet, but my offer stands!" Josef grinned. "We're growing faster than we know what to do with, and the newer entrants to the sport have the money to travel. You could have all expenses paid, my friend, to go and windsurf your brains out in every corner of the globe. Think about it!"

He headed off and Nicki surged forward, scanning the boards and sails with a practiced eye. She spotted the one Josef had picked out for her almost immediately. Sleek, brightly colored and slightly smaller sized, it would fit her frame comfortably and give her maximum lift. The sail seemed to be connected properly to the mast foot, though the hinge configuration was new to her. How long had it been since she'd used equipment this nice? The boards at the Royal Beach had been serviceable and sturdy, meant for beginners. These babies were light. They would totally fly in the wind kicking up over the bay.

"Everyone in! We'll demonstrate beach starts—water starts are better suited for boat trips."

Nicki gave Josef the thumbs up, then lifted her board and carried it down into the water. A beach start was far easier than a water start, though when she'd first learned, it'd been on a large, choppy lake—no beach start beginning for her.

Still, the group that crowded closer to the shore was made up primarily of new surfers, and about a half dozen of Josef's team pushed their boards out past the crashing waves, to where the water reached their thighs. She started with her sail down-wind to keep the beach start easy. She wasn't trying to show off here, merely to reassure beginners how easy a proper beach start was. She walked her hands along the mast, taking it in one hand and the boom in the other. She pulled the sail backward to control the board. Turning upwind, she placed her mast hand on the boom and straightened both her arms. Then she placed her foot on the middle line of the board and pulled the board toward her, extending her arms. Using the power of the wind in the sail she was lifted easily onto the board, and just like that... she was flying.

They stepped off the boards and started again, showing the different ways to mount, common pitfalls, and getting a few of the intermediates into the game as demonstrators. The idea was to be relaxed, moving with the wind, and as Nicki warmed up, she felt more revived, eager to be in the water and moving fast. At length Josef pulled up beside her, waving something in his hands—a freestyle belt.

"You up to showing what you got?" he yelled.

Nicki laughed, grabbing the belt as he tossed. She pulled it around her waist, struggling a bit to keep the sail steady in the wind as she lost momentary contact. They'd practiced this move dozens of times over the years, the goal always to stay upright in the water, no matter the wind conditions or the difficulty of the maneuvers they were trying. She'd become somewhat of an expert and had the belt on quickly enough.

As she twisted the board backward and forward, however, warming up her usual moves, something felt off. She scowled, squinting at the mast foot of the rig. The board was super light and the sail flexible, but she couldn't shake the awkward sense she had. She jerked out of the harness, then jumped over the sail as the board shifted beneath her. After she nailed a clean landing, the board wobbled beneath her again and she glared down, but everything held. So far, so good.

The wind kicked up and she took advantage of it, reattaching the harness and leaning all the way over, her right arm extended wide as the watchers on the shore cheered all the freestyle moves of the instructors. Coming up again, the board skidded awkwardly—and then she saw it.

The mast foot was ratcheting out of its hinge.

"Stupid, stupid, stupid!" she screamed into the wind, but of course no one could hear her. The other instructors were leaping waves, and all she needed to do—all she had to do—was get the boat in safely. It wasn't an issue of crashing, though she sure as hell wasn't about to crash. It was an issue of not freaking out any of the newbies and not letting slip the fact that someone on Josef's team hadn't ratcheted down the mast foot well enough. Shame on her for not checking their work more closely.

She cut the sail quickly and headed against the wind, dropping her speed, a pretty move that had more to do with expediency than finesse. She made the turn easily and realized her adrenaline was jacked more than usual. Not surprising, but she was in shallow water, there was no danger here, no issue. She wouldn't embarrass Josef, but she wouldn't—

Her sight went black.

Nicki whirled around, gasping as her vision cleared then faded again, the dizziness so strong that she could barely stay upright. As it was, the harness was the only thing holding her in place, and she fought the urge to turn and throw up in the water. Her heart was pounding out of control and her breath was tight in her chest—everything was tight in her chest. Dipping crazily, the board whirled and shuddered, and she again was saved by her harness as she caught a hard edge of the wind. The board skittered out of the water, straight once more.

I won't drop, I won't fail, I won't—

The board swung crazily around and Nicki thrust her head up, facing the sky, the sun, the source of warmth and joy that had fed her all those long days as a teenager surrounded by sick people. And as the spray cleared she picked out a point on the shore that gleamed brilliantly white in the sunlight—a reflection off glass. A reflection off a camera lens, she realized blearily, and then she realized who was holding that camera, who was standing in the middle of the crowd as if no one else was there, focused solely on her, videoing her—seeing her.

Seeing her fail.

"Like *hell*," she growled, and she dropped down low, her body skimming the wave that seemed to reach up to pull her down...no. Not to pull her down.

To push her up!

She blinked, squinting through the jumping spray—but she wasn't wrong. A cluster of outstretched hands, all in myriad shades of blues and greens, thrust up out of the waves the next time she swooped down too low, shoving her back upright. She spun and jumped catching more wind, and the sea—or whoever was beneath it—played with her, luring her out into deeper water, helping her soar higher, swoop lower, and stay on her faulty board just a little bit longer. She thought she saw arms—hair—even faces, but after several more turns, fatigue hit her like a brick wall. Her sight faltered again, shimmied and whirled, and her heart shuddered hard in her chest. She angled back toward shallow water, once again feeling the surge of the board beneath her as unseen hands hurtled her and her craft toward safety...but this time, she'd pushed her luck a little too far.

Nicki's head spun, and this time there was no coming back. She cut the sail again and—well clear of everyone else in the group—tumbled into the water.

Thirty-Two

Around Stefan, the crowd burst into spontaneous laughter and applause.

"What a dismount!" breathed a woman beside him, awe thick in her voice. "Honey, did you see that?"

"She looked like she fell," the little girl said, and her mother snorted.

"You don't fall with that much precision—at least I don't. That was planned."

Stefan was inclined to agree with the child. He pulled the camera off his shoulder and stalked to the edge of the water, ignoring the shouts and cheers of the other spectators for the remaining athletes. He didn't want to draw attention to Nicki if she wasn't harmed, but he had no problem jumping into the bay with the entire lifeguard brigade if he thought there was anything wrong with her.

Something had definitely been wrong.

She'd started well enough—slightly tense, perhaps, getting her footing with the unfamiliar board and sail. The other instructors had pivoted and pirouetted around her, their bodies as lithe and built for movement as Nicki's. But then something had changed. He pinpointed it to after she'd gotten the harness from Josef, a freestyle apparatus that allowed her to angle her body more dramatically off the board. At first, she'd seemed fine with it—but she'd kept staring down at her board, at first with curiosity and then with something approaching distress.

Then she'd grasped the boom of the sail hard and from that point on, he couldn't tell what had been intentional and what had simply been her falling with precision and then being tossed back up again, as if the waves were part of the performance.

As if the waves....

Poseidon, what are you up to?

There was no response from the god of the sea, but a chorus of sea nymph chatter erupted from the waves, carried on the wind—laughter, worry, delight, tears. The tears added some urgency to his pace and he jogged up the beach, his eyes on Nicki as she floated for a few moments, her sail arcing out beside her. She'd pulled herself onto the board and her face was turned away from him. At this distance, it appeared as if she was merely taking a break to watch the other athletes flip and whirl, more of them coming off their boards with each turn. The demonstration was winding down.

A few of the surfboarders managed a dismount while angling their boards toward shore, a simple procedure that nevertheless generated applause from the appreciative crowd. Nicki would have done that too, he suspected. She wouldn't have done a flip into the water, no matter what, not with so many kids watching. She would have been more careful.

As if hearing his increasingly concerned thoughts, Nicki finally turned the craft toward shore. With a few quick strokes, she positioned it so she could easily stand in the water and push the entire apparatus forward. Other dismounted boarders were doing the same thing, only a few demonstrating a water mount to guide their boards in.

She took her time, then clearly noticed him standing at the shoreline. A bright, bold grin flashed across her face, and something hard and ugly unclamped from Stefan's chest. For the first time in ten minutes, he drew in a deep breath, and his hands unclenched from their fists as he proceeded casually down to the shoreline.

"You'll get wet," Nicki protested, waving him back. Her smile remained fixed on her face, but her voice sounded thin, thready.

"I'll survive." As the sea nymphs hooted and sang with delight, their distant cries audible to no one but him, Stefan waded into the water and took the edge of the sail. Nicki let him, floating backward as he maneuvered the board and sail around.

"This is all part of the demonstration," he said to her over his shoulder. "Showing how easy it is to pull the unit onto the beach. Go with it."

She didn't respond and he forced himself to focus on the board, the sail, safely bringing the unit out of the water to line up neatly with the other athletes' equipment. As he walked, he scanned the board, and he paused when he noted where the mast foot was secured to the wide, colorful board.

Stefan hadn't spent a lot of time on these toys, but he knew enough to know the mast foot was almost disconnected.

He dropped the board, turning back to the water, and Nicki was beside him. Someone had draped her in a brightly colored beach towel that proclaimed the name of Josef's camp, and she followed his gaze to the mast foot.

"Did it break mid-run?" he asked, as the chorus of sea nymphs changed cadence, becoming more mournful now that their playmate was no longer in the sea. "Or was it damaged when you started?"

Nicki didn't respond for a second, pulling her towel closer as if it was protection. "It didn't break as fully as some I've been on. It just sort of lost connection—it stayed attached, see? But not tightly."

"Right. And how did that affect your sailing?"

"Why, did I look bad?" She turned to him, disappointment evident in her face. He found himself shaking his head quickly, willing to do anything—say anything to reassure her.

"Not at all," he said. "The proof will be on the video footage later, and you can review it for yourself. There was a lot of spray at the end, when I suspect you had trouble with the mast. But it seemed you were in a controlled spin."

"A controlled spin, that's awesome." Nicki's laugh sounded shaky, and her color was off—not as warm or high as he would have expected, following her exertion in the water. "I totally fell at the end, though," she said with a candor that surprised him. "No way around that."

"It was artful enough to leave the question of whether or not you did it on purpose." He shrugged, falling in line with her as they headed back toward the main crush. "Do you need to rest? Are you hurt?"

"Nah. Beat up a little, shook up too, I guess." She shrugged. "I saw that mast foot issue and I could have kicked myself for not checking and rechecking the equipment more thoroughly. Josef's crew is the best, and they work with kids. They're hyper-vigilant. But it's my job to check their work. I'm the one in the water."

Her irritation sounded more like Nicki's normal voice, and Stefan's nerves quieted another few degrees as they re-entered the crowd. Fortunately, Nicki was one of several athletes, and while the older teen girls gravitated toward her, she emerged on the other side of the crowd relatively unscathed. Josef was surrounded by tourists asking questions, and Stefan suspected that she wouldn't tell him of the machinery issue until he was out of earshot of the curious crowd.

"Ambassador Mihal, Miss Clark. You saw much, yes? You have more for your tourism video."

Nicki blinked, but Stefan filled in smoothly. "We have a great deal of footage. You'll be very pleased with the final result."

"Good! Good." Omir scanned up to the ridgeline, his gaze drifting to the southern ridge and the excavation, prominently obvious from this distance. "I think we go ahead and do the tour this evening, as the sun is setting. That will give you good light?"

He slanted a glance to Nicki. It would provide terrible light, but she brightened immediately. "Oh! The light would be absolutely beautiful then," she said. "The sunset views from that location I suspect are stunning, and we could do some fun things with shadows since it's a centuries-old site."

"More than centuries," Omir said, puffing his chest out. "The foundations go back thousands of years. We are only now beginning to uncover its treasures."

"It sounds fascinating." And to her credit, Nicki apparently believed what she said, moving up to her toes as she stopped clutching the beach towel so tightly. "When would be convenient for you to show us?"

"After most of the day's work is done," Omir said, his gaze shifting up to the ruins again. "I will send a car at six p.m.—we'll have time to tour what we can and see the sunset. It will be a sight you will never forget, I assure you."

Nicki nodded enthusiastically, even as Stefan grimaced.

It was certainly a sight *he'd* never forget...especially if it led them to Ari.

Thirty-Three

The short window between the demonstration and the tour was a godsend. Nicki spent longer than any human should in the hotel's shower, which seemed surprisingly big and lonely without Stefan's body surrounding her. But she didn't want to see Stefan right away.

She leaned against the cool tiles. Her dizziness was totally due to lack of hydration, she knew. That and nerves. But it—not to mention her hallucinations of people in the water—scared her anyway. Visions of five years ago flashed in front of her eyes. Her father's gray face the day she'd found him on the floor, her brother's fear. Her mother's descent into petulance and fainting "spells," completely checking out as Nicki had cared for her dad and tried to keep her brother supported and motivated.

And then had come the day of the high school track meet, when her brother John had fallen too—passing out right in the middle of his race. Her worst nightmare come to life. He'd survived, but then he'd received the diagnosis of cardiomyopathy, and not only had his activity level changed...his entire approach to life had too.

Nicki pulled herself back from those thoughts, turning her

face into the pounding spray. If she took much longer, Stefan would be in to check on her, and while ordinarily that would be something she'd welcome with open arms...not today. Today she needed to get the mission done, and convince Stefan that everything was good to go with her—her mind, her body, her heart. If he had one clue that she might have some sort of dizzy spell, he would never take her with him to find Ari. He might not take her anyway, but she had a shot if she remained healthy and alert.

He'd been impressed with her abilities up to this point, and she couldn't screw this up now. Not when she was so close to truly contributing, to truly being part of a team that mattered. She had to pull it together.

She did.

By the time Stefan did knock on her door, she was dressed in a summer dress and walking sandals, her video equipment cleared of all past sessions. She'd downloaded her own run to a memory stick. There'd be plenty of time to review that later and see if she could salvage any of it for use. She had a chance if Stefan had been focusing on her body, not her face. But if he'd had the camera trained on her face, then the viewers would see what he had doubtless seen—her panic, her concern, her stress. Maybe even the point at which she'd momentarily blacked out. Those images wouldn't be good for Josef, and they wouldn't be good for Alaçati. Or windsurfing. Or her.

But that wasn't something she needed to worry about. Not yet.

Stefan knocked again.

"Coming!" Nicki shouted, glad to hear the strength of her voice. It sounded bold and bubbly, exactly how Stefan was used to hearing her. She wouldn't have to put on any sort of show, she reminded herself for the millionth time. She simply needed to be herself.

She opened the door and blinked. "Hey," she managed, taking in his perfectly crisp blonde hair, his piercing blue gray eyes, the sheer masculinity of him, clad in a casual button down short-sleeved shirt and crisp trousers. His feet were shod in tech walking shoes that still managed to look suitable for dining al fresco in some fancy restaurant.

She glanced down at her own attire. "Should I change? I'm a little less formal."

"You're perfect." He leaned down and took her face in both his hands, kissing her gently. "As much as you protest that word choice. Plus, the taxi is here." He noted the camera on her shoulder. "Charged up?"

In more ways than one. "We could shoot for hours and still have memory left," she said, giving him the thumbs up. They made their way down the hallway. "Before we're surrounded by people again, is there anything I should be searching for in particular?"

"Workers, mainly. Men of about six foot three, dark hair. Ari looks...*looked* a lot like Kristos, but he was built on a bigger frame." He shook his head. "They used to joke that Queen Catherine was tired after having such a big baby, so she didn't try as hard with Kristos."

"Ouch!" Nicki said. "Brothers, I guess."

"Kristos didn't mind. He said she had to give birth to a hunk of rock first, before she could sculpt the David." He smiled as Nicki gave a short, coughing laugh. "In addition to the workers, anything you can get of the overseers, or entry points from the warehouse to the outside, up or down the building, would be good. I don't imagine they have extensive security, but there has to be something keeping those men in place at night. In place and quiet. Especially if this feeder camp has been in operation for over a year."

He hesitated. "I also want you to see if you can pick up any evidence of animals—that's still an outstanding question."

Nicki nodded. "Animal-animals or, like, three-headed dogs and all that?"

"All of the above."

She made a face. "I have a hard time believing they could hide animals in a warehouse. Someone would notice that."

"Agreed. But if you see anything suspicious that leans that way, it could be important."

The taxi was waiting for them at the front entrance of the hotel—and not a taxi at all but a personal car of Omir's. Stefan sat close to her despite the roominess of the back seat, and Nicki sensed her calm return. She could do this—she *was* doing this. Stefan didn't appear to be concerned about her health or the safety of the mission. He trusted her to do her job, and her job was a simple one. Take pictures and don't get lost while being sure to comment appreciatively at the right times. She could do this.

The car wound through the pretty streets of Alaçati. Acting every inch the respectful tourist, Stefan drew her attention various villas as they climbed the mountain, as if they hadn't walked through this same district earlier in the day. His chatter served to ratchet down Nicki's stress further.

"Up there—that one," Stefan said suddenly, and she blinked, following the direction of his pointed finger. A villa sat perched on the edge of an outcropping of stone, wide decks open to the glory of the bay and the distant Aegean Sea beyond. "Do you like it? It's similar to the one I own in Oûros."

"Really?" The villa was stunning but not pretentious, with clean lines and vivid blue accents. "It doesn't really hold a candle to the royal palace," she teased.

"Ah, but that isn't mine," he said. "My villa is where I go when all the work is done in the palace, and the royal family is at rest. It's where I light my own candles, and listen to the sea sing her lullabies."

"That sounds nice." Nicki kept the wistfulness out of her voice, but it was a near thing. The thought of Stefan on some promontory somewhere, watching the sunset, lighting candles as the night drew down on the city, was an image she'd have burned into her brain for the rest of her life.

"I like to think so. You're welcome to visit while you remain in Oûros, if time allows."

Nicki nodded, keeping her manner easy. She didn't know if he was maintaining their banter for the sake of the driver or to keep her entertained, but they chatted back and forth for the remaining few minutes as they wound up familiar roads, and finally turned down the street that fronted the warehouse. The gates to the excavation site stood open, and they rolled inside.

Omir was waiting for them.

"Welcome, welcome," he said as Nicki and Stefan exited the car, Nicki already bringing up her camera.

"Let me know what you want me to shoot," she said, staring around as if she'd never seen the site before. "I can't believe you stumbled over this."

"The area was a bit of a blight on our beautiful city," Omir said, warming to her clear admiration. "Overgrown, choked with weeds and brush." He gestured all around them, and Nicki swung around, keeping her camera low as she squinted to the side.

"That building looks old—there had to have been something there."

"The plot of land belonged to an industrial firm who had thought to build. Then the economy crashed, as economies do, only this was in the nineteen fifties. They let their lease expire, and the city bought the land and buildings. We had much to focus on with the beautification and development of the bay, however. It simply wasn't a priority."

"Wow," Nicki said, staring around with appropriately wide eyes. As she continued her expressions of awe, Stefan had turned away, peering intently at the far corners of the site.

Omir caught the movement. "So impatient! But then, we were as well when we discovered the treasures that lay underneath all the brush. You'll see why we're eager to open it as a tourist destination." He brightened as Nicki brought her camera up and repeated his little speech for the good of posterity. He explained the old usage of the land, how it had fallen into jungle, and then declared with excitement how the city had reclaimed the property, only to discover the masterpiece beneath.

"The industrial firm would probably have blasted through the ruins, perhaps not even realizing what they were," Omir continued dourly. "But the fates were not kind to them, and they paid for their hubris."

He waved to the warehouse building. "Soon we'll tear down the last remnant of their operation to make way for parking and an extension building for the ruins. It's a fitting end for a company who sought to deface this national treasure of Turkey."

Nicki didn't look at Stefan, but she knew his attention was once more focused on the Turkish official. If they didn't get Ari out of there on this trip, there was no guarantee he'd be there in another week or month.

If they were going to find him, they'd need to find him tonight.

Thirty-Four

Stefan kept his manner cool and polite as they wound their way through the excavation site. The ruin was a minor one, by Mediterranean standards, but it was impressive enough. A thick, squat, roughly built church was gradually being unearthed, as was a grotto-like area surrounded by columns and the remains of an old well. He could easily see how it would be a tourist draw once completed—so much closer than the more well-known sites such as Ephesus, while conveying the same sense of ancient world wonder and beauty. With a small entry fee, Alaçati would see the return on its investment to unearth the place almost immediately.

And there were still at least a dozen men and women who appeared to be actual archaeologists, mixing in with the remaining construction workers despite the late hour.

"It's a constant push-pull, eh?" Omir said for the benefit of Nicki's camera. "We must move forward quickly, and the intention was always that this would be a working exhibit, with tourists and archaeologists side by side as new possibilities emerge. Yet the archaeologists, they would rather that all our big machines and noise would go away. We can't do that—we would bring this fantastic site to the people as quickly as possible. But they're doing their job."

They toured the grotto and what had been uncovered of the church, with Omir eagerly showing off the visible remains of another, far more elaborate temple set into the rock beneath the primary one.

"Christianity is a bit of an opportunistic religion, yes?" Omir continued. "Its agents come to this place, they see its beauty, its possibilities. Rather than honor what has come before, they build right on top of it, transferring the mystic holiness of the place to their own uses." He flung his arms wide. "Not that you could blame them."

They made their way down toward the church and the temple below it, stopping to talk to archaeologists along the way. Nicki videoed every step and Stefan watched her closely. Fortunately, despite his uneasy feeling whenever he focused on her, she gave no indication of being out of sorts. She chattered incessantly with Omir, appearing almost besotted by him, a reaction the Turkish official gleefully took as his due. Stefan knew she was doing it for the mission—everything for the mission—but he found it strangely galling to watch her play up to the pompous man. When she caught his eye at one turn and winked, he was only marginally comforted.

What was wrong with him? He'd never sought after love—and he was damned glad for it. His earliest advisors, well versed in the ways of demigods, had counseled against lasting relationships when he'd first begun his service. Then, when he eventually did form attachments, he'd had the unenviable role of watching the women he loved gradually age and die. It never got any easier, so he'd prided himself on keeping to short term liaisons that didn't matter. His work was his romance, the Crown's protection his greatest focus. He traveled, he fought, he served. He allowed no time for anything else.

But he hadn't been lying when he'd shown Nicki the villa perched over the cliff. It did closely resemble his own idyll back in Oûros, with all the windows open to the sea and sun. Now he could imagine Nicki there as well, an entirely unexpected but not unwelcome thought. It was pointless to continue down that path, but he found himself straying toward the images he was conjuring forth for himself, if only to pass the time while the Turkish official nattered on.

The final stop on the tour was the most breathtaking by far —literally. Omir led them up to an open-air platform. "Ah! We are here in time to see the sunset. Be sure to take full views! It's an extraordinary sight."

For once, the man wasn't exaggerating. Stefan moved to the side to allow Nicki to step forward and video the commanding view of the ocean, the skyline, and the ridges in the far distance. Then she panned back around toward Omir, while he grinned self-importantly. "We'll reinforce this area in particular to allow for tourists to experience the magnificent view in safety and comfort," he said as Nicki focused on him.

She stiffened as he talked, her body language changing subtly and Stefan looked to where she was pointing the camera. Omir was in full throes of his discussion of the gated veranda decking they'd install to protect the ruins while allowing tourists maximum access, but that's not what held Stefan's attention.

The veranda fell away as the view curved back toward the warehouse, past a rough embankment that had once been an outer arch of the church. They were higher than the warehouse, and were afforded a clear view of the space between the two buildings.

Stefan studied the same thick knot of trees and jungle that he and Nicki had entered earlier that day. Beside those trees, a line of men filed out of the excavation site under the careful scrutiny of two men whose stance indicated they were carrying weapons or had access to them—they were clearly men who held power over these workers. Plenty of other workers remained on the site—and certainly all the archaeologists—so this routine was obviously well established. The men marched to the warehouse, where the building's garage stood open, trucks in place. After the men were safely inside, the garage doors rumbled shut.

None of those workers had looked like Ari Andris, but Stefan was too far away to tell anything definitively.

"Have you had any interest yet from American or European tourist channels?"

Nicki's gushing words distracted him, and he turned around in time as Omir noticed his stare, the official also pulled back by Nicki's question. "What do you mean?"

"Well, gosh—it's so intriguing what you're doing, preserving cultural heritage while doing what's right by the city as well. I'd have to think it would serve as a model for other reclamation or restoration projects." She smiled with yet more earnestness. "Not that you necessarily need to share your success with the outside world, but—if you wanted, I could prepare a video segment developed specifically as a promo piece for those networks. You never know who could check it out. I know you're busy but—"

"Our success is Turkey's success," Omir said resolutely. "I like this idea of yours. How long would it take to produce?"

"I could have a rough cut to you tomorrow, and then you could have anyone you prefer edit the final. That way if you have more footage or interviews, you can add them."

"Yes! Yes, that is good."

As Stefan half-listened to their conversation, he allowed his attention to veer to the right again. To his surprise, a paneled van rolled out of the building—then another one. They turned left onto the access road, then disappeared over the side of the mountain.

He scowled. Were the workers being taken somewhere else? Or was this supposed departure of the vans a ruse to satisfy anyone who was curious at the excavation site? He narrowed his eyes as he looked at the building. It was built solidly, but there were flaws once you got high enough. There were windows in the upper reaches, as Nicki had pointed out. The roofline showed several doors on multiple levels, and even now one of the doors opened, and a man stepped out, a lit cigarette in his hand as he spoke on his phone.

So clearly, not everyone had left the facility. At least not yet.

"How long will you be staying with us?"

Omir's question came as Nicki took the camera off her shoulder, and her gaze slid to Stefan. He nodded to her, then focused on Omir.

"We leave tomorrow," he said, grateful that Nicki betrayed no reaction. "This visit has been very educational, and you have every right to be proud of your achievement here. We're honored that you've shared it with us."

He kept his smile steady. They'd hit the place tonight.

Thirty-Five

Nicki could barely contain her excitement throughout the departure from the ruins and the obligatory stop for a final drink with the Turkish official. She said all the right things in all the right places, but her mind was jumping ahead to the night that was drawing down.

Stefan had said they were leaving in the morning. That was news to her. She hadn't said goodbye to Josef or his crew—hadn't gotten a chance to tell him about the broken board. But that's what email was for.

Besides, they were going to explore the warehouse asylum tonight. That trumped everything.

By the time they were alone again, back at the villa, she'd considered fifteen different scenarios for the exploration of the warehouse, rejecting each one. In the end, there really was only one option.

Stefan, as she expected, wasn't amused.

"None of the men aboard the yacht are expert climbers, Nicki. That's not going to work."

"Of course it's going to work! And I can tell by your voice, you know it too." she protested. "The place is airtight except for the roof, and no one is expecting us there. Chances are they have some sort of guard sweep of the grounds during the night, especially if that's when they dump the trash. If we go in at ground level, we'll be spotted. Or you'll be spotted, if you go in with your operatives. This isn't about me, this is about getting in the best way."

Stefan sent her a withering glare and she grinned. "Okay, so maybe it's a little about me. But you have to admit, it's the cleanest approach."

"It's the most foolish, certainly." Stefan glared at the sketch she'd mapped out on her tablet. The cliff face wasn't completely sheer, but the concrete walls were. "The warehouse is three stories high. That's a lot of flat surface to cover."

"It would be, except for this little detail."

She went to her bag and pulled out her video camera, scrolling backward. "While you were chatting it up with Omir, I saw this." She held it out to him, triumphantly.

He stared. "It's the corner of the building."

"It's the corner of the building with a gutter," she said. "A reinforced gutter, meant to last through any storm. They clearly weren't interested in fixing anything that high up." She zoomed in closer, and he squinted.

"That is not a solution, Nicki, that's a death trap," he said. "You've already climbed once today—and windsurfed."

He was right, but she pushed his concerns aside. "I climbed downhill and I was on the water for, like, a millisecond." When he didn't say anything, she jabbed a thumb at the screen. "Oh, come on! There's a tree line halfway up and then the gutter and its protection. You know it has to extend the whole way, other-wise, what's the point of a gutter? It's all we need for footholds. Our gear will do the rest."

Stefan looked pained. "None of the men are trained in this type of climbing," he said again.

"Well how many were you planning on bringing? This isn't a police raid, it's recon and maybe a rescue. We go in, we see what we see, and if what we see isn't Ari, we get out. There were only, what, a dozen men who filed back into the building? Less than we thought for sure."

"Less than we thought," he said. "But how many more would be guarding them? If there's any truth to the rumors about them harboring animals in there..."

"Yeah, the more I think about it though, no way. Animals make noise and are just inherently messy—I'm talking food, water, and lots and lots of poop. Take it from someone who grew up in Indiana, there would be visible waste if they were boarding anything with four legs in there."

"Unless they were true creatures of myth."

She snorted. "Yeah, not a lot of those in Indiana. But I'm still thinking that sounds like way too much hassle for a building like that. As for actual guards, it's been a year or more that these guys have been at this. They probably have their routine down cold. I bet they have no more than two guys on the building. Probably only one, and he's probably sleeping. I mean, come on. The workers will be locked up, wiped out. Maybe drugged. That'd make things easier. Especially if they were addicts to start."

Stefan still wasn't on board. "Do you have any experience in hand-to-hand combat? I can't believe I'm asking you that. Never mind. If anything like that happens, you'll be a complete liability. And drugged men—even men caught in a stupor—are dangerous. Too dangerous to take you. No. It's not going to happen."

Nicki nodded slowly. She wasn't going to be foolish, and she wasn't going to disobey a direct order.

But that didn't mean she would simply give up without presenting her side of the story.

"Look, you can go up with Tamas or any of the other guys. But you know as well as I do, I'm the best climber. And if you're worried about bulk, I cut that down by about half, right off the bat. Plus, remember," she grinned, "I'm a specialist at being thrown."

It took a few more rounds of arguing after that, but in the end, Nicki won.

Within two hours they were at the base of the cliff, where the trench emptied out over the shallow stream. Nicki experienced a twinge in her chest as she remembered how freaked out she'd been as she'd stuck her landing too hard there, but she resolutely patted her full water bottle hooked to her belt as a talisman. This morning's drop was a lifetime ago, it seemed. Now all she had to do was climb up, hand over hand. It wasn't far.

Nicki had climbed in the dark before, and the Alaçati night was perfect for it, the moon shining full and bright through the jungle. Fortunately, the climb up the wall of the warehouse would be partially covered by trees. They wouldn't be on the open section of the wall for long.

The first leg went quickly enough. She scaled the rocky outcrop ahead of Stefan, adrenaline carrying her up most of the way. She'd need to conserve her energy, but as she'd said to Stefan...the second half of the journey was downhill. That tended to be faster, if not easier.

When they were both at the mouth of the ditch, Stefan leaned down to her ear. "Quiet. If they're on a trash run, they'll hear us. We need to get to the cross-fence line and over. Stealth over speed."

She nodded and he tapped her shoulder. When she looked up, he dropped his head further, taking her mouth in a hard kiss.

"I'm going first," he growled. Then he was past her.

It was a good thing they were opting for stealth, because

speed was almost nonexistent. They crawled forward under brush and over roots, Nicki's tight black tights and close-fitting jersey a welcome layer between her and the thorns, sticks and rough bark they slithered by. It took nearly two hours to cover the tenth of a mile to the warehouse wall—including fully a half hour to scale the fence and climb down and over through the tangle of trees and rock and long-ago construction debris, now caught in the side of the mountain like a future dig site waiting to be unearthed.

Now Stefan reached out and tried the metal framework around the gutter. It was marginally sturdy, threaded through with vines. There was no way to tell what was keeping it to the wall—metal fastenings or organic ties. "I don't like this," he muttered.

Nicki pulled her water bottle free and took a slug. She was thirsty—too thirsty for the amount of water she'd consumed already today. Stupid nerves.

"We'll go up the tree as far as we can, then I'll switch over," she said. "It's three stories, Stefan. If it's not going to work, we'll try to skirt to the front and get in that way."

"Now you're open to another alternative?" Stefan's exasperation was plain, and Nicki rolled her eyes.

"You know as well as I do that if there'd been another way to do this, you would have already come up with it. It's the roof or nothing, Stefan. It's not like there was a ladder leaning up against the near side of the wall. We have to get up there and we have to go quickly, or it'll be freaking dawn already and they'll file the men out for the morning shift. You know I'm right."

"You're right," he scowled at the gutter. "This looks flimsy as hell."

"It'll hold." Nicki's confidence soared with each passing second. They were here, which was the game. Getting in had been a secondary goal after ensuring that she was along for the ride. She was finally in the fray, doing something that mattered. Before Stefan could object further, she turned to the tree. "Boost me up?"

He reached for her at the exact moment she went to reattach her bottle to her belt—and jarred the thing loose from her fingers.

"Oh!" Nicki gasped as the bottle dropped through the trees, wincing with every bounce and clatter. Beside her, Stefan glared.

She gave him a game smile. "Look, we couldn't find that bottle again if we tried. Trust me, they won't either," she said, but her throat already felt too tight.

Before he had a chance to respond, she turned and shimmied up the tree. They moved through the foliage a good fifteen feet before the branches became flimsier and unsubstantial. Taking the nearest one, she swayed toward the wall, trying the nearest gutter brace. It held.

"They don't make them like this anymore," she whispered.

Stefan moved up behind her, his chest flush against her back. His thin suit may have been engineered to keep him from getting cut up, but it was form-fitting, and the touch of his broad chest and abs against her back almost made Nicki's eyes cross. Then his next words really did make her catch her breath.

"Don't move," he whispered. "There's someone below us."

Thirty-Six

S tefan felt Nicki go completely still beneath him. They
were well-braced, and despite his misgivings, there was
plenty of heft to the steel cage around the gutter. Nicki was
right—when this structure had been built, its owners had
ensured they'd have no problems reaching the gutter. It was a
vertical drop, and the top was probably covered to ensure
nothing but water dropped into it, funneled by the slightly
slanted roof.

But the night had been interrupted by the sound of a door
opening, and the muttered Turkish floating his way was the
classic sound of discontent: the nightly garbage run.

"Filthy beasts," grumbled the man over a lit cigarette as he
walked with a long swinging gait, hefting trash that appeared to
be of considerable weight. He crashed into the brush not fifteen
feet distant from them, and his biting commentary followed him
over the ridge.

Stefan wasn't worried about the water bottle, but the guard
presented a bigger problem. There wouldn't be enough time to
scramble up the side of the wall before he got back, and there
was no way to tell whether the gutter braces would remain

sturdy. If one of them squeaked or scraped, the sound would echo for a quarter mile in the quiet night air.

Nicki trembled slightly beneath him, and Stefan snaked an arm around her, ostensibly to brace her further. But he couldn't deny that he also did it to reassure himself that she was steady, she was safe.

They hung like that for several minutes, but Nicki never once breathed a word, not even a sigh. He smiled against her hair, at once protective and proud. She was so determined to prove her worth, though she'd long since done all she needed to convince him she was an asset on this journey.

An asset he was quickly beginning to need for far more than a successful mission.

A flurry of Turkish started up again from the direction of the ditch, then got louder. Nicki and Stefan waited silently, suspended over the open ground, as the man trudged back through the fence, cursing as he got caught on the bared wires. From his vantage point, Stefan watched as the man pulled out a key and inserted it into the lock of the warehouse door far up the fence line. The guard returned the ring to his belt before he shouldered into the building with two large, empty cloth bags.

The door slammed behind him.

"Go," Stefan said, and Nicki instantly surged forward. The path up the side of the wall was quick, but precarious. After testing it the first few steps, Nicki turned back. "Me first, alone. Then you, and make it fast. You should be fine, but—"

He didn't let her finish the sentiment, uneasy for any amount of time she spent on the rungs. "Go," he said again. And she went. He waited until she'd cleared the top before launching himself up, using skills perfected with long years of climbing the palace walls to scramble up the rungs. He reached the roof in less than a minute, but he'd felt the sway and jolt of the rungs, the telltale scrape of pressure.

At the top, he lay flat on the roof for a long two minutes willing his heart rate back to normal. "We're not going down that way," he said. "Especially if we have a body or anything heavy to carry."

To his surprise, Nicki didn't fight him. "Agreed." She waited until he looked at her. "That door, I think. The center one. First tier."

He rolled over onto his side, coming up into a crouch. The door she indicated was only twenty feet away, and cigarette butts and empty bottles lay strewn around it. Apparently trash detail didn't extend to the roof.

"Why come out here to smoke?" Nicki murmured. "Seems a risk."

"Like you said, they've been at this a year. And the man we saw today had his phone. Chances are reception isn't good inside the building, so what started as the occasional call when necessary has since become the standard smoke break." He considered his words. "Speaking of, we should probably get through it before the next round. I suspect smoke breaks happen more frequently then technically necessary."

They reached the door, then Stefan picked the lock with a set of tools he fished out of his suit pocket. Nicki remained quiet —not nervously so, however. She didn't look around the rooftop, panicked, but focused on the door, moving up to the balls of her feet when he opened it.

"Me first," he said. "You stay with me until I tell you to stop. Not too fast. Hand on my waist to gauge my direction."

She nodded and then he was through the door, confirming that it locked again behind them. He hadn't been overstating his concern about the gutter. The rungs wouldn't hold them a second time, not without noisy protest. They'd leave by the front door—or whatever passed as the front door of this place.

The landing they were on shunted down two sets of narrow

stairs, but a door opened to their right, with more stairs beneath. A window was cut out of the door, and the stenciled markings indicated only "warehouse," in Turkish.

Stefan sidled up to the door and peaked through it. There was an open platform, then another room—more of a perch than anything. He couldn't see much from the angle through the window, so he eased the door open slightly.

He'd been right. There was a short open space along the metal platform, and then an enclosed structure with a windowed door. Through it, he could see a guard staring fixedly at the control panel, paying attention to it and the scene below him, visible through a large window.

Stefan eased the door shut again.

"One more." Stefan went down another flight, and this felt more right to him. The doorway above might lead to a catwalk system or the overseers' rooms, but this was the main floor. He turned, and Nicki was right behind him, her breathing tight, though her gaze was steady.

"Alarm?" she asked, and he shook his head.

"Too much hassle, I suspect." He leaned back and glanced through the window cut into this door. There was a large open space in the center of the room, with junk piled against the walls. At the front of the massive room were two intake garage doors, gleaming in the shadows.

But it was the center of the room that held Stefan's fascination.

There were twenty cells lined up in one long row, each separate from the other. Cell wasn't even appropriate—they were more like kennels. Tall enough for a man to stand in—if he was short. Long enough for a man to stretch out in. Opposite the kennel was a long, narrow utilitarian table and a trash can. At the far end, there looked to be a latrine of some sort, but he got the impression they didn't place too high a regard on cleanliness. The place smelled of fried meat, sweat, and urine even through the door. No wonder the guard had referred to them as filthy animals.

Worse, not all the men were asleep. Some muttered to themselves, some rocked, and some had hunched into tight balls, as if to will themselves away. The noise would cover Stefan's approach to the cages, but not do much more.

There were no visible guards on the first floor. Chances were good there was only the guard on the second floor, safely tucked in his overseers room.

He turned to Nicki and smiled. "I have an idea."

Thirty-Seven

At that moment Nicki would have done anything Stefan asked, if it meant she could stay near him. Now that they were here, on site, her tension was ratcheting up to ever increasing levels. She was fine. She knew she'd be fine. But that didn't stop the tension winding tighter.

Relax, relax, relax, she chanted to herself. She focused on Stefan. "Name it."

"These men are being held against their will, and the guard is up top. He has all the guns, presumably. There's no way out without him electrically opening the door. So, there needs to be a distraction while I get that process started."

She brightened. Distraction, she could do. She was an excellent distractor. "Any kind of distraction in particular?"

"Loud, ideally." He frowned at the ceiling, as if trying to determine what might work best with the guard. "You're not big, and you're dressed in black. You'll need to get directly under those lights, on top of the table. Movement and sound. I doubt there will be anything easy at hand to pick up, but that would be ideal. Failing that, if you can incite the men into being louder than usual, which might pull his attention to you, assuming he's not already focused squarely on the men. That would be the best scenario, but I'm not expecting it."

She smiled. "Yeah. I couldn't understand what he was saying, but he didn't seem too enamored with his job."

"That he did not," Stefan said. "So anything you can do to improvise, short of taking off your clothes, would be certainly advisable. With any luck you'll be able to see when I am in the room. Or hear me, which is my intention." He pointed through the window. "Those double garage doors aren't padlocked shut. If a single button will open them, so much the better. Fastest egress and closest to the road. The gate will probably be padlocked, but..."

"But climbing a fence, we can do." She looked out the window, then back to him. "How long do you need?"

He gestured to the window cut into the door. "How long will it take you to get into the center of the room?"

She peeked through the window. "Thirty—make it sixty seconds. I'll count off as I walk."

He nodded. "That's enough time. You distract, I disable the guard and hit the doors, then I go down and make a quick perusal of the pens, and we're out."

"Are you going to let all the men go free?"

He glanced back out to the pens. "If I can, and if they won't pose a danger to us, I will. With the guard out, I should have access to keys and his gun. The moment that door opens, though, you need to run for it. I won't let them free until you're clear of the building. Run and keep running toward the city. Tamas and his team are in the park. They'll find you with their tracking gear, but I want to be sure you're out and safe. Call me as you get into the shadows, away from people. Do you understand?"

"Loud and clear." Her heart kicked up with excitement, but trepidation too. "What if you can't get the door open? All the men will still be losing their minds but there won't be a clear way for them to get out."

"If the door won't open remotely, there will be a box at the units themselves, activated by the guard's key. Failing that, the key definitely opens the exterior push doors—we know that because the guard used it on his trash run. So if the garage door doesn't open, run to the first exterior door you can find, and hunker down there. I don't know how far off reinforcements for the guards here are, but we can't run the risk. I'll find you and we'll get out. That's most important."

"Sounds good." She put her hand on the door. "You ready?"

"Almost."

She looked up at him expectantly, and Stefan leaned down, kissing her hard. He seemed like he would break it off as quickly, but he didn't. Instead, he slid his arms around her, pulling her close. Then he moved to pull away and it was Nicki's turn to grab at him, deepening the kiss a moment more, as if she could take his very strength into her veins, her muscles, and her rapidly beating heart.

And then, suddenly, her heart slowed down. Steadied. The kiss between them reverberated through her, practically shifting her bones—as if her center of gravity reoriented higher in her body. She didn't understand what was happening, didn't know what it meant. But it was good. It was so, so good.

She pulled away and Stefan's eyes were alight with a sea of conflicting emotions. "You're okay?" he rumbled quietly, and she silently cursed herself. She shouldn't have shown weakness —not here, not so close. Nodding quickly, she gave him a fierce smile.

"Yup, but admit it. Bringing Tamas along wouldn't have been nearly so interesting."

He coughed a short laugh. "Go."

Nicki slipped through the door and into the wide space, her

eyes adjusting to the variance of light. A harsh set of fluorescent bulbs hung in a row above the distant cages, causing most of the men to hunker into a ball, trying to avoid the glare. A few had pulled their pillows or shirts over their heads, while some didn't seem to be bothered by the lights at all, instead rocking in a corner or lying against the bars of the cage, staring into the darkness.

None of them were facing her, which was a blessing. Nevertheless, she had to force herself to count as she moved along the perimeter of the room. She didn't want to move too slowly or start her show too suddenly, but she didn't want to leave Stefan hanging, either. Then there was the question of the distraction. It needed to be loud and boisterous, which she could do, but the room was larger than she'd originally thought. If the guard was asleep or listening to music, she could scream her lungs out and it wouldn't faze him.

She slid her gaze to the men. They would be able to help out, if she caught their attention first. Some of them already seemed a lost cause, but if she approached from the other side of the table and stood on top of the thing...maybe. It would be her best bet.

It would also take longer than sixty seconds.

Shit, shit, shit. Nicki picked up her pace, trotting at the edge of the shadows, quietly enough that most of the men didn't notice her. One did, though. The third from the end, an older, bearded man with shaggy white hair who didn't rock but who wasn't trying to sleep, either. He peered up as she padded forward, his face tilting at the sound, like a dog scenting an unfamiliar smell. He didn't cry out though, but simply put his hands on the bars and stared at her intently.

"*Pretty,*" he observed in a low, guttural voice. Nicki blinked at him. She heard the word, understood it. But his mouth moved in an unfamiliar way, the word sounding English but...it couldn't be.

Then the man grinned, his eyes going a little unfocused. "Watch out for the monsters, pretty. They gobble up the weak."

Monsters? She ripped her gaze away from him and kept moving. Was the old man being serious or had he lost his grip on reality? How long had these men been kept here—and who among them were still sane? She scanned the walls, picking out details in the shadows, but though there were several large entryways leading deeper into the building, there were no more cages. Plus, she wasn't picking up on the distinctive reek of animals, just of men. If she could just—

"Aiggghhh!" Another man suddenly shrieked from the center of the cages, the howl so unexpected that Nicki almost jumped out of her skin. His companions seemed to be used to it. The one on the right of the wailing man curled more tightly into a ball, the one on the left said something harsh in return. The man kept crying out, but it was clearly a common occurrence, and Nicki used the distraction to get into position.

She stopped as her toes hit something thick and metal—chains, but far too heavy to lift. Beside her on the table was a cattle prod, and her lip curled to see it. Barbarians.

But there wasn't anything to cause noise, like cymbals or aluminum cans. She was going to have to cowgirl up and do her best work...and she had to do it now.

Drawing in a deep breath, she ran forward and started shouting.

Thirty-Eight

Stefan had eased through the doorway on the second floor when he heard Nicki's cries. He was on an open catwalk that led to an enclosed overseers' room, and though the door to that room was closed, it had a window. He saw the guard jerk up his head from a drowse and lean on the counter, distracted by the chaos below.

Then Stefan burst through the door.

The man half-turned as Stefan smashed into him, but the room was so tight that the guard couldn't get his gun around in time. Stefan sent the weapon skittering across the small space with a fast, jabbing punch. The man wasn't completely without protection though—Stefan's first strike grazed his shoulder and he realized that the thick material overlaid even thicker muscle. The guard had a padded vest and steel-toed boots, and his hands were thick and beefy as he whirled.

He snarled in rage and rushed Stefan.

Stefan dodged his first attack and dived for the control board, rapidly scanning the buttons with the Turkish inscribed beneath them. Unfortunately, complete words had long since been worn off, leaving bare scraps. He hit a few buttons and nothing reacted in the room beyond.

The guard reacted, though. With a snarl he picked up a thick baton and instead of running with it at Stefan he flung it. It arced in a deadly rush and Stefan ducked, the beam crashing through the window and dropping a story to the floor below.

That's when Stefan heard the howls.

His momentary distraction gave the guard an opening. He attacked, his thick, meaty hands clawing up Stefan's clothing and locking around his neck. Stefan flung himself back onto the console and braced himself against it, but he couldn't get enough purchase to dislodge the ox. The man dragged him over the controls and then Stefan saw it—a separate panel with newer buttons and levers. The doors were new, too—that's where the correct buttons would be.

He didn't waste any more time. He caught the man in a round-house punch that knocked him off balance long enough to allow Stefan to flip around. In rapid succession, he hit the buttons on the top and bottom level, everything he could find before he risked a glance out at Nicki again. She'd dashed off the table, yes, but she wasn't alone.

The cages had all sprung open as well.

And deep within the bowels of the building, an unearthly roar sounded.

Thirty-Nine

Oh...shit.

After screaming songs from Broadway show tunes for all of fifteen seconds, Nicki saw Stefan burst into the overseer's cubby—and then had seen the guard attack back, which certainly hadn't been part of the plan.

She'd stopped shouting but stared hard as she watched Stefan and the guard go at each other, jolting out of her reverie only when a thick rod of some sort crashed through the window and came hurtling to the concrete floor. It landed with a loud clang that reverberated off the concrete walls.

The men went nuts in their cages, even more so than when they'd seen her appear, a dervish in their midst. Her gaze jumped from them to the guard and Stefan fighting above her. Then a metallic roar started and she whirled, turning with delight as she heard the immense garage doors lift up.

But that wasn't the only sound of popping and scraping to accompany the screams and howls of the caged men.

She turned back long enough to see the men's cages burst open like toy jack-in-the-boxes. Half the men surged out immediately, the other half lumbering more slowly. All of them were aiming for her, screaming their heads off.

"Shit!" She turned and sprang forward, scrambling off the table as the men surged across the concrete. They were all impaired to some degree, their movements slow and jerky, and she thanked God for whatever inhumane treatment they were receiving that had turned them into shambling zombies. But even shambling zombies were dangerous, and she'd given them a target. She dashed across the floor, the warehouse now lit up with whatever lights Stefan had hit, but her feet betrayed her, catching against another pile of chains. She sprawled to the floor a few feet shy of the open garage door, momentarily dazed.

And then...was that an actual *roar* she heard, over the melee?

She didn't have time to focus on that. She scrambled back, trying to regain her footing as the first man reached her. She got a vague sense of a tattooed, scarred face leering down at her as the prisoner lunged forward, but before he could touch her another man shoved him away, hard. This new man was younger than the first by a good ten years, and looked less wild. When he reached for her, she let him pull her up. "Run!" he shouted—once again his mouth forming the word oddly, for all that she could understand it easily.

But it was too late. The rest of the men were on them, and Nicki turned in the crush of them, dwarfed by the mass of humanity that rushed at her, either trying to stampede over her or grab her hair, her arms, her clothes.

One man swung at her and connected, and she crunched again to the pavement. As she struggled to get up, a surge of dizziness swamped her. She gasped, trying to focus, to fight— but her eyesight dimmed and her throat closed up.

She went down a third time.

Forty

Stefan saw the men surge toward Nicki and rage exploded inside him, so thick and hot he thought he'd choke on it. Forgetting everything but the fact that Nicki was in danger, he surged up toward the guard and cracked his head into the man's forehead, forcing him back. The man tripped and Stefan followed him down to the floor, knocking the guard senseless with a few short, powerful strikes. Then he grabbed the ring of keys at the man's belt and wrenched it free

The outer gate wouldn't have opened—it had been padlocked before, padlocked! Which meant that even if Nicki had gotten free of the warehouse, she'd have remained trapped between the gate and the men. She'd know the way out, but that was a long way to travel around the large building with a dozen men on her heels. Had she reached the gate in time to climb over? Had the men abandoned her and tried the ascent themselves?

Some would, he was sure, but others—

Another burst of rage crackled through him as he raced out onto the catwalk, then boosted himself over the railing to drop to the floor below. He landed in a crouch and launched forward again, running fast, his eyes pinned on the door.

He'd almost made it out when another roar shook the entire building—louder now, clearer, and sounding almost like...lions?

"What in the *gods*—!" Stefan whipped around as a flood of creatures spilled out of a hallway onto the warehouse floor, hooting and crying, talons and hooves scrabbling for purchase on the smooth concrete. The lions took the lead, easily recognizable by their golden fur and clattering, razor-sharp claws as descendants of the Nemean beast Hercules had killed so many centuries ago.

But these lions were far smaller than the way most myths presented their illustrious forebears. In fact, all the mythological creatures pouring into the room looked like they were sized too small. The rooster-headed basilisks, their serpent tails thrashing furiously, were no bigger than pigs. The harpies rushed forward like a cluster of furious flamingos, their wings pinned close to their body, their hair streaming out behind them, and their faces contorted into snarling screams. Even the mighty griffin that galloped forward on its muscular leonine body was only about the size of a pony. Beneath its imperious eagle head, its wings were strapped tight to its body as well.

Stefan realized with a bolt of horror that not only were the winged creatures bound to keep them from flying, *all* the creatures were banded at the neck with electrical collars. Those collars were clearly working overtime to restrain the creatures... and causing them incredible pain. The crackle of singed flesh and crazed howls filled the air, and Stefan wanted more than anything in the world to capture these creatures, to sort out who'd taken them and why. But he didn't have time for any of that.

He could only take them home.

"Fly!" He swept his hands up as the first creatures neared

him, and the combination of his own status as a demigod of the traveling god Hermes and the creatures' inherent magical natures was all that was necessary to pierce the veil between Earth and Olympus. In a blink, the walls of the warehouse fell away, and the entire lot of thirty-odd creatures were surrounded by a lush, rolling field—with blue skies above, and mountains far to the west.

The creatures still screamed and roared, but Stefan stepped back, raising his hands to his mouth to add weight to his own shout above the din. "Hephaestus!"

A moment later, a new figure appeared. Hephaestus, god of every made thing, still held a hammer and smelled of fire, his sturdy body clad in a leather vest and workman's clothes, and his bearded face alight with curiosity.

"What's this?" Hephaestus rumbled, his voice loud enough to break through the creatures' wails.

"Someone took them, held them prisoner with those." Stefan pointed to the band on the nearest basilisk as Hermes appeared just beyond Hephaestus. The tawny-haired god snapped his fingers and all sound dropped away from the animals—they still howled and stamped, but they were silent.

"Gods' *teeth*, you could hear them all the way to the Underworld." Hermes huffed, then he peered closer to the milling creatures. "Why are they constrained like that?"

"Exactly my question. I expect the answer will be instructive."

"Well, you can't just *leave* them here," Hermes countered. "It's against protocol."

"Who created these?" Hephaestus demanded, overriding Hermes's protest. He reached the nearest creature in three strides—one of the lions, now cowering in pain and fear. He reached out and grabbed the collar cutting into the lion's neck. It popped open at his touch, and the lion sprang away.

"I don't know who created them, but you can bet they're tied to Typhon. I need your help figuring out how." Stefan turned to Hermes. "And you need to figure out who the hell is smuggling toy monsters out of Olympus."

"Toy..." Hermes's eyes widened as he swiveled around to stare at the frightened, milling creatures. "Gods' teeth! They *are* toy-sized. Who would have...how..."

The messenger god practically glowed as his nimble mind went to work on the issue, parsing the possibilities. Hephaestus moved swiftly through the silently screeching creatures, freeing them from their bonds, while Hermes's winged sandals buzzed with energy, whipping the tall grass as he levitated up several inches. "Ohhhh, this could be deliciously *bad*—"

"Figure it out," snapped Stefan. "I'll report in later."

Without another word, he spun away and launched himself forward. In another three strides, he soared through the portal and hit the concrete floor of the warehouse at a dead run. A quick glance at his watch confirmed that only thirty seconds and change had passed since he'd left the warehouse—but thirty seconds could be an eternity in the wrong circumstances.

Stefan burst through the garage doors, his brain churning as fast as his legs as he raced into the open courtyard. Where was *Nicki?*

Quickly scanning past a group of prisoners banging ineffectually at the still-closed gate, Stefan blanched as he picked out Nicki. She'd fallen only a few yards from the gate, and was now curled into a crumpled heap on the ground next to a melee of seven fighting men.

Well...six of the men were fighting to reach her, and one was keeping them at bay.

Stefan raced into the fray, plowing into the men from behind. In their impaired states, he shook them off quickly and those who wanted to fight were easily dissuaded with a few roundhouse punches, most of the prisoners willing to give up the fight now that a new champion had arrived on the scene. Still—there were too many of them, and who knew how many more were lurking in the shadows, waiting to join the fight?

Shoving the nearest man out of his way, Stefan took a few precious seconds to sprint over to the enclosure, using every ounce of his gods-given speed. He unlocked the gate in the chain-link fence with the guard's keys and raced back as it swung open, banking on the fact that the men would choose escape over the fallen woman at their feet.

He was right for most of them.

And those that weren't—he swung around and faced off against three men, all of them reeking. One had picked up a length of pipe from the drive and lunged at him, swinging hard. Stefan neatly sidestepped the attack but not before the man who'd been defending Nicki lunged forward as well, blocking the pipe with his arm and stumbling back, shaking his head. Their attacker lunged again. Stefan decked him, hard, dropping him to the ground. Then Stefan picked up the pipe and swung it against the second and third men, who suddenly no longer seemed as interested in Nicki. Instead, they turned on their heels and ran from him, as he turned back to Nicki.

Only she wasn't alone.

A wild-haired, darkly tanned man leaned over her, pawing at her body, speaking to her in raw, guttural gasps. Stefan's gaze turned white with rage. He rushed forward, knocking the man back off Nicki.

"Hurt—!" the man said in English, though his accent was thick with a Middle Eastern inflection. "She's—hurt!"

The garbled voice suddenly became clearer, and Stefan stayed the fist that had been poised to smash into the man's face.

He blinked and stared, too stunned at what he was seeing to process it.

But his fog was cleared away as the man reached forward, grabbing his arm to pull him forward.

"Hurt!" Prince Aristotle Andris cried again, still in English, his voice barely a rasp as he pointed to the crumpled Nicki. "She passed out I think."

Stefan spun to Nicki. While he'd been sure she'd been moving before, now she lay silent on the ground, her face slack. He pulled her up into his lap and growled to Ari. "Help me."

Forty-One

Nicki jerked awake so violently her entire body convulsed. Her eyes snapped open as she took a swing at the man hovering over her. "Get away from me!"

"*Nicki.*" Stefan's voice was intense, focused. It calmed her immediately, though she couldn't understand the events going on around her. "You passed out. The mission is solid. You're safe, but we have to get out of sight. I'm carrying you. Allow me to pick you up. Allow me. Stay awake."

Distantly, Nicki sensed Stefan picking her up but she couldn't control her arms or legs. He lifted her and there was another man beside him, both of them running as he clasped her to him. She filled her lungs with deep, blessed air. Then Stefan was jogging hard right and she felt cool stone beneath her legs as he laid her down again.

"No! I need to sit up—to sit up," she gasped. "To breathe!"

That last part seemed to shake him, and Stefan crouched in front of her, allowing her to sit up while he whipped his phone out of his suit and held it to his ear. He spoke rapidly to someone, ordering them to come pick them up, and she blinked around, trying to make sense of where they were. It looked like a park and she frowned. "We're still on the hill? Near the warehouse?"

Her gaze wandered to the man standing beside them, watching them both with a puzzled frown. "Is that—"

Stefan's sharp glance quieted her voice in her throat. "Tamas is coming. We're heading back to the boat." At her nod, he turned to the shaggy man beside them. "This is Ryker Stavros. He was a prisoner in that warehouse, but he is Oûrois. We're bringing him home."

"Ryker..." Nicki blinked as the man turned to her, an abashed smile on his face. He looked like a vagrant, but she didn't care. He alone out of the wild men had stopped and stood with her—with her, not against her. "You helped me, back there. Defended me. Thank you."

"Those men—they are not bad men." The man spoke English, but his voice sounded rusty with disuse. Stefan stared at him with open admiration, however, and she suddenly knew. This man might think his name was Ryker, might have told Stefan that. But he wasn't Ryker.

This was Crown Prince Aristotle Andris.

"They were penned up like animals," the prince continued in his ragged voice. "The only relief was the work we did with the dirt and the trucks. It wasn't hard work, but it was constant, and they—some of them—had families. They could never work off their debt. It always climbed higher. Some were sick, but they couldn't get better, not in here. And some were merely unlucky." His smile turned self-deprecating. "I was that. It was a very dark place, that warehouse. There were very dark things that they kept further in the back. We didn't see them, but...we heard them."

"Oh, right." Nicki nodded, then rounded her eyes at Stefan. "One of the others warned me about monsters there. He seemed pretty sure that's what they were."

"Someone spoke to you about them?" Stefan asked sharply. He swung to Ari. "Did you see them?"

"Monsters..." Ari swayed on his feet, then stumbled a bit as he put a hand to his head. "I think...I mean I saw..."

Just as quickly, Stefan seemed to change his mind. "Never mind. Don't try to push your memory. We're taking you home."

Ari stepped back, blinking, his thoughts just that quickly derailed. "Home?"

"I know your family." He gave Ari an encouraging nod. "Oûros is not so big that we don't notice when our countrymen go missing, my friend. You were missed. You have a family."

"A family." The idea appeared foreign to Ari, and he stared at Stefan with an earnest confusion that almost made Nicki forget about the monsters. Except Stefan had totally *not* seemed surprised about them, which meant he was totally *going* to be explaining that piece of crazy as soon as she got him alone.

"You're not my family, yet you came here?" Ari asked, his words slurring a bit. "Why?"

Stefan straightened under the direct question but kept his manner easy. "You're my countryman, and you've endured a lot. That's reason enough. There are many people who will be happy to have you back."

"There was..." the man hesitated, then lifted his gaze to the starry night. "There was a crash. I was in a crash. A plane crash. That's all I know. The rest—" he waved his hand in front of his face. "The rest is a blur. I try to remember and there's only pain." He pointed at Nicki. "Then you show up singing songs I didn't realize I knew, and you..." He swung to Stefan. "You come with your fists and keys and—" he spread his hands. "Now we're here."

"The men were sedated every night, we suspect," Stefan said. "Some had been on meds which they had no access to, others were picked up as drunks or vagrants."

That was exactly the story the squatters had told them, and Nicki nodded, trying to keep her voice steady, natural.

"And now we're going back to Oûros," she said to Ari. "Where your family is."

"Yes," Ari said uncertainly. "That..." he turned as a car's lights swept up the road, and Nicki gradually became aware of sirens wailing in the distance. Her eyes widened.

"The warehouse," she breathed.

"I didn't have time to shut down the lights," Stefan said. "There was a guard I left behind who I suspect has awakened and sounded the alarm. The men have fled, though. I suspect they won't be hunted."

Ari straightened, squinting back at the building. He took a half-staggering step forward. "The police...they'll find more than they expect there. It's too dangerous. We have to—"

"I contained the other threats," Stefan cut him off. He held up the keys and rattled them, which made Ari flinch. "There's no more danger. Everyone will be safe."

"Safe..." Ari muttered, still staring at the warehouse with wide eyes.

The long car slowed in front of them and Stefan turned to her. "How are you feeling?"

The sudden realization of what had happened hit her with a rush. "I blacked out, didn't I?" she blurted. "I momentarily got dizzy—I think I might have fallen and cracked my head. My pants are pretty wrecked anyway." She scowled down at her tights, the knees practically ripped out of them and a long snag down one side. "There were all those men."

Stefan bit out a tight curse. "I'm aware. When I hit the console for the garage door lift, I didn't realize it was next to the controls for the men's cages. I tripped those too. I should've realized—both units were new to the building. But I didn't. I put you in danger."

"I was fine—I must have gotten light-headed, then you were there to help me up. You both were," she shook her head, but Stefan didn't appear any less pained. "I was fine. I *am* fine. Really."

"Ambassador." Tamas stood at the door to the limo, and Stefan helped Nicki up, treating her too carefully. She did feel woozy, though, so she didn't argue, allowing him to fold her into the car without protest.

Ari followed, awkwardly getting into the limo and taking the opposite seat, facing them. "I—I'm not exactly fit company for a car such as this," he said, peering around the enclosed space.

Nicki snorted. "Tell me about it."

Stefan remained outside a few moments more, speaking rapidly—but once again, Nicki could follow every word. Was he speaking in English for her benefit? That was nice. It was so, so nice of him.

Why did she feel so tired?

Tamas closed the doors after Stefan joined them, and within moments the car headed out deeper up the ridge.

"We've charted a circuitous course to the yacht. I've taken the liberty of having us checked out of the hotel," Stefan said. He turned to Ari. "There's no one locally you'll need to notify?"

"What? No," Ari seemed to be having a hard time in his seat. He'd begun to tremble. "No one knows I'm here. I don't remember—I don't remember much beyond that." He frowned, staring out the window. "I don't enjoy being in enclosed spaces, I'm afraid."

Stefan hit a button and all the windows of the limo smoothly sank into their slots, the car filling with the redolent air of Alaçati's lush vegetation. That seemed to calm Ari, and he nodded with appreciation.

"There's a spare change of clothes in the bag next to you,"

Stefan said, and Ari blinked down at the crisp cloth bag. "We guessed on the fit, but if you'd like to change, you can."

"I'll close my eyes," Nicki supplied, and immediately snapped her lids closed.

As she heard Ari open the bag, Nicki relaxed too, leaning against the cushions. Man, that was close. She'd almost fainted back there at the warehouse, almost...

Wait. She *had* fainted.

She blinked open her eyes to find Stefan staring at her.

"Just how sick are you?" he asked.

Forty-Two

Stefan sat back in his seat as Nicki blinked rapidly, but the evidence was on her face, and it wasn't as if he hadn't already figured it out anyway. The signs had all been there—signs he could see with his eyes, and signs that he had felt deep within his own body that he'd been ignoring for far too long. Something was wrong with Nicki that had her spooked far more than the momentary terror he was sure she'd faced with those men.

He'd guessed just now about her being sick...but he knew he was right.

Nicki squirmed under his scrutiny. Opposite them, Ari peered out the window, offering them the illusion of privacy. Try as he might, Stefan couldn't call the prince by the name Ryker. Not in his own mind, anyway. It was too jarring to see him so disheveled as it was.

But for the moment, his focus was on Nicki—an American, in his care, whom he had completely failed. Why had he not researched her health more thoroughly? Why had he not looked deeper, searched harder? The dossier on her hadn't included a full medical workup—it hadn't needed to. She wasn't the consort of the prince, as Emmaline had been. She merely was the friend, one of a trio of supporting figures in the drama that had swept up the royal family when the Americans had come to the shores of the seaside kingdom less than a month ago. When that drama had begun, he'd barely registered Nicki's presence.

But she'd lied to him. And, worse—he hadn't caught her out in that lie. He didn't know which angered him more.

He narrowed his gaze on her now. She stayed uncharacteristically quiet, and he knew she was buying time. Whether to come up with a suitable answer or to hope he moved off the topic of her, he didn't know. He suspected the latter, however. He suspected that she'd managed her life quite well with that approach, and that most of her friends and associates had allowed her to get away with it. She was always, simply, Nicki— up for anything, ready for action, the first to volunteer and the last to give up.

Eventually, however, she broke under the weight of his glare. With the rumpled Ari doing his best to be invisible she spoke softly, almost dully.

"It's called a bunch of different things," she said. "Familial hypertrophic cardiomyopathy, inherited cardiomyopathy, genetic—but it all means the same condition. Essentially, my heart muscle has the predisposition to...well, to weaken and die. My dad has the condition, my brother too. I was checked out once, when I was eighteen, and I was fine. Really, I was." Her words picked up speed as she seemed to force them all into the open. "But I'm supposed to get checked every six months or something crazy, and it started consuming my whole life. When I got to college, I stopped getting checked. So I honestly don't know how healthy I am. And, well—I worry, of course. But at least I keep living, too." Her eyes flashed toward him. "I feel fine though. I do. I mean, I passed out, but I'm fine."

"You do that a lot? Pass out?" Stefan kept his words short

and to the point, if only to keep a handle on his fury. At himself, at her, at the gods for allowing someone so vivacious, so full of life to suffer such an insidious threat.

"No!" she shook her head firmly. "Seriously, no. I—I got dehydrated today, and I couldn't seem to catch back up."

"And you dropped your water bottle." Stefan passed his hand over his eyes. "I should have given you mine." Anger and a need for answers swamped him, but the car was already slowing, the lights, smells, and sounds of the marina filling the limo as they cruised toward the yacht. He'd have time to grill Nicki later. And then make sure she got checked out the first moment possible.

He understood the idea of not wanting to live with constant fear. But fear could be managed. The unknown couldn't.

Stefan glanced at Ari and tried again to gently jostle a memory. "You're comfortable traveling with us, Mr. Stavros? You don't need to contact anyone?"

Now Ari's expression turned a bit wan. "There's no one here who will miss me," he said. A look of stark terror crossed his face as a sudden realization dawned. "I don't have a wife or anything, do I? Or a girlfriend—children?"

His anguish was so immediate that Stefan's heart twisted, and Nicki's face softened with understanding and shared pain. To forget everything...

"No," Stefan said quietly. "You weren't married, and to my knowledge had no steady girlfriend. Your work kept you busy. You had no children either."

"Thank God." Ari sank his head back against the limo seat. "I don't know how long I've been gone, exactly. It was summer when I was taken, and it's summer again—that's as close as I can get."

"Almost exactly a year, yes," Stefan supplied, then tempered his words at Ari's wan expression. "But now you're going home."

The car stopped. Stefan stepped out of the limo, then handed out Nicki, his gaze warning her to stay quiet as Ari emerged from the car. She nodded, though she was clearly confused, and she didn't object when he held out his hand for hers.

Good. He didn't think he was going to let go of Nicki Clark any time soon. She'd have to get used to that idea.

Forty-Three

Nicki willed herself to relax as they walked toward the yacht. She wasn't sure why she was so nervous. The danger was past. They had the prince—even if he didn't know he was a prince. She'd succeeded—they'd succeeded.

So why did she feel like she'd failed?

Ryker/Ari drew fewer stares than he ordinarily would because of his casual clothes, despite his unkempt hair and thick, scraggly beard. But when they approached the yacht with its bold crest of the Royal Family, he didn't react. He stared up at the boat with a rueful smile and turned back to Stefan. "It seems I have very good friends. I'm glad of this, though I don't know what I did to deserve it."

"You've been a worthy friend in return, and will be so again."

Ari didn't seem convinced, and they boarded the yacht under the deferent and watchful eyes of the crew. None of the crew referred to Ari as anything specific, using the same honorifics for him as they would any other dignitary. Ari, for his part, didn't recognize any of them either.

"Tamas here will show you to your stateroom, Ryker,"

Stefan said. He'd not moved out of touching distance from Nicki, and she wondered about that, too. "We'll be setting sail at first light, sooner if we must. But it would be best not to draw attention."

Ari nodded. "I don't think the authorities will waste resources searching for me. I won't turn down the opportunity for a shower, though." He lifted his hand to his beard. "And if there's a razor of any sort aboard, that'd be good."

"I think you'll find everything you need in your stateroom. I would have brought a barber too, but we can't risk any information about you getting back to officials here."

"Of course," Ari murmured, though he looked bemused as he went below deck.

Stefan wasn't finished yet. He turned with Nicki to walk her across the deck to the ship's communications room. Instead, of entering that room however, he went another few doors down until he rapped on the door. It swung wide and she stared into the bright space—it was some sort of sick room, with a single raised palette, pristine counters and locked cabinets.

And one of the guards standing in the center of the room... with a stethoscope around his neck.

"What's this?" Nicki said, though Stefan wouldn't let her stop until he'd pushed her into the room and closed the door behind them.

"This is Marco Osman, whom you've met. In addition to his skills as an operative, he is the team medic. I don't want to risk a Turkish doctor here in Alaçati, but it's a twelve-hour trip to Oûros, and I can't risk that either if you are unwell."

"I told you, I feel fine—" the usual panic surged forth as Nicki considered the reality of what Stefan was saying. A doctor would be examining her, and this was only a field medic. When she returned to Oûros, she had no doubt there would be another doctor. Her medical files would be requested, and if her family didn't get involved, it would be a miracle. "Really—I'm good. I'd tell you if I didn't feel okay."

Stefan was immovable as stone. "I can remain in the room or leave, whatever you feel more comfortable with."

Nicki made a face. "Oh, for God's sake, Stefan. Fine." She trooped forward and stood in front of Marco. "You want me standing or on the bed thing?"

"The bed thing is fine," Marco said. To his credit, he didn't smirk, and he didn't glance at Stefan, though Stefan's scowl practically filled the room as Nicki hopped up on the examining table. Before he could ask, she reached up and stripped off her shirt, leaving only her industrial-strength jog bra. To emphasize her irritation, she tossed the shirt to Stefan. She was used to competing in far less clothing than many super models wore. She wasn't shy about her body in front of strangers.

She still flinched when Marco put the stethoscope on her chest. But it was cold.

The tests proceeded from there, the pure basics to determine that her blood pressure, pulmonary activity, pulse and heart rate were normal, with no apparent ill effects from her fainting spell. Her eyes were checked, too, her depth perception and peripheral vision appearing unharmed. Throughout it all, Stefan stared, his glower eventually diminishing to a stoic impassivity that made her more nervous than the checkup did.

"Your immediate vitals are good, and given the limits of our testing equipment, that's as far as we can tell with this equipment," Marco eventually concluded. "You're significantly dehydrated. The climate here is arid, but dehydration can result from other issues too, like stress or adrenal fatigue. You'll want to test that. You don't appear to have suffered a true cardiac event, and I can detect no arrhythmia or fibrillation currently. Nevertheless, we'll want to monitor you for the length of the voyage." He turned to include Stefan in his next statement. "With Miss

Clark's permission, we'll have a full workup done as soon as we return to—"

"No," Nicki said immediately.

"Yes," Stefan snapped. His gaze whipped to hers, but he continued to speak to Marco. "Set it up. For both of us. Full VO-2 Max stress test, echo and EKG testing, and then the same battery of athletic performance tests we put the recruits through at the end of intake training."

"Of course, sir," Marco said as Nicki's eyes narrowed.

"What do you mean, for both of us?"

Stefan shrugged. "If I'm going to ask you to have your physical capacity checked, I should go through it as well. It's been some time since I've gone through the full detail of it, and that's not smart." He nodded to Marco, and tossed Nicki's shirt back to her. "We'll be leaving shortly since you've checked out, and I'd like to put in a call to the king and queen once we clear the port. If you'd join me for that, I'd appreciate it." He hesitated. "Probably best that we're both cleaned up."

Even as he turned to the door, however, his phone buzzed.

Nicki hopped off the bed. "The queen?"

Stefan scowled at his phone. "Regrettably, no. It appears that our attempts to move up our departure may be delayed." He shunted his glance to her, and real regret seemed to color his gaze. "This might take a while. I'll send for you when we're clear."

"Of course," she murmured. He held the door for her and she went through, but to her surprise he didn't touch her, didn't kiss her on the way out. As soon as she registered that disappointment, she clamped down hard on her emotions, and picked up her pace.

"Get a grip on yourself," she muttered, trudging up the hallway back toward the main deck. Stefan was the commander of this yacht. He also was a highly respected diplomat for his country. He did the right thing, at the right time, and when he did it, it mattered. If she was going to stay with him...

Her steps slowed as her brain caught up with her galloping thoughts. *Stay with him?* That wasn't an option—it had never been an option. Stefan hadn't asked, and he'd certainly given no indication that that was what he wanted from her. He wanted her healthy, sure. He was pissed that she blacked out, but who wouldn't be? And...and he did care for her. She knew that. He cared for her as a teammate definitely. As for more than that, it shouldn't matter. It didn't matter.

She'd always gone it alone, out of self-preservation more than anything else. She could handle going down with a busted heart as long as she didn't drag anyone down with her.

Nothing had changed about that.

Nicki continued to her stateroom. Of course, until now, all her concerns had been hypothetical. Maybe her heart would go out on her one day—maybe it wouldn't. But they were beyond hypotheticals at this point. She'd passed out. Her heart hadn't stopped, sure, but when the going had gotten tough...she'd flaked. No matter how she tried to talk her way out of it, the truth of the matter was—she was sick. She was broken.

The tears started before she made it to the shower. Nicki stripped off her clothes woodenly, pausing in front of the mirror to survey herself. Other than the usual assortment of bruises, she appeared to be whole. Normal. She didn't look like a ticking time bomb. She turned and switched on the water, grateful for the cocoon of noise and warmth as she stepped beneath the heavy spray.

"It doesn't have to change anything," she muttered, but the reality wasn't as easy as that. She had proof now. Who knew what was really wrong with her? At a minimum, she'd be prescribed a laundry list of drugs, and if things got worse, her whole life could change. She could end up walking on eggshells, and that still wouldn't ensure that her heart wouldn't give out one day anyway.

She didn't want surgery. She didn't want more pills. And she didn't want to tell her family, especially her mother, who seemed to have been rooting for the family to stay in crisis since her father had been diagnosed. Nicki didn't want to hear the latest treatment options, didn't want to get forwarded even more articles about athletes dying on the field.

The water pounded down around her, and she leaned against the wall, finally giving into sobs. She didn't want to be broken, a liability. Didn't want to live her life like she was the walking wounded. But now people would know. The staff at the castle. The royal family. Stefan.

She could keep it there, maybe, she thought. If she agreed to the tests conducted in Oûros, there'd be no record of those tests to follow her back home. She could manage her care quietly, away from her family's prying. She wouldn't be stupid—couldn't be, not anymore. She'd care for herself so she never left anyone in the lurch again. But she'd go somewhere that would be easy. Maybe to Josef's teaching school after all, down in Texas. She'd be close to hospitals and clinics there, if needed. She could manage. She would adapt.

Nicki huddled beneath the pounding water, and never felt more alone.

Forty-Four

Stefan was only about fifteen feet from the bridge when his heart squeezed so hard that he stumbled—and a wave of blackness rushed up to shrink his sight down to a pinhole. He gasped and went down on one knee, his hands coming up automatically to his chest, as if he could rip out the offending organ and throw it into the ocean. Everything hurt—his breathing, his blood, his muscles and bones—and he pitched forward again, nearly sprawling this time before catching himself.

"Ambassador Mihal!" He vaguely heard the alarmed cry of the sailor, the familiar sound of his own name refocusing him... and suddenly he knew.

"Get away!" He snarled, and surged up so quickly, turning with his arms outstretched, that the small knot of men who were coming to his aid abruptly fell back. His sight cleared, his heart beat freely, but he took no solace in that. For the pain to go away so abruptly, could only mean one thing.

"*Nicki.*"

With the speed allowed only to the fastest of demigods, servants and soldiers of the winged god himself, Stefan raced below decks, so fast he may as well be flying until he reached

Nicki's stateroom. He bypassed the lock with a wave of his hand, gaining entry with the skill that had proven useful many times throughout his long years of service to the Crown.

But when he pounded into Nicki's suite and he couldn't see her right away, panic seized him anew. He couldn't sense her, couldn't feel her. He hadn't realized how much of a presence she had become in his own waking awareness until now, when she'd been ripped away unexpectedly.

"Nicki!" He shouted, but there was no response, and it took another second for him to hear the water of the shower running. He didn't hesitate further. He sprinted forward, yanking open the bathroom door, and stepping into the steam-filled chamber. Nicki was slumped against the wall of the shower, motionless, water raining over her.

Stefan lunged for her. Sweeping up her compact form in his arms, he whirled back toward the bedroom. Before he'd even completed the full turn, he whispered "*Fly,*" and dropped into the Underworld.

Darkness flooded around him, hugged him close, and he felt the passage of earth and time speed by him, plunging through the planes of existence. The fact that it was so easy gave him no relief. Among his many roles, Hermes was a psychopomp, a ferryman of the souls of the dead across the River Styx. But Nicki wasn't—couldn't be dead. She'd just been examined by a doctor! She'd been cleared. She'd been...

The world around him abruptly brightened, blackness turning to shadows, shadows giving way to rolling mist. He landed in a crouch, Nicki still huddled close to his body, then straightened and turned. At first he could see no one, and he threw his head back in a defiant roar.

"You will not take her, Hades. Not yet!"

"Won't I?"

The response was heavy, cold, and sneering. Stefan turned

again to see a large, hulking figure coalesce from the rolling mists, a dark form against the shifting grays. The landscape of the Underworld never got more visible than this, in Stefan's experience, but then again—he'd never had an occasion to spend much time down here. He wasn't planning on doing so now.

Hades drew more sharply into form. His broad, muscular frame was clad in a long robe of inky black over an equally dark tunic and pants. His stark, chiseled features, etched with the harshness of his realm, betrayed not even a hint of concession. Hades met Stefan's gaze across the open space, while in Stefan's arms, a tiny spark of energy stirred within Nicki.

Stefan's knees nearly turned to water. She still lived. He realized for the first time that some small part of him had feared he was already too late.

Hades' smile was cruel, his black, gold-rimmed eyes glittering. "You come down here to my realm, making your demands," he mocked, his words almost a drawl. "Do you know how many demands like this I hear every day? Year after year, millennia after millennia? Why should I grant yours, demigod? You of all people know that human lives are short. They were born so that they die."

"Not her. Not now." Not ever on his watch, if he had anything to say about it.

"Most especially her," Hades countered. "She was given the gift of fragility in this lifetime. She should have taken better care, stewarded her resources. Instead, she did the opposite, stretched too far, too often. Laughed in the face of death." He gestured around him. "My face. Eventually, there's a price to pay for such boldness."

"Not your face," Stefan insisted, willing the tiny leaping flame of Nicki's consciousness to keep flickering, to get stronger. He tightened his hold around her. "If anything, unlike most mortals, she *honored* you when we discussed your rule—as you well know, I suspect." The tiny shift in Hades's expression told Stefan that he'd guessed correctly. *Good.* He would be more than happy to tug any lever, push any button in this conversation to get what he wanted.

He pushed on. "What she fights is the fear that's taken down those around her. She fights to live, so that she can do and be everything possible in her life. Unlike most mortals, she fully understands her frailty, or her potential for it, anyway. But also, unlike most mortals, she pushes against it every day, not willing to let it define her until it absolutely needs to. She's bold, yes. She's brash. But she isn't foolish. She takes what precautions she can, then she uses her body to its outer limits, to strengthen it however she can to protect the parts of it that aren't so strong. You could let the cup of mortality pass her this once, should you choose. The fates of mortals aren't written in stone, but in a fabric that's constantly being rewoven. We both know it."

"What I know and what I care about are two different things." Hades shrugged, his gaze once again stony with cynicism. "Humans die."

A surge of panic clawed up the back of Stefan's throat. The gods wanted nothing more than to be feted and honored, and he had never taken the time to honor Hades. Few did. Among all the major gods, Hades had the fewest demigods that agreed to serve him as his emissaries on earth. Would Hades take his anger over that out on him, a mortal who'd spent so many years in service to another god? "This one doesn't have to, not right now," he said.

"Doesn't she though?" Hades's smile was as cruel as his tone. "You gatekeepers have grown smug in your role of guarding the world from us, and arguably, you should. We're the ones who gave up our freedom to roam your world all those centuries ago. We were tired, and we yearned for the separation, the retreat. You built your walls stronger than we expected you to. But if you choose to separate yourself from the pitfalls of our involvement in your lives, why do you think you can pick and choose the graces that we might bestow upon you? Your very ability to stand here and have this conversation is an example of that grace. Is it not enough? Do you pretend to know how the fabric of existence will be woven if I allow the fire of this one woman to burn on in your world instead of mine?" He gestured lazily at the swirling mists surrounding them. "You can't deny that she'd bring brightness to a place that sorely needs it. Perhaps I deserve that brightness more than you."

Fury boiled through Stefan. "I have given my life several times over in service to the gods. I do so willingly, by my choice. You can take anything you want from me, Hades. But you can't take her simply because you crave her light. It's not yet her time."

"And I say again, how do you know? Perhaps her death is exactly the next stitch that is required. But come." Hades once again waved an indolent hand. "Lay her down more comfortably, and we can discuss this like civilized Olympians. You can't keep clutching her to you like she's a prized goat. Give the woman some air."

"Not hardly," Stefan scoffed back, redoubling his hold on Nicki. No self-respecting demigod of Hermes would miss this trap. "She won't grace your realm with so much as a footfall until it's by her choice—whether a deliberate choice or the consequence of the choices she makes. That's only fair, Hades."

"And I'm supposed to get lectured about fairness from the demigod of liars?" Hades squared his shoulders, his form growing thicker, heavier, until he appeared nearly seven feet tall to Stefan's eyes. The mists surrounding him rolled back further, and Stefan caught a glimpse of Hephaestus's forge behind Hades, a fire burning within it, a slab of thick stone to the right. "I should rip your tongue out and have Hephaestus forge a new one for you of lead. He owes me a favor, and he'd do it the second I asked."

"Hades, I—"

"Stefan."

Stefan jerked his gaze down to see Nicki, beautiful Nicki staring up at him, her green eyes bright with tears, her red hair wild from the damp heat of the Underworld. The face that had been etched into his mind so sharply he didn't think he could ever live without it broke into a shaky smile, and her eyes searched his, seeming to focus and steady as he willed his strength into her. Her lips trembled, and a long breath gusted out. She shifted in his arms.

"Please, set me down," she said. "I...have a request to make of Hades."

Forty-Five

Nicki could feel Stefan's muscles contract, as if her words had turned him to stone. Could that possibly be a thing? She didn't know, but at this point, she decided that anything was possible with these people, in this place.

She was in freaking *Hell*—or the Underworld, whatever that meant, but she was pretty sure it served as a proxy for freaking *Hell*—and Stefan was talking to Hades! Hades, who'd just threatened to rip her beautiful demigod's tongue out and replace it with one made of lead. Like that wouldn't be a crime against humanity. She really liked Stefan's tongue. She really liked every last inch of him.

"No, Nicki," Stefan said, his grip still a vice around her. "That's exactly what he wants. If you set foot in his realm, you're his."

"She's mine anyway," Hades put in. He seemed to be pitching his voice a notch louder to make sure they heard him. "I'm only granting her the illusion of talking to you because I can. Surely, you have to know that."

Nicki would have smiled at the almost petulant comment except for the way Stefan's expression changed. He went pale, his skin turning almost ghostly, his eyes haggard. He believed what this asshole god said, believed that she was dead or on the brink of it.

Screw that. She knew she wasn't dead. She had too much to live for, too much to do. But seeing Stefan stare fixedly at Hades, his jaw clenched, fear and loathing mixing together in a potent stew of emotions, tugged at her in a way she'd never felt before.

"You have a bargain you'd like me to drive, Hades, you have only to say the word," Stefan said, his words dripping ice.

"And again, bargaining with an acolyte of Hermes is a fool's game," Hades retorted. "You don't have anything I want."

Nicki rolled her eyes. "Yeah, well, I do." She craned her head to the side, and peered at the hulking man—god—whatever he was, who stood maybe thirty feet away. "Will you grant me permission to stand up on my own two feet without turning my request into some sort of weird Greek riddle where I can't leave if I do it? Will you give your word and not cheat me on this?" She wriggled a little in Stefan's grasp.

"Nicki..."

Nicki glanced up toward Stefan again, but he wasn't looking at her. His glare was still solidly on Hades. Still, she turned her face in time to flinch at the single drop of water that splashed onto her cheek. Her eyes widened. Was Stefan crying? Over *her*?

Hades grunted, then waved a hand. "You may stand. It will not be the reason why you'll stay here."

If anything, the cryptic response made Stefan's arms tighten further.

"Oh, for heaven's sake," Nicki wriggled harder. "So that we're clear, *I* decree that *you* won't be a dick about me leaving footprints on your precious underworld carpet, and no matter what, you won't keep me if it's not my time. Stefan—please."

Looking like he'd sooner trade his tongue in as Hades had suggested rather than give in to her request, Stefan nevertheless let her stand.

Nicki planted her feet on the solid surface, grateful that the swirling mist seemed to cover something that felt like actual ground. A wave of dizziness stole over her, and she steeled herself. She sure as hell wasn't going to show weakness now.

"Thank you," she murmured, turning and lifting up a hand to Stefan's cheek. He grabbed it and held it tight, then turned his mouth into the palm, kissing it hard.

When he pulled away, he stared at her with eyes gone flat and hard. "He's a god, Nicki. An actual god. He doesn't have power on Earth anymore, but this is his home. He could kill you here."

"I could kill her anywhere," Hades observed, again sounding bored, and this time she did smile.

"I like him," she told Stefan, and then—before she could think too much about it—she lifted up on her toes and brushed her lips against his. "And I love you, my beautiful, fearless man. As far as I'm concerned, you're an actual god, too."

She turned away before she lost her nerve, and faced Hades squarely.

The man—god—whatever was a veritable beast of a guy, big and deeply tanned, with a thick mane of dark hair that was tied back with a heavy leather strap. He wore a cloak over a black tunic and pants and heavy boots, and he folded his arms over his chest as she took him in.

"You said Hephaestus could make you a tongue?" she prompted, reveling in the long steady beats of her heart. She could almost feel her blood rushing through her veins in this place, feel the energy of her prickling nerves, the spark of her synapses snapping. She felt alive, vibrant, real. "Like, smite one up in his forge or whatever?

"He can make anything." Hades glowered at her. "And anything would be an improvement over listening to a demigod of Hermes prattle on."

"Okay, fine." She drew in a quick breath, released it. "Can he make me a new heart?"

Stefan, to his credit, didn't fully gasp behind her. It was more of a furious hiss of air that he choked off before it could make a sound.

"A new heart." Hades echoed, but she could tell the god was as surprised as Stefan.

"That's what I said." She took a few steps forward, if only to keep Stefan from clutching her back to him, though she certainly didn't mind the impulse behind that move. How had she gone from feeling so alone in that stateroom shower, to blacking out under the pounding water, to waking up in the arms of a man who was defying a god to keep her safe? Whose life was she even living?

She didn't know, but she was in no mood for it to end anytime soon.

"The way I see it, your magical kingdom needs people to defend it. People like Stefan here, who are willing to go the extra distance. I could be one of those people. I could serve. Even if I can't be a full-on demigod because I wasn't born with the right blood, I could serve fierce and strong. If you've been watching me at all, you know I'm telling you the truth."

"Nicki..." Her name sounded strangled on Stefan's lips, but Hades merely stared at her.

"You'd pledge yourself in service to me for a new heart?" he rumbled.

"I mean, as long as you're not an ass about it, sure." She winked. "But more to the point, I'd pledge myself to Oûros, to the gatekeepers, and I'd absolutely be willing to serve as your ambassador there. I understand from Stefan that you scare the shit out of most all your descendants, and that's really too bad, because people should face their fears, not run away from them. I don't run away. But I can't solve this heart thing on my own. And maybe you can't either, and that's okay. I don't think healing is one of your fancy powers, but I wanted to try."

"I also don't bring back people from the dead," Hades growled, showing some teeth. "That's the domain of the demigod Asclepius, more the fool he."

"And yet, I'm not dead." Nicki lifted a hand. "No, no, don't try to deny it. We wouldn't be having this conversation if I was dead. We're having it because you're getting impatient to liven this place up a bit, pardon the pun, and because you want my awesomeness on your team already. And I get it—I'm amazing."

Behind her, Stefan coughed a half-swallowed laugh.

"But I'm not ready to die yet, so I think my offer is a solid one. I help keep Oûros safe, get plenty of windsurfing in, and have a heart that isn't quite so tricky—assuming Hephaestus knows what he's doing. As a bonus, I serve as your ambassador—doing whatever it is that your demigods do, as long as it isn't anything too squicky. Stefan here can enter your realm at will, and he can pop me over for a chat whenever it's convenient, so the communication channel between us will remain open. Far as I can see, it's a win-win."

"And when you do pass on, mortal?" Hades asked, his words a rumble. "Nothing I can do can fully stop the passage of time. The lives of mortals are short and fierce."

She shrugged. "Only when we do it right. But I need your help, I think, to stay the course. I've done about all I can on my own, and I just need things to break my way on this one."

Hades shifted his attention to Stefan. "Step forward, demigod," he rumbled.

Stefan did, his body ramrod straight, and the god of the

Underworld looked between the two of them. "You agree to teach her to serve?"

"No."

"Stefan!" Nicki protested. Without thinking, she turned and punched him in the arm, hard. The sudden strike made him flinch and Hades' booming laugh rolled back the mists, revealing a wide, verdant patch of green grass beneath him, with peeks of light breaking through the swirling clouds high above.

A second later, the mists swept back, and Nicki put her fists on her hips, scowling at the intractable demigod. "Oh, come on, Stefan! I can't believe you're not willing to—"

"Enough." Hades cut her off, suddenly sounding happy enough that she glanced his way. To her surprise, he grinned at her. "But it is the demigod's choice as to when and how you will begin your service to the gods. You, fiery comet, will not remember this conversation until that time. There is no other way."

"Right." She snorted. "Pretty sure I'm not gonna forget this."

"Hades..." To her surprise, Stefan sounded choked up again, but the god merely crossed one fist over his chest, tapping his heart.

"You honor me by bringing her here to plead for her life, demigod. She honors me by offering to pledge it to me. I honor you both for your steadfast hearts. Begone before I change my mind."

Everything went black.

Forty-Six

I t was another several hours before the yacht slipped out into the Alaçati Bay, and Stefan turned away from the sunrise peeking over the horizon. The delay had been tedious, but not dangerous, in the end. Typical bureaucratic nonsense to ensure they had signed the right papers and paid the right fees before Turkey was willing to let them go. There'd been no mention of Ari or of the vagrant escape on the southern ridge, not a peep from Omir or any other Turkish official about anything going awry on the sleepy June night.

Sleep wasn't something he'd had much of through it all—catnaps only, with reports coming in from all directions... not to mention the gift that Hades had given him. What in the world was he supposed to do with that? Nicki had woken up in his arms in her stateroom with no memory of what had transpired in the Underworld, and a subsequent check of her vitals—which he'd pushed her on since she'd fainted again—showed absolutely no change in her readings.

They wouldn't show any change, he thought. Hades might not end up doing anything regarding her heart that she couldn't have done by medical doctors, the god simply wasn't going to accept her into the Underworld until she was ready. He did have some sway over such things, as Lord of the Underworld. And if he really wanted more ambassadors in Oûros...

He shook his head. He needed to work through all this *after* they safely delivered the prince.

The weather for sailing was clear. There should be nothing to obstruct their speed. They wouldn't race home, wouldn't draw attention, but at least they wouldn't run into any storms. He didn't know how Ari would handle a storm at sea, given how his odyssey had begun nearly a year ago.

The royal family had been put off with a convenient lie about the timing of the rescue operation—and more lies about the precise nature of the facilities they were infiltrating. Cyril knew the truth, but if the king and queen had received word of the possible conditions Ari had been enduring, it wouldn't have helped matters. It probably would've complicated them, in fact, with Jasen and Catherine's natural tendency to want to intervene using diplomatic channels.

As to the other victims of that unfortunate holding pen, the mythological beasts that had been restrained with electronic devices, Cyril was pursuing that on this side of the gates to Olympus and Hephaestus was pursuing it on his side. The electronics were devoid of any barcodes or identification, but they would eventually track down where they were made. The smaller-than-ordinary beasts were a more puzzling issue. Was someone breeding monsters for mortal use, somehow? As pets or protection or the gods only knew what else? If so, the monster god Typhon had to be involved, there simply was no other way around it.

Stefan pinched the bridge of his nose, trying to sort all the moving parts.

And then there was the prince himself. Ari was being monitored in his stateroom, with surveillance cameras installed in his sleeping quarters and even the bathroom for this purpose. Not to invade his privacy, but to ensure he didn't become disoriented again or harm himself either by accident or misguided design. Stefan grimaced. The crown prince wouldn't be affronted to learn of the surveillance, merely bemused. But that man in the stateroom wasn't the crown prince. He might never be.

The final piece of information was the most disquieting. The name Ryker Stavros had to come from somewhere, but Stefan couldn't for the life of him deduce where. And all attempts to quietly ascertain that answer had so far met a dead end. Had Stavros helped Ari escape the wreckage of his plane? Had he attempted to harm Ari in some way, imprinting on him indelibly?

"Sir. The communications room is ready."

"Good," he said. "Miss Clark?"

"Already present. She was waiting for us when we knocked."

That did finally ease Stefan's tension, for all that it intro-duced another round of concerns. Hades' intercession or not, Nicki would undergo exhaustive tests when they returned to Oûros, but he wasn't fooling himself into believing that she'd necessarily act on the results. She wasn't a child, or in his command. He couldn't force her to take the information they would provide her and care for herself appropriately. He couldn't force her to stop taking so many risks, to stop pushing herself so relentlessly.

There were so many things he couldn't do.

Shoving those thoughts out of his mind, he followed Tamas down to the communications room and pushed inside. As Tamas had indicated, Nicki had already arrived. She stood against the far wall, fresh and ready for anything in a tee-shirt and khakis. Her color was good, her eyes bright.

She'd hate that he was even thinking of her in those terms,

as if she were an invalid in any way. Too bad. She may not remember anything she'd said in the Underworld, but he did.

She'd told him that she loved him.

Stefan's heart gave a strange little leap in his chest at that thought, his blood seeming to flush through his body, his nerves crackling with anticipation, but he schooled his features to neutral and gave Nicki no more than a brief nod before turning to Tamas, who stood at the controls. "Patch us through."

The screens came alive and Cyril Gerou was the first to catch his attention, but multiple screens flickered and Stefan sighed. The king, queen and Prince Kristos were also on the video screen. Their expressions indicated that they were braced for the worst.

"Report," Cyril said crisply, giving no indication that Stefan had already been in contact with him. Probably wise.

"Our reconnaissance trip proved successful sir, Your Highnesses," he said, focusing on Cyril and pushing on as all three members of the Andris family surged forward, brimming with questions.

"Ari is alive," he raised his hand sharply, making the royal family flinch, though it didn't stop Catherine from bursting into tears. "He appears to be suffering from a severe case of amnesia. He doesn't know who he is or how he came to be in the airplane. He knows that he crashed, and that he's some sort of pilot. He believes his name is Ryker Stavros. We have not—"

"Ryker Stav—you're *joking*." It was Kristos who spoke, and Stefan flicked his gaze to the screen depicting the young prince. Kristos stared at him wide-eyed, while Jasen turned to his wife and drew her close. "That name—that was a character Ari dreamed up when we were kids, an alter ego or whatever. Ryker Stavros was an international mercenary bounty hunter kind of guy, able to go anywhere, be anyone. We would role play games for hours where he was Ryker and I was an equally capable

Drake Quinn or something like that." He smiled weakly. "Only I wasn't a pilot. I was a special forces operative."

"He's healthy though—he's healthy?" Catherine turned from Jasen's embrace and stared into the screen. "He doesn't have his memory, but we can help him with that. We can help him."

"He appears healthy, yes." Stefan nodded. "He's submitted to a basic medical review aboard ship, but we'll need a more exhaustive examination when he returns to Oûros." He paused. "If his return to the capital city is considered advisable immediately, that is. I'm not certain."

"Why not—" Catherine's anguished cry was quelled by King Jasen's snapped response.

"You think it will delay his recovery? It will overwhelm him?"

"There's simply no way to tell, Your Highness. He believes quite firmly that he was concussed in the crash, but he knows with a certainty his name and his trade. If we suddenly take that out from under him, I'm not sure how he'll respond." Stefan grimaced. "Further, I'm not sure we want to manage the press once they learn that the prince has returned, but that he is in any way impaired."

"He's *not* impaired," the queen protested hotly. "Don't even say that. He's injured—but he will recover."

"He *might* recover, Catherine," Jasen said. His words were stern, but not unkind. They had the result of making the queen go pale. "Ari is alive, and for that we are eternally grateful. He appears to be responding normally otherwise?"

"Yes, Your Highness." Stefan nodded. "He appears in good health and of sound mind, other than his memory. I have no idea if that will change."

"Agreed. But if we have the prince here on site, the media

will learn of it. It could be overwhelming for him, and that won't be helpful."

"But how can we—how can he—" the queen's throat worked as she tried to get hold of herself. "We have to be able to see him," she whispered. "Surely that can be arranged somehow?"

"Ask Fran—she might know."

Nicki's voice sounded from the corner of the room, and she took a step back as everyone's eyes turned to her. She still seemed a little disoriented, which was a fair enough reaction. He still hadn't fully processed everything that had happened in the last twenty-four hours, and she had had her memory blanked on top of that. But she wouldn't betray any weakness to the queen, he knew. She wouldn't want to betray weakness to anyone.

The queen leaned forward, breaking away from Jasen. "What do you mean, she might know?" she demanded.

"Well, she worked with vets—active military too. That was her thesis study, the effects of PTSD on general cognitive something or other." Nicki flapped her hand, clearly warming to the idea. "I don't know the specifics, but she spent nearly a year on it so she would know. Heck, maybe she could talk to Ryker—Ari. Maybe she can help him remember who he is?"

The queen seized on the idea with both hands, turning to Kristos. "Where are the girls now?" she asked, but once again Jasen was the voice of reason.

"We have time, Catherine," he said, his words calm. "It's another several hours before the yacht reaches our shores." He flicked his gaze to Cyril. "Do you agree with Stefan's concern about where they should dock?"

"I do, Your Highness," the chief advisor said carefully. "It might be wise for the yacht to dock at Asteri for a few days. We can send a medical team there. If there's a reason to bring Ari to the mainland, we can. If there's a reason for him to remain, it's a comfortable location."

Stefan nodded. Asteri was a private island owned by the royal family but rarely used except as a getaway for esteemed guests seeking a safe haven in the tiny country. The king and queen had long preferred to remain in the thick of the action in the capital city, but the island was isolated, pristine, and the facilities there—while more than suitable—were not as elaborate as the palace.

"It's a good idea," Stefan said. "Whether you recruit Miss Simmons or a more experienced psychologist, I would advise you to keep the circle of the informed quite tight. This is not something we want in the news."

"No," Catherine spoke before Jasen could. "No, we do not. We'll find someone we trust," she said. "Take him to Asteri, Stefan. Thank you for bringing him home."

He let his mouth soften into a brief smile. "I'm not the only one you should thank."

Forty-Seven

Nicki stiffened as everyone focused on her once more. "Hey, I simply followed orders," she said, lifting her hands. What was Stefan doing? She needed more attention like a hole in the head.

He kept talking over her protest. "It was an excellent decision, Your Highness, to insist that Nicki accompany us on this mission." Stefan's words were impossibly polite and neutral, which somehow increased the impact of what he said next. "She was instrumental at every turn, from fulfilling her requirements as a travel videographer to stepping in where needed with the windsurfing community in Alaçati. She interacted capably with the Turkish officials and made suggestions that enabled us to complete the mission quickly and effectively. Without her, the mission would probably have been completed, but I'm not certain we would have recovered Ari as seamlessly." He turned to her. "The kingdom of Oûros is in your debt."

Nicki blinked, startled out of her own spinning thoughts by the formality of his language, but the king and queen were focusing on her with renewed interest. "I have a feeling that will make a very interesting story," the queen murmured, her brows lifted.

King Jasen merely looked concerned. "Everyone is safe? Uninjured?"

Nicki's stomach knotted, but Stefan continued. "The entire team is safely aboard the yacht, unharmed. We do need to rechart our course for Asteri, but we expect to reach that port in approximately eight hours. It would be best if the team you were assembling was in place before we arrived. There are enough unoccupied villas there, I suspect, to ensure the prince's privacy?"

"The guests we had on the island left yesterday. No one else is scheduled?" Jasen quirked a glance toward the queen, and she shook her head, her expression indicating that her thoughts were already on a dozen different topics.

Nicki stifled a grin. Of course the royal family would have a private island for their personal use, and of course they'd be able to staff it in a matter of hours. Poor Ari might not be walking into the palace, but she had a feeling he would be in for a dramatic welcome all the same. "We'll be there before you, but keep us updated on your progress and any developments that will impact our personnel."

"Of course, Your Highness."

They talked for a short while further, then Stefan signed off. He spoke quickly to his men, and while she knew he wasn't speaking English—it once again sounded like English to her. She didn't just know how to speak Oûros, it was like the language was encoded in her DNA. Could that even be possible?

Stefan turned to her. "We need to move quickly now. There's a lot of preparation to take place in a few hours."

She nodded briskly. "I can totally make myself scarce—"

"What? Oh—no," he said. "There's still the matter of the

debrief. We'll want to ensure our stories match before you're interrogated by the queen."

He gestured her out the door and she lifted her brows. "Interrogated?" she asked, though she obligingly exited in front of him.

"It will probably include a liberal helping of *tsipouro*," he said. "You would do well to be prepared."

His words were light—much lighter than the tone he'd used with the royal family, and Nicki found herself grinning in response. To her surprise, Stefan didn't take her to another of the small conference rooms, however, but up the corridor to the main deck, then across to where the sleeping cabins were situated. He stopped at his stateroom.

"The veranda here is more private and protected from the wind. We can talk," he said, ushering her inside.

"Of course." She pointedly did not glance toward the doors that led to the bedchamber, and instead headed outside.

Stefan was right. The small sitting area was wonderfully comfortable, open to the sky but with walls high enough to cut most of the stiff breeze coming off the ocean. Nicki ducked under the shade to sit at the table, and Stefan joined her, their chairs angled to make the most of the view.

The view and decided proximity to each other.

Stop it, Nicki reminded herself again. Her time with Stefan was rapidly nearing an end, and she needed to focus on what was real, not what was wishful thinking. He'd become even more protective than ever since she'd gotten dizzy and passed out in the shower, but she supposed she only had herself to blame for that.

She pushed all those thoughts from her mind, and refocused on the issue at hand. "So," she said, leaning forward to put her elbows on the table. "What do I need to change about the story? Or is it a matter of not giving specific details?"

"The queen is cagier than that," Stefan said. He also leaned forward, and Nicki fought her shiver. He was so—competent. Strong, vibrant, masculine, smart, sexy as hell—the total package. She was going to miss that.

She was going to miss a lot of things.

"Primarily, though, it's a matter of what you should omit."

"Yeah?" she asked, refocusing. "Like the part where we broke laws, or the part where we had sex?"

His gaze remained steady. "I think she'll be unfazed by either of those revelations. In fact she'll give herself full credit for the latter." He shook his head at her quick grin. "Specifically, though, the accounts of the squatters on the nature of Ari's arrest—the timing, the details. Those can be left out. The queen will learn easily enough that he was rounded up as part of a work detail, but she would take issue with the way the Alaçati authorities handled Ari's incarceration, and that's not useful at this juncture."

"That makes sense." Nicki said. "Anything else?" She narrowed her eyes. "Are you going to tell her about me passing out? Because I certainly won't."

"I won't share that directly with the queen, but with Cyril and King Jasen," Stefan said. "What they choose to tell the queen, I can't say."

"Well you could *choose* not to tell Cyril and Jasen anything either. That would solve that problem."

He shrugged, "I could, but there is the matter of the, ah, medical tests we'll be running. I've already set those arrangements in motion, and they aren't secret."

"Fine," Nicki said, sitting back in a huff. "I'm still not bringing it up."

"There's no need to do so." He quirked her a glance. "Unless you're feeling poorly?"

Irritation crested. "I'm feeling *fine*. I told you that. I don't know why you're making such a big deal about this."

Stefan lifted his brows. "Because you nearly died?"

She scowled at him. "I didn't nearly die. I passed out! That's it."

"Which begs the question. Why did you willfully keep such a vital piece of information about your health hidden from me for so long?"

"Gee, Stefan, maybe so I could avoid this exact conversation?" Nicki found herself dangerously close to tears, so she converted her annoyance to anger. "Maybe so we could focus on the mission and not on something that might or might not have been a concern—and even then, only for me?"

"Only for you?" he snapped, and she watched him visibly struggle with his temper. He looked away, his jaw working as he stared out to sea for a long moment. Then he spoke again. "If I had known you might be put at risk because of an adrenaline spike or dehydration, or that your body might not respond well to stress, you're correct. I wouldn't have put you at risk."

"You wouldn't have taken me on that last mission, for sure. And I helped! You said yourself that I helped."

He gave her a curt nod. "You could have helped in other ways, though. Just because you're not on the front lines doesn't make your role any less vital."

"But the front lines is where I belong. It's where I've always been. And I was fine—right up until I wasn't. There was no way to predict that."

"There were ways to work around it though. Ways to manage through it. And when I found you in your room..." his words trailed off and she saw the tightness to his jaw, the way his hands clenched. "I only had a sense something was wrong. I didn't know for sure. If I hadn't reached you in time..."

"You did reach me, though," she said. "It all worked out and I'm here. I'm fine."

"You're fine." He sighed heavily and turned to her, and to her surprise he lifted his hands to either side of her face, drawing her close for a long, searching kiss. "You're fine."

His voice trembled with emotion, and Nicki's own heart trembled in her chest—not with anxiety, but with a surge of excitement that swept through her like a cleansing fire. Stefan desired her—still. She held on to that realization with both hands. He wanted her.

And she wanted him back.

Then Stefan pulled away and stared at her. "I need you to be more than fine, Nicki. I want you healthy and safe. I want you to be able to do whatever you want, for as long as you want."

She smiled, her hands shaking now, too. "Well, it looks like you got your wish."

Forty-Eight

I *want you as mine*. Stefan shouldn't have said the words. He'd monitored Nicki's emails closely since they'd returned from Olympus. He knew she was in conversation with the American windsurfing instructor. He knew she'd responded to his overture for work. And she was aware of his knowledge, he suspected, since she knew the protocols for email monitoring on the mission. It didn't change the truth of things: she was already planning her exit from the shores of Oûros, and from him.

Without ever knowing that she'd bargained with Hades... without ever knowing what she'd said.

"You know, I'm never going to be completely out of danger," Nicki said, her eyes wide, searching his. "That's not who I am. If I can't do the things I want to do without breaking, then what's the point? Like now." She leaned forward and kissed him again, then whispered against his mouth. "Stop worrying over me, Stefan. We don't have to think about the future, only this minute, nothing more. And this minute, I want you. Only you."

Stefan went very still, every muscle on high alert. "Nicki—you're supposed to be resting."

"That's true." She pulled back and grinned at him. "But I

have it on very good authority that what I have in mind frequently happens while the participants are lying down. So really, you'd be doing me a favor if you lay down with me, say— on your bed. And since we wouldn't want to mess up your clothes..."

She stood and stepped away from the table, and Stefan shook his head. Even as he did so, however, his resolve weakened. "I don't think this is a good idea," he said, but Nicki pulled him into the stateroom, then immediately turned and headed for the interior cabin.

"Well, I'm taking off my clothes and climbing into your bed. You're more than welcome to join me. If you prefer to stand watch outside, that's also fine."

He watched, startled as she stripped off her tee shirt and shimmied out of her khakis before she reached the bedroom door. Without pausing, she reached for her bra-strap...

Stefan was behind her in three long strides. "You really shouldn't exert yourself unduly," he said, gripping her shoulders in his hands.

Her hands fell to her waist as he unhooked her bra. "In fact," he murmured. "I'm pretty sure you should let me take the lead from here."

She gave the faintest protest as he leaned down and lifted her into his arms, but her smile was wide as she gazed up at him. "No wonder they picked you as team lead. So strategic," she said, but he wasn't fooled by the wry humor in her voice. Equal parts relief and need shown in her eyes, and he leaned down to kiss her softly on the forehead. She was so fierce, and wanted so much to be strong, that showing vulnerability was nearly impossible for her. She had to be in control, had to be active, had to take charge of the situation.

But right at this moment, he knew, more than anything, that she needed something more. She needed to know that someone craved her. Needed to know that someone saw her not as an invalid, but as someone who was powerful, desirable...intoxicating.

She was all that and more.

"I'm going to forego tossing you, if only this once," he said as they stepped into the cool confines of the room. Nicki laughed, but her expression sobered as he laid her carefully on the bed.

"I'm not going to break, Stefan," she said. He leaned down, kissing first her collarbone, then her cheek, and then softly, gently, he pressed his lips against hers, his gaze resolute. She must have seen something of what he was thinking because her eyes widened in surprise.

He rose, his mouth slanting into a soft smile. "You're not the one I'm worried about breaking anymore." She blinked, and he stood again, pulling off his shirt before shimmying out of his trousers. He freed the condom packet from his pants pocket and tossed it on the bed, then stripped off his shorts.

Nicki reached for her own clothes, and he lifted a hand. "Don't move."

"Stefan, I can—"

"That's a direct order," he murmured as Nicki froze, but he didn't give her long to puzzle through his intentions. Reaching up, he slid her panties down her legs.

"You missed a spot," Nicki said, hooking her thumb into her bra strap.

"I missed nothing," Stefan said. He knelt on the bed between her legs and traced the curve of her functional bra down its sleek lines, sliding his fingers under the soft swells of her breasts. Nicki's breath caught, and her pulse jumped in her neck, but her eyelids drooped, and she sighed as he teased her nipples through the fabric.

"I think you should have a new supply of lingerie as part of your payment for this job," Stefan said, and her gaze flicked to him, sharpening with focus.

"Lingerie?"

"You tend toward serviceable gear—which I appreciate—but I can't help but imagine you in something a little less... practical."

Nicki's snort of laughter cut off abruptly as he snaked his hand behind her back, loosening the catch of her bra. He slid it over her shoulders and leaned down, following his progress with his lips as he traced kisses down over her trembling skin. While he drew his tongue over the peak of her left breast, he allowed a hand to close around her right breast in synchrony, the dual pressure causing Nicki to arch off the bed.

"Yes," she muttered, and the soft urgency in her voice was the only motivation he needed. Pulling back from her, he sheathed himself quickly, then returned to her body, leaning down for a kiss.

To his surprise, Nicki held up a hand. "Permission to take the lead?" she asked, and when he nodded, she reached up, pushing at his shoulders until he rolled to the side, then onto his back.

He quirked her a bemused glance. "You were supposed to take it easy."

"This position improves oxygen flow," Nicki said, but what she was doing was decidedly damaging the flow of oxygen and blood to *his* brain, that was certain. She straddled his body, naturally coming to rest over his shaft. The compression as her body settled made his jaw tighten, but he couldn't take his eyes from Nicki's face. She was so intent, so beautiful—her expression focused, her eyes clear, and the soft smile on her face something he would never tire of.

She slid over him and his attention fractured. He had the vague sense of her expression growing far more triumphant.

"Better?" she asked, with a twist of her lips, throwing his own words back at him. His breath escaped in a tight hiss, and he lifted his hands to her hips, seating her more firmly against him as her body rocked. He found his gaze darting everywhere, her breasts, her face, the tight knot of her abs as she flexed to hold herself in place—and then further up, to where her precious heart lay safely beneath skin and bone. An unreasonable tide of possession surged inside of him, and the message traveled straight to his groin.

Nicki's gaze riveted on him as she felt the difference. "Oh," she breathed, and he grimaced.

"Yes. Oh." He tried to loosen his grip on her hips, but then she lifted her chin, her body stretching taut as she dropped her head back. He watched as her eyes drifted shut while she absorbed the complete experience of him—and the sheer joy of her expression added exponentially to his enjoyment. They moved with increasing speed and strength, her body flexing, tightening around him until there was no way to tell where she ended and he began. The symbiosis of their movement was as timeless as the sea and filled with laughter, light, and sunshine, like the smile on Nicki's face.

The sudden orgasm rushed up on him so quickly that he growled. Nicki's eyes flew open as she fell forward, her hands bracing on his chest, her lips parting as he bucked with sudden, frenzied need beneath her. She cried out, too, with sudden, unfettered happiness, and he gripped her even harder, wanting to hold her, keep her, and make her his far beyond this moment, far beyond this day. Within that moment, they shared thoughts, they shared emotions, they shared sensations, they shared *all*. In a flash, Stefan knew the truth: that was the gift and the curse of their connection; that was the future he faced. Whether they stayed together or he let her go, Nicki would remain linked to him...as long as she lived.

How could he let her go, knowing that?

With a great, gusting sigh, Nicki rolled off him, sprawling onto the jumbled sheets, her body appearing as boneless as his felt.

"See?" she murmured, curling against him. "That wasn't stressful at all."

Their quiet, shared laughter flowed easily into the sea-bright sunshine.

Forty-Nine

Nicki stared in wonder as they pulled into port. The yacht was greeted by a small army of workers who marched out of a bright-white boathouse and trotted down an equally white boardwalk to greet their ship. The entire mini marina appeared freshly scrubbed, and as Stefan handed her off the boat, she squinted at him.

"No one lives on this island but the royal family and their guests? It's literally a private island? And they own it? Like... they *own* it, own it?"

Stefan glanced at her, his face looking a little bemused. "Technically, the country of Oûros owns it, but it's in the royal family's name, yes. For use as they see fit, whether for guests or extended members of the family." His lips quirked. "If you stay in Oûros for any length of time, however, you'll find the family extends...quite a long way."

"But all of these people—"

Stefan cut off her confusion. "The island isn't all that isolated. We are actually not too distant from a larger island with a robust fishing village—Miranos, home of Dimitri Korba's family. The staff for Asteri draws heavily from Miranos—and supplies are shipped over weekly when guests are in residence."

"But they don't live here." Nicki shook her head. The island was everything she could imagine in a tropical paradise—lush vegetation peeking from high cliffs that surrounded impossibly tranquil turquoise waters. Beyond the boathouse, a manicured road wound off into a thick overhang of trees. "No one lives here permanently."

"They could if they wanted," Stefan shrugged, as if deciding whether or not to live on a remote Greek isle was an everyday occurrence. "Most of them prefer the community of Miranos. There is a staff who stay onsite, primarily when there are—"

"Yeah, yeah, I get it. When there are guests on the island."

More voices sounded behind them, and they turned to see Ari emerge on the deck. Stefan had wanted them already off the boat when Ari saw the dock for the first time, and he observed the prince keenly as Tamas escorted him to the gangplank. Ari appeared happy, animated, and not at all familiar with the location.

Beside her, Stefan tilted his head. "I don't know anything about memory loss or the effect of a concussion on the brain. He doesn't appear to be damaged otherwise, but...it's impossible to tell."

"He doesn't recognize anything, but he's not upset about that," Nicki said. "That has to help, right?"

"One would hope. We've arranged for three different specialists to examine him, once we have the island equipped with the proper scanning devices."

Nicki blinked. "You're shipping a cat scan machine *here*? To the family's pleasure island?"

"There's a fully outfitted medical facility here. For the immediate future, the family would prefer not to let Ari's condition be revealed to anyone. Oûros is a small country, but our media is persistent. Especially when it comes to the royal family. In the end, the cost of shipping equipment and personnel is far less onerous than enduring a twenty-four-seven newsreel on the health of the crown prince."

"Fair enough." Nicki let her smile broaden when Ari joined them on the dock. He stared around in appreciation, then grinned at Stefan.

"You have friends in high places, Stefan," he said, speaking flawless English. Nicki hadn't let drop that she could speak Oûrois yet. She wanted to keep that her little secret for the discernible future. "But I'm not about to believe I do. What is this place?"

"A private island—Asteri," Stefan said, watching Ari with deceptive ease. "How much do you remember of the Aegean?"

"Standing here right now? Not a damned thing." Ari shook his head ruefully. "I know my name, that I was flying on a job—but not for who. I think I know how to pilot a plane, but I wouldn't want to get behind the controls unassisted anytime soon."

Nicki laughed. "Well, then at least your sense of personal safety isn't impaired."

They turned toward the main drive as a car cruised to a stop and Stefan started walking. Ari and Nicki followed behind him, and Nicki had to force herself not to catalog Ari's every move. It's not as if she knew what she was looking for. Ari could start quacking like a duck and she wouldn't know if that even meant anything.

"Who will we be meeting?" Ari asked, a note of apprehension creeping into his voice. "I assume—my family?"

"Not at first," Stefan said, and Nicki didn't miss the flash of relief on Ari's face. "I'm afraid you'll have to go through a battery of medical tests before anything else."

"Here?" Ari asked doubtfully. "This looks like a resort island."

Nicki snorted. "Once again, nothing wrong with your powers of observation. But yeah, here. As it turns out, really good doctors don't seem to have an issue with house calls to islands. I can't say I blame them."

They piled into the SUV and Nicki peered at the driver, disappointed it wasn't Dimitri Korba. But then, she supposed that made sense. Dimitri was Ari's best friend. Chances were good that seeing him would trigger some sort of memory event, and until they understood where Ari was in the recovery process, it made sense to go slow.

Conversation continued as the SUV wound its way through the lush forest, definitely heading uphill. "I have a feeling we're going to have one hell of a view when we're done, aren't we," Nicki put in, and Stefan's glance was amused.

"It's a favorable one," he said.

"And beaches too, I suspect? But a long way down." Ari peered out at the heavy forest but showed no sign of familiarity with the place.

"There is a beach below the main house, but it's a fair distance—there's an access road to it and I believe a zip line now."

Nicki turned to stare at Stefan. "A...zip line?"

He smiled back at her, lifting his brows, but just then, the trees gave way and they rolled into the bright sunshine once more. The lawn spread before them and Nicki's eyes bugged out as she took in the royal family's compound—a large white villa with several tiers, and multiple additional villas and buildings scattered over the grass. From her viewpoint, the Mediterranean sun reflected off no fewer than three pools, and fountains lined the crisp white stone walkways.

"Wow," Nicki breathed, but when Ari didn't respond beside

her, she turned to glance at him. Stefan had turned as well from the passenger seat.

"Ryker?" Stefan asked. "Everything okay?"

"What? Oh—yes. Yes, of course." Still, Ari sat forward as they approached the building compound. "I remember seeing this place—I'm sure of it. Not from the ground, though." He frowned, glancing upward. "I must have flown over this section of the island at some point. That's possible, isn't it?"

"Eminently possible," Stefan said crisply. "I'd be surprised if you hadn't, really. It's not on the commercial airlines flight path, but for smaller craft it's completely reasonable." He turned back forward as the vehicle rolled to a stop. "We'll be staying in the main house, if that's acceptable." Without waiting for a response, he continued. "We'll have a medical team here as quickly as possible. By tomorrow morning, I expect."

Ari swung out of the car, then eyed Stefan with the first hint of doubt. "I really don't want to put you to all this trouble. I—if I have work, a life, I should be getting back to it."

"It's a precaution for everyone." Stefan lifted a hand. "Nicki and I are also getting full medical workups tomorrow, so we're stuck here, anyway. You, of course, are not obligated to be examined. But if you wanted to rule out any physiological reasons for your amnesia, it would be best."

Ari's smile was wry. "As in, perhaps my skull got cracked in the wreck? Probably not a bad idea." He shook his head. "I don't remember a hell of a lot from the time before they picked me up in the nature preserve. And what little I once thought I knew— it's gone now. That happened a few months back, the memories of the time immediately after the crash fading away into the same blank soup as the rest of my history."

Stefan froze, but he kept his voice calm enough. "You've lost other memories?"

"No—I don't think so. Only that period between the wreck

and the park. I...I don't know. I could have been drunk, hurt worse than I thought—high on something, I don't know. I picked up food and a boat but otherwise...it's simply sort of faded."

Stefan looked like he wanted to say something more, but he gestured them all into the house instead. A group of smiling men and women greeted them, all dressed in casual uniforms—shifts or pants sets for the women, khakis and polos for the men. Stefan waved Ari along. "We'll serve a late dinner on the veranda, if you'll join us?"

Ari snorted. "I'll check my schedule." He gave them a jaunty salute, then ambled off down the hallway. The rest of the house remained as still as a tomb.

Stefan turned toward her. "Brace yourself," he murmured. "The family is waiting for us in the sitting room. We've been monitored since we boarded the SUV."

Fifty

Stefan entered the room first, but Nicki was right behind him, and he had the sense of the two of them presenting a united front. It was an odd but welcome feeling—and it vanished the minute they cleared the door.

"Your updated report, Stefan," Cyril began, but before he could fully get the words out, Queen Catherine strode forward.

"He's so thin!" she exclaimed. "You didn't tell us that he'd suffered—what happened to him? Where was he, and who was holding him?"

"Catherine—" the king's voice cut across his wife's but he stepped forward as well as she turned on him.

"Did you know? Am I the only one in this family who isn't being kept in the loop—"

The two other men in the room remained silent, but it was clear they were bursting with questions as well. Kristos about his brother, Dimitri about his best friend. But they were too well trained to interrupt when Cyril had given him a direct command, and too polite to shush the queen.

"Your Highnesses, sir," Stefan said, nodding to the royal parents and then Cyril. "As you no doubt saw, Ari is physically healthy—and yes, thin." He lifted a hand again as the queen fought to maintain silence. "He survived the aircraft crash and came ashore at a small barrier island off the coast of Turkey in a confused and disoriented state. He was apparently uninjured other than having no recollection of anything beyond his name —he did not know his nationality, his purpose for being in the plane other than for, as he termed it, a 'reconnaissance mission,' and he had no memory of his family, friends or associates. He approached a scavenger and traded debris he had recovered from the plane for a boat and supplies to get him to mainland Turkey. He landed in a nature preserve and made some contact with the squatters there, again making trades for supplies. The city of Alaçati was, at the time, conscripting vagrants and drunks for work crews. They picked up Ari as part of this effort."

The queen hissed, but said nothing as Stefan continued. "For the next eleven months, Ari worked on a construction detail for the city of Alaçati, and was kept in a holding pen with other men at night. He endured the trial remarkably well, it appears." Stefan made a dismissive gesture with his hand. He and Cyril had agreed on this part. Until they knew more about the creatures that had been kept in the warehouse, there would be no mention of them to the queen. She'd demand details, and they needed to be able to provide them. "A medical analysis will provide better information on how well."

The queen stood rigid in Jasen's grasp, but it was Cyril who spoke next, his words crisp and controlled. "The last of the medical team will be in place tomorrow morning. Depending on what they find, we'll transport Ari to a clinic in Zurich for further evaluation. We appear to have slipped the bonds of media notice for the moment, so moving him quickly will be of paramount importance, if that is judged to be the safest course for him."

The queen nodded. "When can we see him, then?" she demanded. "It will obviously take time for him to recover, but perhaps if he saw one of us..." she shook her head, discarding the idea as quickly as she had it. "I guess that's something we simply won't know until he gets evaluated. Who do you have coming in?"

Cyril gave her the names of the specialists, then detailed the equipment being transported as well.

She frowned. "What about Francesca Simmons? I thought we'd agreed she would be part of the evaluation team."

Stefan's brows shot up and Cyril grimaced. "Your Highness, we discussed this."

"Don't you 'Your Highness' me. Yes, we discussed this, and you agreed to think about it. We've not shared another word, and I continue to think it's a good idea." She swiveled to Stefan as both Kristos and Dimitri exchanged a glance. Apparently, the queen had been quite vocal about the idea, and not only to Cyril.

"Francesca has had multiple interactions with US servicemen recovering from PTSD endured after military-related traumas. She's written her thesis on it. I've read it. It's quite good. She should be part of the evaluation team."

King Jasen sighed. "We have some of the best neurosurgeons in the world on that team, Catherine. They are more than equipped to do their job."

"But they haven't been working with soldiers."

"And Ari is not a soldier, not anymore." Jasen's voice was terse, but stopped shy of a snap. "He's a pilot, at most, locked in his current delusion."

"A pilot whose plane *crashed*, and who then was *imprisoned* without recourse and made to work in a *camp* for nearly a year, Jasen. All of which sounds fairly warlike to me, regardless of whether or not everyone lined up in uniforms against each other." She shifted her glare again to Cyril. "Tell me, are any of the neurosurgeons you've called in under the age of fifty?"

The advisor frowned. "I fail to see what their age has to do with anything."

"Ari is a twenty-eight-year-old male, Cyril. Stop being so dense! A woman closer to his own age with actual skilled training in working with traumatized soldiers might be someone he's willing to endure far more easily than a fifty-year-old pinhead in a white coat."

Jasen winced. "I'm sure no one would describe these doctors as pinheads."

"I suspect I would. Ari certainly would." She turned her glare on Kristos and Dimitri. "Wouldn't he?"

Both men spread their hands, but it was Dimitri who spoke. "There's no way to tell how he will react, Your Highness. The man who walked away from that plane is not the same man who went up in it." He hesitated. "But Ari certainly had a healthy appreciation for beautiful women."

Kristos snorted, and Stefan tightened his jaw as Cyril's irritation broke. "We are not setting these people up on a date," the advisor protested. "Ari is potentially in a very fragile and suggestible state. We must proceed with caution, following the guidance set forth by the medical professionals we are sparing no expense to bring to Asteri."

"Exactly!" The queen's response was almost defiant, and Stefan suspected he wasn't alone in feeling like they'd lost some ground, somehow. "If the medical professionals agree that having Francesca here—a trained counselor who will serve in a non-official role as simply another connection point for Ari—if they agree that she is a better solution to help Ari find his way back to himself, then we'll go that route. I could not agree more, Cyril. Thank you."

Cyril blinked, and Stefan fought a smile as Jasen sighed and shook his head. "Agreed, then," the king said. "Stefan, tell us about the conditions of this work camp. Is it something we need to respond to officially, in some way?"

"No, Your Highness," Stefan said crisply. "The work detail to which the camp was assigned was very specific. The building where the holding cells were located is slated for demolition within the next several weeks. The night that Ari was recovered, the remaining detainees were also released."

Jasen's brows went up, and his expression lightened. Cyril would fill him in later, Stefan knew. At some point when the queen wasn't around. If possible, she was even more fierce in her veneration of the gods than King Jasen was. She wouldn't look kindly on anyone attempting to enslave and profit off the creatures of Olympus—so, again, Stefan knew they had to tread lightly here. There was still more to learn.

King Jasen's gaze shifted to Nicki.

"Another item I would like to clarify. You helped Stefan on this mission?"

Nicki was clearly startled by the sudden change in his focus. "I—well, yes, I did. Of course," she said, but Stefan could hear the note of caution in her voice. So could the rest of them, and their attention on her only intensified. "I uploaded videos of a diving experience off the coast of Turkey, and more videos of the expo. I participated in a windsurfing demonstration to solidify my cover while I was there. That's pretty much it."

Jasen must have sensed her prevarication because he clasped his hands at his waist almost casually, rocking up on his toes.

Kristos and Dimitri went still, and even the queen blinked, staring more curiously at Nicki. "I believe you did a bit more as well," the king said. "The queen hasn't been fully informed, and I think she would be grateful for the update."

"Oh, I—" Nicki paused as Stefan turned toward her, a blush

steadily climbing her cheeks. For all that she was used to being in the spotlight, she didn't know how to trumpet her own horn, he realized yet again. She always let her actions do the talking. She gave and gave and gave until her body—literally—gave out. "I didn't really do anything else special. Truly. I simply helped where I could." The glance she threw Stefan was panicked. "Wouldn't you agree?"

He nodded, grateful that she'd given him the opportunity to share what she wouldn't. Then he turned back to the royal family.

"I've given you a partial accounting of Nicki's actions to help free Ari, but I wanted to be fully clear. Her life was endangered on the barrier island when a miscommunication threatened the negotiations with the scavenger dealer. Still, she reacted with commendable calm, placing her trust in the team and following their lead. With her resourcefulness and past connections, she helped facilitate our conversation with the Turkish official and convinced him to give us a guided tour solely in the hopes that it would gain us visual access to the site where we suspected Ari was being held. When that suspicion was confirmed, she helped identify likely methods of access to the building, which involved using free climbing abilities."

The queen gasped, and Nicki audibly groaned. "Stefan..." she said.

"That's not all," he continued, inexorably. "Once we achieved access to the building, she willingly put herself in harm's way by distracting the guard at a crucial moment. Then, when I mistakenly released all the locks in the main holding cell area, she found herself in a footrace, being chased by several detainees."

"They weren't chasing me." Nicki protested. "They were trying to escape, that's all."

"Most were," he said. "Ari wasn't. He reached Nicki first

and turned to protect her." He paused as the queen clasped her hands to her mouth. "He succeeded in doing so until I could reach her. By then, Nicki had overtaxed herself and had collapsed."

"Stefan!" Nicki's voice was like a whip crack, overrode only by the queen's cry of Nicki's name. "You don't—"

"She recovered quickly enough, but there's no denying that the state of Oûros—and I personally—put Nicki at mortal risk. It was a risk she willingly took on to rescue Ari. Even after it was clear that her body had failed her, she wouldn't give up until we were able to get her to safety."

"That's more than enough—" Nicki started.

Stefan turned to her. "I don't think it's anywhere close to enough."

Fifty-One

Nicki's flare of anger shorted out at the intensity in Stefan's face. Then the infernal demigod kept talking. "I've arranged to have a medical evaluation tomorrow that both Nicki and I will undergo, and if there is any reason to be concerned, she will be transferred to a cardiac facility in Zurich at the same time we transfer the prince."

"Cardiac!" the queen nearly shouted, aghast. Nicki turned in time to see the woman go pale.

"Really—it's *nothing*."

"It is potentially nothing to be concerned about," Stefan agreed. "However, Nicki's family has a history of cardiomyopathy, and Nicki has not undergone the required screening for several years, so her condition remains in question." His gaze was like granite. "It will no longer be in question, shortly."

"You knew—" the queen seemed to have trouble breathing. "You knew that your heart wasn't stable, and you insisted on going on this mission? Why?"

"I—" Nicki tried to speak, she did. But her heart felt too full all of a sudden, and she would have given a lot to fake a dizzy spell at that moment. But the thing just kept happily beating along—not too fast, not too slow. That threw her for a loop as well, and when she didn't respond fast enough, Stefan was there once again, ready to step into the gap.

"Because she knew she was the best equipped to help the prince," he said. "She had the contacts and the training. She knew the city. She had the best reason to be there and therefore provided the best cover."

"But, you could have been killed." The queen's soft words drew Nicki's attention back to her, and when Catherine walked forward, it was all Nicki could do not to run away.

"You sacrificed yourself willingly, for a family you didn't know existed until a few short weeks ago," the queen said. "You..." She swallowed. "You helped bring my son home to me. I can never repay that—ever."

"You don't have to repay me," Nicki said, lifting her hands to slow the tide of emotion flowing out from the queen.

"Yes, I do," Catherine said, shaking her head. "You will receive the Rite of Oûros, with my blessing. And my eternal, desperate thanks." She closed the final feet to Nicki, and then her tears did give way. This beautiful, serene woman, so strong in all her actions and words since the moment Nicki had met her, crumpled in front of Nicki like the relieved mother she could finally allow herself to be. Nicki automatically put out her arms and the queen stepped into them, though Nicki was unsure as to who was giving and who was receiving the greater grace in that moment.

"Thank you," the queen whispered. "Thank you, thank you, thank you."

Around them, there was movement—talking, walking, industry. But Nicki paid no attention to anyone but the queen for a few more moments, giving her back all the strength she had left in her body, giving her every beat of her heart, broken or not.

"Of course," Nicki said. "He'll be okay—he's going to be okay."

"I know." The queen leaned back, and her expression had totally changed in those bare moments. Despite being streaked with tears, her face was stronger, almost ebullient. "He's surrounded by those he loves, and that love will sustain him, even if his mind has forgotten why."

She squeezed Nicki's shoulders. "And now we have to make sure you're healthy, too."

Nicki nearly groaned. "I'm good. Really, I'm good."

"You *are* sick though?" the queen asked, and the question was so gentle, so unexpected, that Nicki blinked at her.

"I'm...I'm maybe sick, though I don't feel sick anymore," she said, the admission almost a relief. "I definitely have a disconnect going on. I get too dizzy, and I sometimes black out. I—my family has a history of heart problems, as Stefan said. I guess..." She shrugged. "I guess I didn't want to find out I did too. I wanted to live my life going full out."

"Being smart doesn't mean being an invalid, you know," Catherine said, and though her voice was stern, her eyes were soft. "And I'm not pressing you on this for only your benefit, although of course that is important."

She turned, still not quite letting Nicki go, until they both could see the cluster of men at the far end of the room. Dimitri and Kristos were practically coming out of their skin with electric energy, Stefan was arguing with Cyril—and Jasen, now that no one was watching him, had allowed his expression to soften. He gazed across the room at his wife, vibrant with joy, and a hope that Nicki hadn't ever realized she'd missed firmly reflected in his face. Queen Catherine gave Nicki's arm a squeeze, her smile radiant as she beamed back at her husband.

"Love is too important to squander, too precious to miss out on," the queen said. Nicki turned to her in surprise, and she nodded to the men again. Specifically, to Stefan.

"Oh—you have the wrong idea." Nicki shook her head sharply. "Stefan and I—I mean, we barely know each other. We couldn't fall in love, not that quickly. We're just...friends."

"Friends," the queen said soberly. "And do you regard all your friends with your entire soul in your eyes, ready to give and give and give until there's nothing left? Do you stand as if your hands are reaching out to connect with the other, ready to offer your whole life up in that one touch, when you haven't even moved?"

"I..." Nicki winced. "I didn't realize I looked like that."

"You don't," the queen said. "He does."

She hugged her more tightly as Nicki froze. "I have known that man since Jasen first began courting me—back then, Stefan served Jasen's grandfather, like he'd served generations of kings before. Then Jasen's father—and then, finally, Jasen. Over those many years, I have seen him look at women—beautiful women from all over the world. And none of them can compare with how he looks at you."

She turned to Nicki, and her eyes were filled with tears again. "Ari wasn't the only man you've helped find his way home again, Nicki. You've brought Stefan home, too. Please, don't ever let him go."

Fifty-Two

S tefan glanced up as the queen finally stepped away from Nicki, his stomach churning over what the queen might have said to her. She obviously hadn't explained the Rite of Oûros, since Nicki hadn't fainted dead away again.

He excused himself from the knot of strategizing between Kristos, Cyril, Dimitri, and Jasen, which he suspected would go on far into the night, and strode across the room. The queen smoothed her hands over her eyes, whisking away tears, and took her leave of Nicki, stepping toward Stefan with purpose.

He knew Catherine's ultimate goal was the men behind him, but her focus was fully on him, her stare intent as he met her in the center of the sitting room. She paused briefly, then speared him with a glare.

"If you don't tell that woman that you love her, I will personally make your life miserable for the rest of my life and then instruct all my heirs and their children to do the same," she said. "She's a national treasure, and I expect you to make her *our* national treasure, Stefan Mihal."

Then she was gone.

Stefan didn't break stride, sparing only a moment to blink a few times as he assimilated the queen's words. He'd known from the start that the queen had an incurable penchant for matchmaking, but he hadn't expected it to manifest so...clearly. He waited for the flash of resistance to come in the wake of the queen's high-handed command, just as it always did when she made completely unreasonable requests with complete confidence that her dictates would be followed.

But no resistance came. If anything, his mind instantly set to work, going through the possibilities, considering the angles.

Nicki, for her part, was grinning gamely at him as he reached her.

"So it's going to be okay, right?" she asked, and he quirked her a smile.

"They're—happy," she said, waving at the knot of people across the room. "Glad that you found the prince, that he's here safely, despite that he's not quite right yet. He will be normal again one day, or whatever will become the new normal for him. And he's safe."

Stefan nodded. "They're happy. They're beyond happy. Their son is safe, he is returned. I suspect that even if he's unable to remember who he is—who they are—that disappointment will pale in comparison to the reality that he's alive and there remains a lifetime of new memories to forge." He glanced back to where the royal family stood, arguing exuberantly over the best course of treatment for Ari's recovery. "The queen will win her battle to ensure Francesca Simmons becomes part of the therapy team. Do you know if she'll be prepared for that?"

To his surprise, Nicki didn't answer right away. Instead, she frowned thoughtfully.

"I think she will," she said at last. "Her natural tendency would be to say yes, of course—especially if she's not acting in an official capacity. But Fran has always been the quietest of us all. She studied a lot and didn't really go out much, even when she was done with her training and thesis work overseas. I don't know as much about her as I do about Lauren and Emmaline, that's for sure."

Stefan frowned, and Nicki rushed in with reassurance. "But she'll be great in whatever the family and doctors decide what her role should be, honestly. She's dependable, really, she is."

"There seems to be a fair amount of that going around."

Nicki's smile was genuine. "What can I say—I've got good friends."

"And they're lucky to have you," Stefan said. They'd moved to the far end of the room, where the windows overlooked the sea—a dim patch in the darkness as the night fell swiftly over the island. There were several more beautiful locations in the villa, but few that were so private. And privacy had been critical for this conversation. The entire family would retire to the other houses soon, keeping out of sight of Ari.

But Stefan found he couldn't wait another second for what he wanted to say—what he needed to say. He turned to Nicki and took her hands in his. "I've been very lucky to find you, too," he murmured.

Fifty-Three

Nicki froze in Stefan's grasp, the light hold of his fingertips somehow too strong for her to escape—but she didn't want to escape, if she was honest with herself. Stefan seemed to be waiting for her to say something though, and she stammered out a response. "Well—I mean, thank you. I'm lucky to—"

"No, I don't think you understand." Stefan squeezed her hands, seeming to send warmth directly to her, through her fingers, into her veins, swirling in a tight protective whirl of strength and focus. "When you first walked into my life, you turned it upside down. Inside out. I'd never met anyone like you, and I didn't want to know you."

Nicki blinked. "Oh," she managed, stung to the quick. She tried to pull her hands away, but Stefan wouldn't let go.

"You see, I realized almost instantly how much you would change me," he said instead. "How you would smile at me and brighten my whole world, how you would challenge and provoke me, irritate and frustrate me. And most of all, how you would make it impossible for me to live for even one day without knowing that you were safe, you were healthy. And that you were mine."

Nicki jolted, jerking her gaze up to meet Stefan's when she realized she'd been staring at his mouth as if she couldn't quite process the words coming out of it. His eyes were the color of a winter sea, a turbulent blue-gray, and she felt her heart kick up its pace. Not frantically, not erratically...but as powerful and true as Stefan himself, standing like a rock in the storm that was building around her.

"I—I don't—I didn't mean to upset you," she finally said, and Stefan's fierce expression wavered, a warmth coming into his eyes as his lips curved into a tender smile—a gentler smile than she'd ever seen on his face.

"But you did upset me, Nicki. You changed everything for me by walking into that room. I know you have a life beyond these walls, beyond the four corners of this kingdom. You have an entire world of adventures to live. But I'd be lying if I told you that I didn't want you to share those adventures with me. I'd be lying if I said I didn't want you to stay with me—by my side— to see what we could find if we explored this world together. Not racing each other to the finish line, not seeing who reaches the top of the hill first, but learning how fast and how well we can run together, pulling and pushing each other, if need be, or simply holding each other close. Because I love you, Nicki. I think I have since the first moment I saw you. And that's..." he swallowed, and his smile faltered a little, his expression suddenly a little dazed, as if he hadn't expected to say all those words at once. "That's what I wanted to say. To ask you if you'd consider remaining here in Oûros. With me."

Nicki wanted to respond—she really did. She wanted to speak with the same flowing and beautiful words that Stefan had. Words that no one had ever said to her, no one probably even *imagined* saying to her, even if she'd slowed down long enough to let them. But the tears welled up in her eyes and she shook her head, hard, her voice barely a rasp as she finally managed speech.

"I—yes," she said, her heart overflowing with its own set of tears, breaking down and dissolving the tight web of protections she'd built up around it for so many years. "Yes, Stefan. I can live anywhere in the world, I think, as..." She let her gaze fix on his, his beautiful eyes steady and true, staring back at her. "As long as you're there with me. Because I love you, too."

Her words were barely a whisper, but it didn't seem to matter as Stefan bent toward her, claiming her mouth with his.

"It's going to be all right," he said, when he finally broke away from her. "You'll have to trust me on this."

Only then did she hear the sound of applause.

Nicki's head came up, as Stefan turned with her, his arms around her as if he thought she would fall. But he stood with her, not before or behind her, as she looked out at people she had come to care about impossibly much over the past few weeks. The king and queen, standing together with hands clasped. Dimitri, Kristos, and even Cyril, all of them watching Stefan as if he had six heads.

And Queen Catherine, her face radiant with delight, her hands clasped to her heart as if her every wish had somehow come true.

Epilogue

Nicki lay collapsed on the chaise beside a crystal blue pool, every muscle in her body screaming in muted agony. Beside her, Stefan lay with a towel draped over his head. A tray between them held fruit juices and a collection of sugary pastries, but neither of them had the energy to stretch that far, not even for food.

"Those people were barbarians," Nicki groaned.

"They were...certainly thorough." Stefan sighed as he pulled the towel down his face, his starkly beautiful features appearing untroubled, as if they hadn't just run the equivalent of a marathon uphill carrying bricks. "They'll have preliminary results soon, I suspect, but I consider the fact that neither one of us collapsed a good thing."

She didn't miss the concern threading through his wry comment. If it were possible to hover from a treadmill across a gym floor, Stefan had hovered. First through the bloodwork, then through the VO2 max stress test, and finally through the window as they'd been taken in separately to be scanned. Nicki had undergone an echocardiogram test, sort of an ultrasound for the heart, and the techs had retained professionally neutral expressions throughout the entire procedure—the same kind of expressions that the diabolical personal trainers had worn as they put them through every muscle, sprint and endurance stress test Nicki had ever heard of, and a few she hadn't.

But Stefan was right. She hadn't passed out or gotten dizzy. She'd taken every challenge up to the point where she felt uncomfortable and then backed off, determined to do only as much as she could without pushing herself to a limit that no one asked of her—a limit no one wanted her to hit. It was strange, not going all out, but it was right too. She had a reason to protect herself.

She smiled at Stefan. "It's been one good thing after another, it seems."

He nodded, but his expression turned more serious at her words. "It has," he said. "And there's something else I really do need to explain to you."

As if on cue, all of Nicki's neuroses leapt to the fore. She and Stefan had retired to separate rooms the night before, but she hadn't been able to stop thinking about his words in front of the royal family. She opened her mouth to tell him it was okay, that he could take it back, that he could—and then he said something that made the words die in her throat.

"You're going to receive the Rite of Oûros, Nicki. Do you know what that means?"

She frowned at him. "The what?" Then her eyes widened. "Oh, right! The queen said that yesterday."

"Do you know what it is?" he asked again.

From the severity of his face, she decided honesty was the best policy here. "Umm...no. Is it bad?"

He shook his head. "Not at all. It's—it's perhaps best stated as an honored position within the borders of Oûros. You're not a citizen, but you'll enjoy the benefits of one."

"Oh." Nicki considered that. "That sounds good."

He eyed her closely, almost expectantly, but she didn't know why. "What?" She prompted. "What am I missing?"

"You'll also receive a yearly stipend," Stefan continued, holding her gaze. "And a home, fully paid for, in your name—that is, if you didn't want to move in with me."

"A..." Unaccountably, Nicki's eyes felt wet. She blinked, hard, to clear them. "Are you insane?" *Was he asking her to live with him? Was that even possible?*

"I'm not." His smile was infinitely tender. "Whatever you want, whatever you crave, it's yours. I swear it."

"I want to serve Oûros," she blurted, then felt her cheeks flush. "I know that sounds weird. I know I can't be a demigod like you are. But I want to serve. Like *really* serve. Like, be an ambassador for...for..." she broke off, biting her lip as she tried to form the words that were clanging around in her head, desperate to be spoken. "Wait, I'm sorry. Obviously I couldn't—"

"You absolutely could," Stefan cut her off. "If you want it, we can make it so. Nicki Clark, liaison to the gods. Well...one or two in particular."

"Oh..." A little sunburst of joy buoyed up within her, like a cork bobbing in the ocean. "I'd really, really like that. Maybe a god who doesn't get much press, you know? Like Hephaestus—or Hades even. He always gets a bad rap."

Stefan nodded sagely. "I happen to know he'd be honored to have you take the job."

"You're serious." Nicki gaped at him a moment longer, then stiffened as Stefan's expression changed, his gaze focusing over her shoulder.

"It's a doctor," he murmured.

As one, they sat up on their chaises, and Nicki did reach for the juice then. If she was about to get bad news, she deserved some sugar in her system.

The doctor who strode up was part of the medical team assigned to Ari, not one of the techs who'd worked on them, and Nicki went cold inside. This wasn't someone who knew her. This was someone who could only see tests and numbers and statistics, who could make decisions without knowing her spirit or soul, who—

"Nicki Clark?" The man asked crisply. "I'm Doctor Tanor, head cardiologist at the Klinik Im Park in Zurich. I had the opportunity to review your test results, and the queen asked me to speak with you directly as soon as I did." He barreled on without pausing, his gaze steady on her. "You don't have any current signs of cardiomyopathy in your heart muscle."

"I—" Nicki blinked, but she couldn't seem to see correctly, her eyes not focusing. "I don't?"

"You do not. You have a slight arrhythmia that's worrisome and will require some monitoring, and I'd like to have you track your blood pressure more routinely. There are also some diet and exercise recommendations I'd prefer you to follow to ensure you don't tap your system unnecessarily. But the bottom line is—you're healthy. You can do nearly every activity you might want without concern other than, potentially, sky diving. And while I recommend testing your heart again in six months and consistently thereafter, you're otherwise free to carry on." He smiled, at last, his eyes softening. "I can't speak to all your fitness evaluations, but your heart is in a very good place."

The doctor accepted her stammered thanks then took his leave quickly afterward, heading next to Ari, she suspected. Nicki stared after him for a long minute, biting her lip to keep from crying as Stefan reached over and slipped her hand into his.

"It's in a good place," Nicki whispered, and he leaned toward her to brush her lips softly with his. "He said I'm fine—

I'm fine. I'm in a good place." She looked up at Stefan and he pressed his fingers against hers, pulling her close.

"You're also here...with me," Stefan said. "For as long as you wish to be. That feels like a good place as well."

"It's the best place I've ever been," Nicki whispered, squeezing his hand tight. She didn't bother trying to keep the tears from falling anymore. "The best place in the world."

~

Thank you for reading CLAIMED...Nicki and Stefan will have more to contend with in the next installment of The Gatekeepers of the Gods series. In CROWNED, a lost prince returns home, both new and very old secrets are revealed, and true love takes a magical turn... now available for pre-order

I'VE BEEN ROTTING *in prison my entire life...the life I can remember anyway, which began a year ago in fire and pain. It's as if the gods themselves tossed me aside and forgot me, leaving me to burn.*

Then a vision sent from Poseidon himself steps out from the surf and into my world with maddeningly cool hands and gentle words that light up my soul in a whole new way.

With each touch she reawakens arcane knowledge within me, with every whisper she stirs in me the call to fight. Only this battle won't be waged solely to defend my country, but to avenge the gods of Olympus against an ancient, cunning foe.

I'll take on that fight, too. I'll serve, I'll sacrifice, I'll bleed.

I'll do whatever the gods demand to make this precious sea nymph mine.

~

Learn more about CROWNED—or turn the page for a sneak peek!

Keep the romance going! Sign up for my mailing list at www.jenniferchance.com/newsletter (signup at the bottom of the page) to learn about upcoming books, giveaways and more. Other places you can find me online include my website and Facebook.

I appreciate your help in spreading the word about my books, including telling a friend. Reviews help readers find books! Please leave a review on your favorite book site.

Turn the page for an excerpt from CROWNED!

Excerpt: Crowned

The roaring speedboat smashed headlong through the white-capped waves of the Aegean, apparently deciding today was the day it would pick a fight with the open sea. Fran Simmons knew exactly how it felt.

"Isn't this *great?*" Beside her, Nicki Clark gripped the side of the boat, her bright red life jacket more a formality for her than any sort of needed protection. Nicki lived for any ocean-adjacent adventure—the more outrageous, the better. "The island is even more gorgeous—you'll see!"

"Great!" Fran echoed, glad the gale-force wind meant she didn't have to carry on a conversation with Nicki. She needed the time to think, to plan. To figure out how she was going to unravel this newest vacation tangle that had wrapped up her and her three best friends.

A vacation! That's how this trip had been described to her originally. She wouldn't have agreed to it otherwise. A few weeks traveling through Europe, ending in Paris and starting with the tiny seaside country of Oûros, nestled between Greece and Turkey. The aquatically challenged Fran hadn't even minded the idea of them all vacationing next to the ocean—as long as *next to* never ever meant being *in*.

The trip had offered the perfect chance to reconnect with the three women who'd become Fran's rock. Six years ago they'd all helped Fran become the person she was today in more ways than they'd ever know. She'd lost a bit of that person over the past year. Her grad thesis work with traumatized soldiers had shown her exactly how much she could help others, but it had also revealed some cracks in her own hard-won self-concept. She needed to re-establish her base before she could launch herself into her next challenge: life after grad school.

But the relaxing girls' trip through all the tourist meccas of Europe had gotten derailed almost immediately once they'd set foot in the idyllic seaside kingdom of Oûros. Within what had seemed like thirty seconds, Emmaline had fallen in love with the newly minted crown prince of Oûros. Then Lauren had taken out her whack-job ex-boyfriend with the help of a gorgeous captain of the Oûros National Security Force. After that? Nicki had set out on a grand rescue adventure with the royal family's icy cool ambassador. The fact that one of these men was royalty and the other two were straight-outta-Greek-mythology *demigods* was just icing on the crazy cake. Their entire adventure now felt like a wild delusion brought on by too much tsipouro and too little sleep, except every morning Fran kept waking up to the *same* delusion.

Now it apparently was her turn to get roped into the chaos, and she had to play it smart. The royal family wanted her help for a very legitimate reason—and she would give that help. But only on her terms. She couldn't afford to make any mistakes.

"Oh my god, Frani, look! Dolphins!"

Terror seized Fran's heart, and she gripped the side of the boat so hard she thought the rail might break in her hands.

"Wow!" she shouted back, fixing her gaze on a point far beyond where the pair of shark-like mammals leapt out of the sea.

She could not—*would* not—betray her abject fear of freaking dolphins, of all things. Dolphins! Possibly one of the most beloved sea animals on the planet, and they made Fran's legs practically shake to pieces whenever she so much as thought of the creatures. Her baseless horror of dolphins was so absolutely, unforgivably ridiculous, she'd never breathed a word of it. Today didn't seem like a great time to start.

The engine throttled back abruptly. Fran flinched back as a spray of water splashed over the deck of the speedboat.

"Man! We were flying." Nicki beamed at her. "Hey, don't be nervous. I'm telling you, there's nothing serious you have to do here, other than, you know, help."

"I can't truly add value here, I told you that already." Fran tried to take the sharpness out of her tone, but this wasn't a lie, at least. "I'm not anywhere close to being licensed to work with anyone, and from everything you've said, Prince Aristotle—or Ryker or whoever he thinks he is—needs the care of a medical doctor. He's the king and queen's oldest son! Surely they can afford the best medical care in Europe."

"He has plenty of doctors. And neurologists and shrink people too," Nicki said, her grin not dimming a fraction. "But they're all a hundred years old. The queen thought, you know, maybe having someone his own age who at least had some background in PTSD would be good. Someone who wasn't a doctor. Or about to die."

Fran quirked a glance at her. The idea sounded no less lame than when she'd first heard it. "So she wants me to be his playmate."

"His *companion*," Nicki corrected. "And come on! You'll be great at this. Ari has been through hell this past year, and you've worked with tons of guys like that. With this job, you're not seriously working. More like, you know, hanging out. How hard can it be?"

Fran grimaced. A hundred distinct faces slid through her mind...haunted faces, worn and weary and forlorn. Soldiers with expressions that seemed to have been taken carefully out of a box and worn like a mask until at last, these men and women could hide again from the real world, returning to the place inside that both soothed and tormented them.

Nevertheless, Fran could help Aristotle Andris, she suspected. If she'd learned nothing else from her year-long study of traumatized soldiers, it was that sometimes merely sitting with a survivor in comfortable silence, letting him know he or she wasn't alone, was the best gift you could possibly give.

She could do silence, right? Anyone could do silence.

Especially someone with so much to hide.

Fran stared at the private island they were puttering toward and went over her story again. She was a grad student...true. She had a year of working with military personnel enduring Post-Traumatic Stress Disorder under her belt, as part of a psychology thesis program for which she'd earned a scholarship...true.

She'd met Lauren, Nicki and Emmaline during her undergrad years and they'd all struck up a friendship that had profoundly strengthened over the years...also true.

Then came the rest of her bio. Her name was Francesca Simmons. She'd spent an idyllic childhood in suburbia. She had a cozy middle-class blended family back in Michigan with her father, his wife and Fran's two step-brothers, basic cable, hot dogs on the deck every summer weekend, and absolutely no run-ins with the law.

False, false, and false again.

"You said Prince Ari had been held prisoner?" she asked

finally. She turned back to Nicki who bounced on her toes, her satisfaction at winning obvious.

"Yup!" Nicki said, glancing to the dock as the boat cruised in. When she spoke again, her words were lower, more hurried. "He took off from the municipal airstrip in Oûros one night last June and crashed his plane in a storm somewhere off the coast of Turkey. He washed ashore, delirious. Then he got caught in some kind of vagrant round-up and put into a work camp. He still has no idea he's the heir to the kingdom of Oûros. He thinks he's some pilot. But according to the doctors, his prognosis is good. There's nothing physically wrong with him. He's simply sort of...forgotten who he was."

Fran couldn't help her half-choked laugh. "Sometimes that isn't so bad," she said wryly. "Though maybe not when you're a prince."

"Hey!" Nicki waved furiously at a new target, and Fran pivoted as well, shielding her eyes from the brilliant Aegean sun to take in the rapidly approaching dock, and the two men standing on it. She recognized the Oûrois ambassador Stefan Mihal, of course. He and Nicki had been charged with traveling to find the errant prince.

Fran didn't much like Stefan, but it wasn't because of anything he'd done to her. The man—*demigod*—was simply too smart. He'd run dossiers on all of them when Emmaline had been in the middle of her whirlwind courtship with Prince Kristos, Ari's younger brother. Fran hadn't been able to breathe for a few days until everything on her had checked out. She'd covered every base imaginable to create her new life, and it appeared that hard work was paying off.

She knew more than most, however, that it could all be yanked away in a heartbeat. The faster she got out of Oûros and back into the rhythm of her own anonymous life, the better.

Stefan caught one of the tie ropes at the prow of the boat,

while the second man grabbed the edge and stabilized it. With a delighted "thanks!" Nicki accepted the second man's outstretched hand and mounted the step halfway up the side of the speedboat. Then she leapt out of the boat, clearing the short distance to the dock like she'd been born to the sea.

Fran, on the other hand, widened her stance as the boat rocked, then clutched the back of the passenger seat to steady herself, rigidly not focusing on the water surrounding their craft. *Breathe in...breathe out.* She just had to step out of the boat and on to the dock. If she fell into the water *where dolphins lived*, she was going to drown. She knew she was going to panic and drown, there were no two ways about it. So she couldn't fall into the water. She could only step off the fucking boat and on to the deck, without falling, without drowning. There was no other option, so that's what she'd do.

The unfamiliar man turned toward her and she steeled her nerves, unable to look at anything but the dock.

"Easy there, it's a short step," he said with a thick Mediterranean accent. The boat tipped precariously again and Fran's balance shifted. She flashed a grateful smile in the man's general direction, focusing on the step in front of her as she lunged for his hand.

The moment the man's rough palm closed around her fingers, a zip of awareness rushed through Fran, sharp enough to make her forget her fear for a split second. She glanced up and found herself staring into the face of quite possibly the most gorgeous human she'd ever seen—which was saying something, since Oûros was chock-full of beautiful humans. But this one was tall, broad-shouldered and intense, his dark hair streaked by the sun. He had a deep tan, dark chocolate eyes and high, sculpted cheekbones above a neatly trimmed beard. His face broke into a broad grin as she stared.

"You good, miss?" The impossibly gorgeous man asked as another wave rocked the boat.

She blinked, recalling herself. "I'm good, I'm just a little—"

Before she could finish her words, he tugged her up out of the boat...and into his arms.

Want to read more? CROWNED is available for pre-order now!

A Note From Jenn

In researching Nicki's illness, I realized very quickly that heart conditions can vary widely, manifesting in many different ways. I found myself understanding Nicki's hesitation in getting regularly tested, but knew that ultimately, she would have to face her fears and learn the truth about her condition, so she could manage it properly. While I was writing this book, I was also diagnosed with a physical condition in my own body that requires ongoing medical testing—a condition I'd apparently had for some time, without significant symptoms. While I was momentarily tempted to forego testing—after all, I'd gone this long and was okay, right?—I knew I had to be certain, both to ensure my own safety and to prepare my family no matter what the results were. There are many ways to treat a physical ailment, but you have to have full information before you can make any sort of decision about your health. So I urge you—if you're ever recommended for medical testing, follow through on that recommendation. What happens after is totally your call, but at least you'll be prepared.

And here's wishing you amazing health, no matter where your adventures take you.

Acknowledgments

As always, my thanks to my original editor, Linda Ingmanson, and proofreader, Toni Lee, as well as the tireless efforts of Holly Thompson, who took the updated book and made it shine. Additional thanks to Judi Soderberg for her epic last-minute copyedits. Any remaining errors are definitely my own. To Sabra Harp, thank you for being with me on this crazy journey —I couldn't do it without you! To Jennifer Dickey and Laurie Clark, thank you for your thoughts and suggestions on some of the factual elements in this tale. I won't share what, so as not to incriminate you in the inevitable event that I have gotten anything (everything!) wrong.

And to those readers who have continued the journey with the gatekeeper royals of Oûros, thank you. And keep on dreaming.

Also by Jennifer Chance

About Jennifer Chance

Jennifer Chance is an award-winning author of magical modern romance and romantic fantasy. She is also the urban fantasy and paranormal romance author Jenn Stark. For free reads, news, and a magical escape from the ordinary, connect with her at jenniferchance.com.

link: https://www.jenniferchance.com

fb: https://www.facebook.com/authorJenniferChance/